DUNGEONS & DRAGONS®

ALEX IRVINE

THE SEAL OF
KARGA KUL

Wizards
OF THE COAST®

Dungeons & Dragons
The Seal of Karga Kul

©2010 Wizards of the Coast LLC

Published by Wizards of the Coast LLC

DUNGEONS & DRAGONS, D&D, WIZARDS OF THE COAST, and their respective logos are trademarks of Wizards of the Coast LLC in the U.S.A. and other countries.

Printed in the U.S.A.

Cover art by Wayne Reynolds
Map by Robert Lazzaretti

Appendix reprinted from *Player's Handbook Races: Dragonborn,* by James Wyatt, Wizards of the Coast, January 2010, ISBN 978-0-7869-5386-8

First Printing: December 2010

9 8 7 6 5 4 3 2 1

ISBN: 978-0-7869-5572-5
ISBN: 978-0-7869-5811-5 (e-book)
620-21444000-001-EN

U.S., CANADA,
ASIA, PACIFIC, & LATIN AMERICA
Wizards of the Coast LLC
P.O. Box 707
Renton, WA 98057-0707
+1-800-324-6496

EUROPEAN HEADQUARTERS
Hasbro UK Ltd
Caswell Way
Newport, Gwent NP9 0YH
GREAT BRITAIN
Save this address for your records.

Visit our web site at www.wizards.com

The road ended in a tumble of scree that fell a few dozen yards to the lip of the gorge itself. Remy couldn't see its bottom from where they stood. Around them reared up impassable walls of stone, with the narrowest of ledges on the left side of the scree.

And ahead of them, hanging impossibly in the empty air, was the Bridge of Iban Ja. Remy tried to count the stones, but could not. Some of them were larger than the house where he had last taken a meal in Avankil. Some were no larger than a man. Gathered together, they were a mosaic impression of a bridge, the gaps between them sometimes narrow enough for a halfling to tiptoe across and sometimes wide enough that no sane mortal would endeavor the jump without wings. Bits of cloth on sticks fluttered from cracks in some of the rocks, the guideposts of long-past travelers. All of the stones moved slightly, rocking in the winds that howled through the Gorge of Noon as if they floated on the surface of a gentled ocean, or a wide and flat stretch of river. Snow clung to some of them, and drifted in sculpted shapes across the flat edges of others.

"Well," Kithri said, "now we've seen it. Biri-Daar, what did you say the other way across this gorge was?"

"It involves traveling fifty leagues off the road to a ford," Biri-Daar said. "We have no time. I have crossed Iban Ja's bridge before. It held me. It will hold you."

"And by this point, crossing it is no longer a matter of choice," Keverel chimed in.

"Is that so," Kithri began. She saw Keverel pointing back up the road, turned to see what he was indicating, and saw— as Remy did at that exact moment—the band of tieflings standing in the road behind them. As they watched, the band of perhaps a dozen was fortified with ten times as many hobgoblin marauders.

DUNGEONS & DRAGONS®

**Additional titles in the new
DUNGEONS & DRAGONS® novel line**

To Gary Gygax, for the game,
and my Pop for introducing me to it.

In the shadow of empires, the past echoes in the legends of heroes. Civilizations rise and crumble, leaving few places that have not been touched by their grandeur. Ruin, time, and nature claim what the higher races leave behind, while chaos and darkness fill the void. Each new realm must make its mark anew on the world rather than build on the progress of its predecessors.

Numerous civilized races populate this wondrous and riotous world of Dungeons & Dragons. In the early days, the mightiest among them ruled. Empires based on the power of giants, dragons, and even devils rose, warred, and eventually fell, leaving ruin and a changed world in their wake. Later, kingdoms carved by mortals appeared like the glimmer of stars, only to be swallowed as if by clouds on a black night.

Where civilization failed, traces of it remain. Ruins dot the world, hidden by an ever-encroaching wilderness that shelters unnamed horrors. Lost knowledge lingers in these places. Ancient magic set in motion by forgotten hands still flows in them. Cities and towns still stand, where inhabitants live, work, and seek shelter from the dangers of the wider world. New communities spring up where the bold have seized territory from rough country, but few common folk ever wander far afield. Trade and travel are the purview of the ambitious, the brave, and the desperate. They are wizards and warriors who carry on traditions that date to ancient times. Still others innovate, or simply learn to fight as necessity dictates, forging a unique path.

Truly special individuals, however, are rare. An extraordinary few master their arts in ways beyond what is required for mere survival or protection. For good or ill, such people rise up to take on more than any mundane person dares. Some even become legends.

These are the stories of those select few . . .

THE SEAL OF
KARGA KUL

BOOK I
THE WASTES

Remy lay *dying*, the poison of stormclaw scorpions burning its way through his veins, and while he died he tried to pray. Pelor, he called out, save me. The god did not answer. Remy tried to look around him, but dark was falling and his eyes were sticky and dry, whether from the venom or something else he didn't know. He fell into a fever dream as beside him, the horse he had ridden past the Crow Fork breathed its last.

◆━━◆━━◆

He was a boy of twelve, weaving through Quayside with a message for the captain of a river barge. He was barefoot because his mother forbade him to wear shoes on warm days. The stones of the Quayside wharves were familiar to him, as were its smells: stagnant water, woodsmoke, sun-baked mud. Avankil stood at the head of the Blackfall Estuary, which slowly opened out for a hundred miles or more. The Blackfall itself was meandering and brackish there, a creature of tide and commerce three miles wide and studded with vessels of every description. Remy found the barge captain smoking a pipe on the deck of his vessel, sharing an uproarious joke with one of Avankil's custom-house clerks. Silver and what looked like a snuff tin appeared briefly in the captain's hands before vanishing into the clerk's pocket. Permission to board, Remy called out. I have a message for the captain.

Board then, the captain answered.

Still out of breath from the run—he'd come all the way from the Undergate of the Keep of Avankil—Remy delivered his message. Is that right, the captain mused. He worked the stem of his pipe around in his teeth. Well. Here is something to carry back.

He wrote on a sheet of paper, in an alphabet that Remy—who could read Common well enough—could not decipher. Show this to no one but the vizier himself, the captain said. Or, if you must, his double.

How will I know the difference? Remy asked.

The captain laughed. The customs clerk joined in. Remy burned silently, not understanding the joke. If you ever figure that out, tell me, the captain said. He gave Remy a piece of silver. Go now.

The seventy-ninth vizier of Avankil, counsellor to kings and keeper of the library, unchallenged lord of the Undergate and all that passed through it, was named Philomen. It was rumored that he had once spent a hundred years perfecting an enchantment for creating doubles of oneself, and that he lived on in those doubles, moving his spirit from one to another as each body aged beyond its prime. Philomen was rarely seen in public. Remy had seen him twice, and to Remy the vizier seemed impossibly old. If he was moving his spirit into new bodies, he wasn't doing it nearly soon enough.

Where does a man learn such magic? he asked his mother once.

The Abyss, she answered. Don't ask again.

Remy had mistrusted magic ever after. His mother was kind but not foolish, imaginative but not superstitious. If she believed that Philomen's magic came from the Abyss, Remy believed it too.

He came to the Undergate bearing the barge captain's message. A guard at the gate, big as a dragonborn and just a bit less ugly, demanded the message.

I cannot, Remy said. It is for the vizier only.

The guard caught Remy's arm and squeezed until Remy could feel the bones of his wrist grinding together. He stood it for as long as he could but eventually he cried out and dropped the slip of paper on the ground. The guard picked it up and squinted at the writing. He looked at Remy. What does it say?

How should I know? Remy answered. I can barely read, and I don't know those letters.

Remy snapped briefly out of the fever. Cold sand against his cheek, cold stars overhead in a cold, cold sky. Remy shivered and knew he was going to die. This was what he got for going beyond the Crow Fork. All the world was darkness and cold. Something was eating the horse. Remy tried to look over and see what it was. He couldn't lift his head. He tried to crawl away but couldn't move his arms. With a sigh that was meant to be a scream he faded back into his delirium.

———— ◆◆ ————

At the Crow Fork, the North Road splits, one arm reaching across the wastes toward the fabled Bridge of Iban Ja, where the Crow Road begins. There stands Crow Fork Market, an ancient trading post and bastion against the hobgoblin raiders who harry and destroy civilized outposts throughout the wastes between the Blackfall and the Draco Serrata Mountains to the north. Over the centuries the market had grown from a collection of tents to a fortified settlement and staging area. It sprawled and wound behind timber walls and beneath the pitiless sun of the wasted lands that stretch from the North Road away from the Blackfall toward the mountains. Remy had gone there for the first time a month before his father died, on a trading excursion in the company of a dozen other men and boys, of whom Remy was the youngest by more than a year. On that trip he had learned most of what he knew of the folklore of the Crow Road and the Draco Serrata. Those were stories for the campfire on the trip from Avankil; by the end of the trip, when the timbered walls had heaved out of the hazy glimmer at the horizon, Remy had been ablaze with the desire to see the world beyond the city he had known.

As he had fallen asleep that night, within sight of the glow of great fires and magical illumination inside Crow Fork Market, Remy had dreamed of going there again. And that night he had dreamed of taking ship and seeing the cities and towns of the Dragondown Coast: Karga Kul the largest, but Furia, Toradan and Saak-Opole each with their own histories and points of interest to an urchin who had rarely ventured beyond the walls of Avankil.

He had never dreamed it would be six years before he saw Crow Fork Market again, or that when he saw it he would ride by, his errand too pressing to admit digression.

❧

The vizier Philomen had found him soon after his mother's death, which had occurred not long after the death of his father. Orphaned, Remy squatted where he could and fed himself how he could. Philomen's guard—the one who a few years before had ground the bones of Remy's wrist—caught that same wrist one afternoon as Remy was dashing off with a message from a ship's captain to the woman he kept in apartments overlooking the Inner Pool. The vizier has messages that need carrying, the guard had said. Remy had never been certain whether it was an invitation or a demand; it had never occurred to him that he could refuse.

He heard the muted clop of horses' hooves on hard earth. The road from Avankil to Toradan—the road at whose side Remy would shortly die—was laid down of stones cut flat and placed so that in most places a knife blade would not slip between them. Hooves made a different sound there. Someone was riding off the road.

To me, Remy thought. *Someone is riding to help.*

"Stormclaw scorpions." The voice drifted down through the veils of Remy's fever. He tried to answer but could not.

"The horse is dead."

"Notice that, did you?"

Something prodded Remy's hip. "This one isn't, though, I don't think." That voice came closer. Remy vomited and tried to speak as several voices joined in rough laughter.

"Not quite. Got some life left in him."

"Late. Maybe we should camp anyway, see if he makes it through the night."

"And then what?" The voices blurred together, too fast for Remy to follow. The last clear thing he heard was, "We should leave him."

He dreamed in his fever of catching fish in the shadowed water under the wharves. Sometimes when one of the wizards or alchemists of Avankil disposed of failed elixirs, remnant trickles found their way to those slack waters, producing monstrosities. Once Remy had caught a fish with tiny hands. He had been about to throw it back when a passing woman, her face hooded by a dark cloak embroidered with the constellations of summer, bought it from him for thirty pieces of gold. It was that money Remy had used to buy his first short sword, an unadorned blade whose hilt Remy had re-wrapped with wire and leather scavenged from dockside rubbish heaps. He had enough left over for a month of lessons with one of the drillmasters who trained the garrisons of the keep. He had taken to wearing the sword, but not everywhere. Avankil had laws about which of its citizens could be armed and when. Remy had no desire to break them, and no desire to provoke random belligerents who might swagger across his path from the docks or the Ferry Gate.

Despite his discretion, he had crossed swords more than once and had killed a man the year before. A drifting sword for hire, killing time on the Quayside, had seen Remy receive a message and a few coins. Catching up with Remy in one of the twisting alleys between Quayside and the downstream terminus of the Outer Wall, he had left Remy no choice. Since then Remy had moved with more caution through streets he had once thought he owned. When he was a boy, he was just one more boy flitting through the streets of Avankil; as he became a man, he attracted more notice.

Once a year, perhaps, he found some oddity dangling from his hook. Some of them died as soon as he brought them up. Some frightened him enough to drop the whole line into the water. Some were pathetic, freakish, fit only for an afterlife suspended in amber fluid on the top shelf of some distracted alchemist's study. All of them were mysteries Remy didn't particularly want to solve.

What's in the box?

"No," Remy moaned. "Don't."

The vizier had warned him. If you open the box—if you so much as crack the seal that holds it shut—you might not die, but you will wish you had. And if you don't die from what the box contains, you most certainly will when I find you again. You are a good messenger, Remy. Do not disappoint me in this.

With that, the vizier Philomen had disappeared through the curtains into his inner chambers, leaving Remy with the box he dared not open and a letter to present at the stable just inside the Undergate, in return for which he would be given a horse. Toradan was a week's ride. Perhaps ten days if he made excellent time and encountered no trouble along the way.

Remy woke to the smell of stew. The odor of cooking fat hooked him and hauled him up from the depths of his fever into waking life. He shivered and opened his eyes, confused at first by the angle of the sun. Long shadows lay across the wastes and behind he heard conversation in low voices. He rolled over, legs tangled in a blanket that was not his. He blinked the sleep from his eyes and pinpointed where the voices where coming from.

Like most residents of Avankil—or any of the settlements along the Dragondown Coast—Remy had only seen a few dragonborn. They kept to themselves, by and large, and their travels—for the dragonborn were a rootless and wandering race—tended to pause only in the company of other dragonborn. From time to time, Remy had seen them on board ships that docked Quayside. Once he had run a message from one such seafarer to the dragonborn clan enclave upstream of Quayside, near the Outer Wall in the oldest quarter of Avankil. On the whole, dragonborn didn't spend much time in the settled coastal cities, preferring to spend their time in places more likely to yield adventure.

And there was one—a female, no less, armed and armored—stirring a small pot over a campfire off the road between Avankil and Toradan. She looked over at the motion and said, "Ah. So you did live. Praise to Bahamut."

"Or to Keverel's medicines," cut in a halfling woman sitting at the dragonborn's left. She nodded at a human wearing the holy symbol of Erathis and the sunburn of someone who spent most of his time under a roof.

"The cleric is honest in his worship. Bahamut does not consider the followers of Erathis enemies of the Law," the dragonborn returned. "Be flip about something else, Kithri."

The halfling stood and somersaulted backward. "I am flip," she announced, and went over to Remy. "So. I'm Kithri." Pointing at each member of the party in turn, she introduced them. "The humorless dragonborn there is Biri-Daar. Keverel there saved your life with his clerical ministrations. He and Biri-Daar will bore you to death with their notions about Bahamut and Erathis. You ask me, there's not much difference between a god of civilization and law and a divine dragon dedicated to justice and honor. The sourpuss with the bow is Lucan, and the quiet one in the wizard's cloak is Iriani."

She squatted and tapped Remy on the shoulder. "Now you know us. Here's what we know about you. You were traveling from Avankil. You were attacked by stormclaw scorpions. You killed several of them. After they killed your horse and you slipped into your fever, something else came along and ate the horse."

"You should feel lucky it didn't eat you," Lucan said from the other side of the campfire. He was an elf. His dress, leathers, and muted colors marked him as a ranger with long experience in the trackless wilderness of the Dragondown. Iriani, sitting quietly at the edge of the campfire's light, also had the elongated, angular features that bespoke elf blood, but his aspect was more human. A half-elf, Remy thought. They were known to be drawn to the magical arts. Iriani had acknowledged Kithri's introduction with a nod in Remy's direction but had not yet spoken.

Already it was brighter, the shadows were shorter, and Remy realized with a shock that it was not evening but morning. He sat up and thought that he might attempt to get to his feet.

"How long have I been . . . ?"

"Before we came along, who knows?" Kithri said. "A day, probably. And another half day since we found you. Probably other travelers passed during that time but didn't think you had anything worth taking."

"She and I disagree about that," Lucan said.

"Lucan and I disagree about everything," Kithri said. "It passes the time."

"If there are stormclaws around, probably there's a ruin nearby," added the cleric Keverel. "They tend to congregate in such places. I believe this road dates from the times of Bael Turath, before the great war. There could have been an outpost . . ." He trailed off, looking around. "The land reclaims what the higher races abandon."

"Higher races," Kithri said drolly. "Speak for yourself."

"Wonder if there's anything to be gained from having a look around for that ruin," Lucan said.

"Depends," Biri-Daar said. "Are you taking our mission to Karga Kul seriously, or are you adventuring?"

"You say adventuring like it's a bad thing," Kithri said.

"Wait," Remy said. He was having trouble following everything they said; it seemed like he was still feeling the effects of the venom. "I have to get to Toradan," he said.

"It's that way," Kithri said, pointing down the road. "Maybe five day on foot. Not that it matters. If you go walking alone in this desert, you won't live a day."

"My errand is urgent. I—I thank you for saving me, but the vizier of Avankil will—"

"String you up by your thumbs? Run a ring through your nose and lead you around his chambers? Put you to work in the kitchen?" Kithri winked, but Remy had no time or patience for jokes. He was frightened and confused and very conscious of the time he had lost on his task for Philomen.

"Please," Remy said. "I have to take this to Toradan." He showed her the box. Reflexively his fingers traced the runes carved into its lid.

"What exactly is the errand?" Keverel asked. His fingers traced the outline of his holy symbol, a silver pendant worked in the gear-and-sunburst motif of Erathis. "What does the box contain?"

"I don't know," Remy said.

"No one told you?"

Lucan tsked. "Never take anything anywhere for anyone unless you know what it is," he said.

"And why they want it to go where they want it to go," Kithri added.

"I already did," Remy said. "And now that I've said it, I have to do it."

"Admirable," said Biri-Daar. "It is too rare that one finds that kind of commitment. But unless you want to walk the rest of the way by yourself," the dragonborn went on, "you're going to be traveling with us for a while. And scorpions are hardly the worst things you're going to find out here."

Having no choice, Remy went, at least until he could think of a better plan. He wasn't going to get a horse from them unless he stole it, and he didn't think that he could steal a horse. When he was a child, he'd stolen things here and there, but to steal a horse from a party of adventurers in the wilderness . . . for one thing, they would hunt him down and kill him if they could. For another, it was wrong.

So, with the option of theft removed, Remy turned with Biri-Daar's group—it was clear that the dragonborn, a paladin of Bahamut, was the leader of the group—and followed the road back toward Crow Fork. The sun burned down and morning haze lifted, replaced by the glimmer of mirage at the horizon. "Sometimes," Iriani said, "you can see the mountains in a mirage. Then when you see them with your own eyes, you fear that it's magic."

Remy guessed that he wouldn't mind seeing the mountains whether by magic or other means. Anything to get him out of the wastes. Around them, flat, salt-stained sand stretched to the horizon, broken only by the occasional small heave of a hill or protruding stone. No bird sang, no lizard crept. If life was there, it kept to itself.

Like stormclaw scorpions, perhaps, hiding under the earth until they emerged from their ruined lair in the cool and darkening evenings.

The welts left by their stingers still puckered angry and red on Remy's legs and the back of his left hand. He had survived. He felt stronger, not just because of his five companions but because he had fought off stormclaw scorpions. They had not killed him. Whatever came next on the road—before he could finally get to Toradan with Philomen's box—Remy felt that he was ready for it.

After the first day of travel, trying to keep up with a party on horseback, Remy was also more than ready to get a horse again. Biri-Daar's idea was that they would see what was on offer at Crow Fork Market, which they would reach the next morning— "If you can keep your pace up," she added with what on a dragonborn's face passed for a smile. "If not, it'll be two days."

As night fell they built a fire. "Just like last night, except this time you're not rolling around sweating in your sleep," Kithri joked to Remy. The evening meal was dried fruit, cheese, and bread; they'd had meat that morning, and would again the following morning. Then, with any luck, they'd arrive at Crow Fork Market and replenish their supplies before continuing the trek.

"Where are you going again?" Remy asked at the end of the meal.

"Karga Kul," Lucan said. "The great cork stuck in the bottle that would pour the Abyss out into this world."

"Sounds wonderful," Remy said with a grin.

"It is," Biri-Daar said. "I was hatched there. It is the city of my dreams, the city I would grow old in. The city I would die in, if I had to die somewhere."

"Listen to Biri-Daar talk about dying," Iriani chuckled. "She's yet to meet the foe that can nick her sword, and yet she thinks about dying. You dragonborn."

"Bahamut will decide," Biri-Daar said.

At the mention of the god's name, Remy caught a gleam of pale light beyond the glow of the campfire.

"You better hope something interesting happens between now and Karga Kul," Kithri said. "And by interesting, I mean something that ends with some kind of booty. Otherwise you're going to owe Biri-Daar for a horse. She's not forgiving when it comes to debt."

"I'm not going to Karga Kul," Remy protested. "I must get to Toradan."

"Then go right ahead back the way we came. Give the stormclaws and the hobgoblins our greetings," Kithri said.

Remy stewed. He knew he wouldn't survive the road to Toradan on his own. Kithri was right about the hobgoblins. They controlled everything on the map between the few points of civilization, of which Avankil and Karga Kul were the largest. Even the substantial towns such as Toradan were on constant alert against hobgoblin incursions, and the roads between settlements were heavily preyed upon by the creatures native to the wastes.

"Erathis has brought us together, Remy," Keverel said. "Whatever worldly errand you contemplate, remember that the gods dispose and we must follow."

Again, as Keverel mentioned the god's name, something shone briefly just beyond the light. "Did you see that?" Remy asked. He pointed into the dark, in the direction of the gleam.

The others looked that way. "See what?" The elf-blooded had better night vision; Lucan stiffened as he caught sight of something.

"Stay close to the fire," he said, as a chilling cackle came out of the darkness.

"Hyena," Keverel said. He was shoulder to shoulder with Remy. "How did you see it?"

"There was a gleam when you said the god's name," Remy answered. He had the presence of mind not to use the name, since he was not a worshiper. Some gods looked dimly on hearing their names in the mouths of unbelievers.

The leather grip of Keverel's mace creaked as he brought it up. "Then it's no ordinary hyena," he said over the cackling, which got louder and seemed to come from several directions at once. "It's a cacklefiend. There will be gnolls with it as well, and perhaps worse than gnolls. Erathis!" he called out, holding up his holy symbol.

Light washed out from the symbol, washing over the hulking shape of a cacklefiend hyena. It was nearly man-high at the shoulder, with a row of serrated spines where an ordinary hyena had bristles down its back. Its fur was mottled green, gray, and black. Behind it loomed the hyena-like humanoid silhouettes of gnolls.

"This is why I hate the desert," Kithri said.

"Me too." Lucan unsheathed his sword, which gave off a silvery light similar to the glow of Keverel's talisman. Iriani too created light, with a complicated pattern of snapping fingers that popped small flares into life over their heads. The cacklefiend ducked its head and chuckled demoniacally, swaying its head back and forth as the gnolls skirted the perimeter of light, timing their rush to the cue the cacklefiend would give.

It was a tricky situation for the members of the party used to having an advantage because of their superior night vision. The gnolls had it too, and the cacklefiend could see the way demons did because it was a demonic perversion of a hyena. So one advantage Lucan, and Iriani were accustomed to had vanished because of circumstance and opponent—yet for Remy and the others, the campfire and the various glares of magical light were a leveler. They could see the cacklefiend and the gnolls perfectly well, or at least as well as the enemy could see them. And the first thing Remy saw after Iriani's light flashed into being was the gleam of Kithri's throwing daggers, flickering their way to their target out at the end of the gnoll grouping. She was trying to prevent the gnolls from spreading out and surrounding them. In the uncertain light, Kithri's attack—unusually for her—wasn't fatal. The gnoll, a burnished steel dagger hilt sticking out from its shoulder and one of its ears carved to a flap, charged. The rest followed, the giggling cacklefiend skipping around to flank the party and keeping to the edge of the firelight.

Biri-Daar stood to meet them, Keverel and Lucan flanking her. Behind them, Iriani and Kithri used the campfire itself as a defensive structure. Remy stayed up with the fighting front rank, not sure what he should do but knowing that when push came to shove, he was more good with a sword than he was dancing around and waiting for a clear shot from a distance.

There were perhaps a dozen gnolls. Lucan cut down the first as it got within range of a sword stroke, while it was still raising the chain-slung morningstar it carried. The spiked ball thudded into the packed earth between his feet. Biri-Daar took a single step forward and broke the charge, knocking a gnoll aside with her shield while slashing another to the ground. The gnolls hesitated, sidestepping away from her into Lucan's blade and the crushing head of

Keverel's mace. Light shone more fiercely from the cleric's holy symbol as the misbegotten enemy drew closer, and Biri-Daar's sword too glowed with Bahamut's power. Remy saw that, and was nearly distracted enough that when a gnoll bore down on him, its weapon a steel bar that thrummed past Remy's head with the promise of a backswing that would shatter his skull, he barely reacted in time. But his training both casual and formal, from Quayside brawls to those first precious lessons in the courtyard of the Keep of Avankil, took hold; before he could think about what to do, Remy had stepped inside the sweep of the gnoll's brutal mace, pivoting along with the backswing until his head was practically in its armpit—at the same moment the blade of his sword scraped along its bottom rib as he spitted it with the momentum of its own charge.

He looked up to see the cacklefiend slavering not six feet away. It chuckled and raved, and the drool from its yellow-toothed maw hissed and crackled when it dropped to the bare earth. The clashes of blade against steel reached him, but Remy did not look. The enemy that he could see was the only enemy he could fight, and to turn his back on that enemy would bring only death. His sword caught on the gnoll's ribs. He wasn't going to be able to get it out in time. The cacklefiend's eyes glowed with a hunger sharpened in the Abyss. It sprang as Remy kept hauling on the hilt of his sword, throwing his other arm up as he wished for a shield. Anything. Even an armored sleeve.

A blast of magical energy from an angle behind Remy and above his head knocked the cacklefiend off to one side.

It hit the ground, legs splayed, and skidded. Iriani came into view, brewing another spell between his two hands as Kithri kept watch on his back with throwing daggers fanned out in one hand and a short sword in the other. Like a marketplace magician, Kithri flicked the daggers one and two at a time without ever seeming to move her hand.

She couldn't keep all of the gnolls away, though. One of them had outflanked their position, Remy saw as he finally dragged his sword free of the dead gnoll. It was behind Kithri, behind Iriani; Biri-Daar and Lucan were still back to back against the main group of marauders. He could not see Keverel.

"Behind you!" Remy shouted. At the same time he broke toward the gnoll as it leaped over the campfire. Behind him, the cacklefiend got its feet under it and tensed to spring again.

The gnoll landed within reach of Kithri and dealt her a two-handed blow that she partially deflected at the cost of her own sword. Its blade snapped and the head of the gnoll's mace glanced across the top of her helm. Kithri went down, and in the firelight Remy couldn't tell how badly she had been wounded. The gnoll was poised for another blow, this time at Iriani, whose focus was still and solely on the cacklefiend. Remy hit the gnoll from the side, his blade cutting through its leather cuirass and deep into the muscle below. The gnoll roared and tried to bring the butt of its mace down on Remy, but he danced away. The mace thudded into the ground and Remy thrust over its guard, feeling the point of his sword strike home at the base of its neck.

Rearing back with this death blow, the gnoll swept upward with its mace, catching Remy in the pit of the stomach and knocking him flat on his back. His mouth was open but he could make no sound, couldn't breathe. It felt as if the mace had caved in his ribs. He rolled over onto his side and looked for his sword. As he put his hand on its hilt he looked up to see the cacklefiend bat Iriani aside and keep coming toward him.

He got to his knees but could not stand. The cacklefiend came closer. Off to his left, Remy heard the crunch of Keverel's mace splintering bone. He saw Lucan come at the cacklefiend from the side, plunging his sword down into its back. It rounded on him, snarling, and bit into the edge of his shield. Smoke poured from its mouth as its saliva ate away at the wood and steel of the shield. It shook its head like a dog with a rabbit, unbalancing Lucan and knocking him down. He still held his sword and struck out at it, opening a wound on its snout. Blood ran and mixed with the acid that dripped from its open mouth. It shook its head, spattering Lucan with blood and saliva.

The elf started to scream as the cacklefiend's fluids ate into his skin and burned holes through his armor. He dropped his sword and shield, trying to strip his tunic and jerkin before the rest of the blood could get through them.

The cacklefiend laughed, high and maddening. It came after Remy again.

He still could not get to his feet. The dying gnoll had knocked the wind out of him so badly that he still couldn't draw a full breath. Lucan was screaming *Melora, Melora, Melora*, drawing on the strength of his god to keep the pain from driving him mad. He got his jerkin off and stood barechested, burns showing across his arms and face. Past the cacklefiend, Remy saw him run around to the other side of the campfire.

No. He couldn't believe Lucan would abandon the fight. Remy got one foot under him and found the strength to point his sword at the cacklefiend. Iriani was stirring. Kithri lay still. Keverel spoke an incantation and energy flowed through Remy, loosening his throat as the clash of armor and weapons lessened in intensity. Remy glanced from side to side. On his right, Iriani scrambled to his feet.

On his left, Biri-Daar was surrounded by the sprawled bodies of gnolls, her face wreathed in smoke from her mouth and nose. She struck down the last of them and stepped over it to finish off the cacklefiend . . . but Remy wasn't sure she would get close enough before it got to him, and he had nothing to protect himself against its corrosive blood.

But he would die trying, if it came to that. Aided by Keverel's blessing, he got his feet under him and stood to meet it. It tensed to spring.

Two arrows, one after the other faster than Remy could follow, struck it in the chest, an inch apart just inside the joint of its right shoulder. Bolts of eldritch power peppered it from Iriani's side. Keverel was running to its other side, winding up with his mace as Biri-Daar came on behind him.

For me, Remy thought. They're doing this for me. A new kind of strength rose in him. He raised his own sword and stepped forward. Another arrow from Lucan's bow buried itself in the cacklefiend's neck. One of its feet slipped. Keverel got to it first, bringing his mace down on its head with a crunch. Blood splattered onto the ground and across the font of the cleric's mail shirt. He raised the mace again.

The cacklefiend kept coming at Remy. He met it head-on, sword thrust out at its chest. The blade went deep and Remy planted his feet, keeping the cacklefiend's jaws away from him. From the corner of his eye he saw Biri-Daar hacking down on its back, twice before Keverel caved in its ribs with his mace. It slumped to the ground, the awful giggle dying in its throat as the Abyssal light went out in its eyes.

Remy walked to the nearest dead gnoll and wiped the blade of his sword on its fur. The cacklefiend's blood ate into the flesh. Before sheathing his sword, Remy scrubbed it down with sand. The other members of the party did the same, not talking for the moment as each of them came slowly down from the pitch of battle. Keverel broke the silence, murmuring healing charms over Lucan's wounds and then ministering to Kithri as she stirred and wakened. The unscathed members of the party dragged the bodies of gnoll and cacklefiend far enough away from the campsite that the night's scavengers wouldn't be tempted to add adventurer to their menu.

It was some time before anyone said anything to Remy, and when the words came he wished they hadn't. He had just finished cleaning his sword and was oiling it and wiping it down, looking forward to a few hours' sleep before the sun would come up and the wastes breed new monstrosities for them to face. He heard someone approach and stop. It was Lucan, fresh bandages showing through the holes in his tunic and jerkin.

"How come the cacklefiend wanted you so badly?" the elf asked him. "It fought its way through us to get to you. What is it you have there in your little box? Care to show us?"

"I told you I can't."

"Perhaps I can." Lucan nudged Remy's pack with the toe of his boot. "Come on. Let's have a look."

Remy knew bullying when he saw it, and he knew that if he didn't put a stop to it now it would grow into something far worse. He stood. "We just fought together," he said. "I don't want to fight against you now."

Lucan was taller than he was, but Remy was broader and had one other advantage. He was ready to fight, and he didn't think Lucan was.

Biri-Daar stepped in before things could get any more tense. "Lucan," she said. "Remy swore an oath. Would you have him break it?"

Lucan didn't answer. His gaze remained on Remy, who looked back.

"Lucan," Biri-Daar added. "Even if we wanted to open the box, would you do it without knowing what those charms on its lid might unleash?"

There was a pause. After a delay, the common sense approach appeared to work. Lucan looked away from Remy at the group's dragonborn leader. "The cacklefiend was looking for him," he said to her, pointing at Remy. "Because of what he carries. That endangers all of us."

"Perhaps," Biri-Daar said.

Remy was suddenly and uncomfortably conscious of the fact that the entire group was looking at him. Something permanent was being decided about his status within the party, and how it affected their mission.

"What endangers us is you breaking away from the group when the gnolls had us surrounded," Remy said before he could stop himself. He was a stranger to the group, perhaps, but he was damned if he was going to be made a scapegoat.

"You dare," Lucan growled. A dagger appeared in his hand, the motion too fast for Remy to follow.

"Hold," Biri-Daar commanded. "Remy, you will not question Lucan's stomach for a fight while I am here. He and I have faced down creatures the like of which you cannot imagine. And Lucan, the gods have brought Remy into our group. We will not cast him out while their reasons are still unclear to us."

"If the creations of the Abyss are following him," Keverel said quietly, "I'm inclined to think he's on the right side."

"Enemy of the enemy is my friend, is that it?" Iriani said.

"Something like that," Keverel said. "Remy, would you mind if Iriani and I took a closer look at that box? The sigils might tell us something that we need to know the next time creatures come out of the dark looking for it."

"If we just left him here, we wouldn't have to worry about it," Lucan grumbled. His good-natured, jousting demeanor was utterly gone, as if the brief battle had killed off his sense of humor and left him with an inexplicable hostility toward Remy. For his part, Remy could only wonder whether Lucan was ashamed of how he had reacted in the fight or something else was happening that Remy couldn't detect.

"True," Kithri said from a little distance away. "But if he's not around and horrible monstrosities stop following us, we are going to have a lot less of this."

Everyone turned to look as she came back into the firelight. "I know they're only gnolls," she said, "but all of you need to sharpen up your looting instincts. Look what we have."

On a flat rock near the campfire, she spilled a number of objects she had bound up in a cloth.

"Trust Kithri to distract us with gnoll trinkets and trash," Lucan said—but he went right along with the rest of them. "What wonders have you found? And which ones went into your pockets before you told us about the rest?"

"Ask me no questions, I'll tell you no lies," Kithri said as she spread her findings out on the rock. There was nothing in the way of coins—gnolls had no use for them—but there were four things of interest. An armband worked from silver in the shape of entwined snakes, with tiny jewels as their eyes; a human jawbone with its teeth replaced by cut gems; a gold ring set with a square green stone; and a pearl, a single pearl, worked into an earring with gold wire.

"And this was tied around the cacklefiend's neck," Kithri said, drawing a pendant from her pocket. "I thought I would save it for last."

Biri-Daar took it and handed it to Keverel. "Do you see what I see?"

"Demon's workmanship," Keverel said with a nod. "I can feel it even if I can't see it. Erathis knows." The god's name brought a pale gleam from the pendant and Remy realized that gleam was what had first alerted him to the presence of something beyond the firelight.

"This pendant is a demon's eye," Biri-Daar said. "It guided the cacklefiend and the gnolls to us."

"Or to him," Lucan said, pointing at Remy with the dagger he had not yet put away. Remy began to feel that a fight between him and the elf was inevitable, and he did not feel confident of winning it.

Biri-Daar's response made him even more uncertain. "Or to him," she echoed. "Which means that we need to know more about what he carries, and why. But the wilderness is no place for such investigations. Lucan, we didn't rescue this boy just to kill him. Put the blade away."

Lucan did, with a last cold glance at Remy, who was a bit nettled at being called a boy. Yet now was not the time to challenge the group any more than he already had. He bit his tongue. Biri-Daar swept all of the treasures into cupped hands. "We'll sell this, or have it appraised at least, when we get to Crow Fork Market," she said, holding her hands out to Iriani. "Iriani, is any of it of use to you?"

The mage floated a palm over the items and closed his eyes. "There is some power in the jawbone," he said after a moment. "But nothing I would dare use. Corellon would turn his back on me, and for good reason. There is evil in it."

"Then we must be careful who we sell it to," Biri-Daar said. "But maybe we can wring some good from it."

Everything went into a pouch at her belt. "We ought to sleep now," she said. "First watch to the unwounded. That means me and Remy."

———◆———

"For someone without much experience fighting in a group," Biri-Daar said after everyone else was asleep, "you did well."

Remy nodded, accepting the compliment.

"And it's a good thing you can fight," the paladin went on. She looked from the campfire to Remy. "Even though you should maybe have been more careful about picking a fight with Lucan. He was right that the cacklefiend was looking for you. That's what the demon's eye was for."

The fire was burning low. Remy poked at it and watched the swirl of the glow in the embers. "I understand if you're not sure what to say," Biri-Daar said.

"I said everything I know," Remy said. "I don't know what's in the box. I only know that Philomen wanted me to take it to Toradan."

"So you don't know what it is and you don't know why Philomen gave it to you. Let me ask you this: what do you know about Philomen?"

"That he's the vizier in Avankil, and has been since well before I was born." Remy said nothing about the darker rumors of sorcery that Philomen's enemies propagated throughout the city.

"Do the people of Avankil trust him?"

"If they don't, they're shy about saying so," Remy said.

"With good reason." Both of them watched the fire for a few minutes. Remy wondered what Biri-Daar was thinking behind the roundabout questions about the vizier.

Out in the darkness, something growled and there came the sound of tearing flesh. "Scavengers are out," Remy commented.

"Worried?" Biri-Daar looked at him and he shook his head. A bone cracked. "Why do you think Philomen gave you something so important?" she asked.

Remy bristled. "Because I've carried things for him before. I've never failed him."

"And you don't ask questions," Biri-Daar added. Remy didn't challenge this. "Because if you did," the dragonborn added, "you wouldn't be here." She lapsed into thought again until Remy broke the silence.

"What are you getting at?"

Still the silence went on. Remy yawned. Finally Biri-Daar said, "If someone is looking for what you carry, and that someone is powerful enough to make a demon's eye, then you ought to ask yourself what the vizier thought was going to happen to you out here."

Now it was Remy's turn to fall silent.

"There are two possibilities, Remy," Biri-Daar said after some time. "Either Philomen has enemies who are after what you carry, or the vizier himself is using you to get the box out of Avankil and he planned to have you killed in the wastes. Either way, more is going on than you or I understand. And either way, someone wanted you dead. That means that what you carry is important." The dragonborn shifted her weight, her armor creaking. "And now you should sleep. One thing you learn when you leave the cities is that when a chance for sleep comes, you take it. No questions asked."

Remy knew he should keep watch with Biri-Daar, but he was too tired to argue with this small kindness and too confused to assess everything she had said. He lay down where he was and was asleep so fast he couldn't even remember touching the ground. He dreamed of fighting a battle and winning, only to find that another battle awaited and another victory, and another, and another . . .

In the morning, the bodies of the gnolls were gone but the cacklefiend lay untouched except by flies that appeared as the sun rose.

The next morning passed uneventfully except for minor bickering among members of the group who wanted to spend a few days in Crow Fork Market and those who wanted to stop just long enough to replenish their supplies and then get on with the trip to Karga Kul. Lucan and Kithri wanted to delay, Lucan for the gaming and Kithri for the possibilities of a little recreational purse-cutting; everyone else wanted to get on with it. "You two are agreeing on something?" Remy needled them, seeing a chance to perhaps mend some of the fences broken in the aftermath of the previous night's battle.

Kithri laughed, a high pure bell of a laugh slightly at odds with her fundamentally larcenous nature. Lucan, by contrast, didn't crack a smile. Remy had the feeling that the elf still bore him a grudge; his ready wit seemed to appear at all occasions and conversations save those involving Remy. This preoccupied Remy as he backtracked along the section of the Toradan Road he had followed in the last day before the scorpions had found him. He found he had few memories of that day; between passing Crow Fork and waking up in the care of Keverel, all Remy remembered were general sensations of heat and dust and endless broken landscapes where no living thing moved. There was a dreamlike quality to those sensations, and Remy lapsed into that dream. His task was going unfulfilled, Biri-Daar had raised troubling questions about Philomen . . . Remy had to wonder what he was getting himself into.

Perhaps the thing to do was take his share of the spoils from the gnolls, buy a horse, and traverse that stretch of the Toradan Road for a third time. He owed them a debt for saving his life, but he didn't think it was a debt any of them were especially interested in collecting.

And either way, he would finally make his first trip inside the walls of Crow Fork Market.

Its walls reared up just then like a mirage on the horizon, shimmering and flickering with the promise of everything civilization had to offer in the midst of the endless empty wastelands. A sandstorm had prevented Remy from seeing those walls on his way east toward Toradan; he enjoyed the fine clear day not least because it showed him the sight of the market, resolving and solidifying as if it were actually becoming real.

Remy knew part of the story, the part that any child who grew up along the Dragondown Coast would know: In an age forgotten even by the time of Arkhosia and Bael Turath, a market had sprung up around an oasis at the intersection of two roads. Perhaps it had sprung up because a freak desert rainstorm had bogged a caravan down in mud so deep that when it dried, the merchant could not dig his wagons out and all of his beasts had died. So he stayed, never arriving at his destination—which might have been any of the ancient cities that since lay in ruins along the shores of the Gulf. It might even have been the ancient city that lay below Karga Kul.

At first it was a collection of tents, a way station for caravans skirting the edge of the desert but wary of coming too close to the bandits and worse that haunted the Blackfall's banks. There was water there, and safety in numbers.

Over the centuries, the market had grown. Walls had sprung up around it, and earthen berms. Cisterns had been dug, and cellars to store goods that would not survive long in the Fork area's heat and dust. As Remy walked through its road gate, it was larger than any town he had ever been in except Avankil. Above the ground, awnings and tents that had once stood by themselves now fronted permanent stalls and rows of wood-frame houses. Remy wondered how much the builders had paid to get that much wood all the way out here. The nearest tree was forty miles away. At the center of the market stood a citadel built of sandstone. "More than once," Keverel said, "Crow Fork Market has stood against an army. Below that keep, there are cellars. Below the cellars, dungeons. Below the dungeons . . ." He trailed off. "One hears stories."

"Who invades a place out in the middle of a waste?" Remy asked.

"Recently?" Kevel said. "The hobgoblin warlords who ravage these wastes have had their eyes on this market since before you were born."

Around them surged the activities of commerce, a storm of getting and spending. Crow Fork Market stood at the crossroads of the southern Dragondown. Any land route between Toradan, Avankil, and Karga Kul passed the Crow Fork.

Iriani stopped a passing fruit seller and spent a piece of silver on a basket of apples. Holding them up to everyone, he said, "Apples in the wastes. Who wouldn't fight to control this place?"

"Me," Biri-Daar said. "I wouldn't. I wouldn't waste a goblin's life on this place."

Keverel looked around, taking in the chaos. He had mentioned to Remy that morning that he, like Remy, had never been inside the market's walls. "History is long. One imagines that the actions we find baffling made sense at the time," he mused.

"Or that people were just as stupid then as we can expect them to be now," Lucan countered dryly.

"At least once, it was an elf army that marched on the market," Biri-Daar reminded him. "Which by your formulation would mean that elves can be stupid just as humans can. Or halflings."

"Or dragonborn," Kithri added cheerfully.

"The propensity for foolishness knows no racial boundaries," Keverel commented. "Shall we eat?"

The area immediately inside the gates of Crow Fork Market was reserved for the staging of caravans and merchant missions. From there, grooms took their horses and walked them along the wall toward the stables that were set away from the main bazaar spaces. To the left and right were rows of stalls offering every kind of foodstuff found within three months' journey. These stalls were hotly contested, and handed down across generations. Few things in commerce were certain, but one of those few certainties was that a caravan arriving was hungry and a caravan leaving thought it might be. In both cases, food was desirable.

Remy ate skewers of fried squid from the Furia coast, where the waters were deep and wracked with storms. He washed them down with a strong tea chilled by ice brought down from the glaciers high in the Draco Serrata. It was said that some of those glaciers contained the preserved bodies of warriors and mages from the age of Arkhosia, and that so powerful was their magic that when the ice melted from around them they walked and breathed as if they had never spent frozen millennia beneath the alpine stars. There were those who believed that ice from those glaciers had healing properties, as did the water that remained when the ice melted. Remy didn't know about that, but he would willingly have stated that the tea itself had restorative properties after ten days spent in the wastes.

Tieflings down from the mountains mixed with their ancient adversaries, the dragonborn; members of warring nations and clans haggled over the same goods; zealot and unbeliever poured and drank from the same tankards. Crow Fork Market, by tradition and decree, was a place where the only permissible violence was that done to a customer's purse.

Spiretop drakes flitted from the gate towers and nestled under the eaves of the keep at the center of the market. They were an irritating scourge of some cities, threatening unlucky citizens and stealing anything shiny that caught their attention. In Avankil, Remy had earned bounties from the Quayside neighborhood constabulary for killing spiretops. It was how he had learned to use a sling. They were the rats of the air, only smarter and more vicious than rats. Remy was tempted to take a shot at them now. Instead he sipped his tea and crunched the last of the fried squid, spitting their beaks onto the stones. "All of this came from somewhere else," he marveled.

"Most of it, yes," Iriani said. He was rebraiding his hair and pausing every time he finished a braid to take a swallow of distilled liquor from a bottle he'd bought the minute they came through the gate. "When this place was founded, the stories go, all they had to work with was rocks and sand."

He turned to Remy. "So. Are you staying with us?"

Remy blinked. His conversation with Biri-Daar the night before had unsettled him. On the one hand, he felt that of course he would go with them; they had saved his life. On the other, he had an errand to complete.

On a third hand rested the questions Biri-Daar had raised.

"No," he said. "I will buy a horse and go to Toradan. I committed to this errand."

"Let him go," Lucan said.

Keverel took a swallow of Iriani's liquor. "Lucan, bury your grudge," he said. "It is no right act to let a boy go off and die out of an overdeveloped sense of obligation."

"I am not a boy," Remy said. "You didn't think I was a boy when I fought with you."

Iriani laughed. "As a matter of fact, we did. You fought as a boy fights, all arm and no brain. But that's good. At least you have the strength in your arm. The brain for the fight comes later."

"Where are you going to get money for a horse?" Kithri asked, eyes wide and expression so serious that Remy knew he was being mocked. "If you leave now, you aren't entitled to a share of the spoils."

Remy couldn't quite tell if she was serious about this. "That is the code," Keverel said. "But surely we could make an allowance given the circumstances."

"Ha! The boy who called me a coward is finding his own cowardice," Lucan said. "At least that's what it seems like to me."

Coming from Lucan, this stung. Remy bit back his first reply and considered the situation anew. "Biri-Daar," he said. "Do you still think that—?"

"Yes," she said. "If you go into the wastes alone, you will not survive to reach Toradan. And if you do, you will not leave Toradan alive. Bahamut has brought us together.

Keverel would say Erathis. I believe we should show your box to the Mage Trust at Karga Kul. We can trust them, and their magic is powerful enough to discover what lies inside."

"So he draws demon's eyes and we're going to invite him along," Lucan said. "Biri-Daar, one of these days you're going to take in a stray and get us all killed."

"I would sooner die doing the right thing than live an extra day because I failed what I know to be right," Biri-Daar said. "Remy, I will say it again. The gods have brought us together."

Remy's childhood had not featured much in the way of devotion to gods. His mother was a quiet worshiper of Pelor, in the way that many citizens of Avankil whose recent ancestors had come in from the fields still followed that god of harvests and summer. Her devotion had become perfunctory, a matter of occasional holiday sprigs and leonine sunburst emblems stitched into the hems of the tunics she made. In the Quayside, religions mixed and turned into a kind of hybrid river creed, a constant barrage of hand gestures and muttered oaths, holy symbols and superstitious stories told over tankards of ale. Remy had soaked it all in without ever developing a firm idea of which god he would follow.

Even so, Biri-Daar's idea that the gods had brought him together with her party gave Remy pause. He had been on the brink of death, and now he lived, thanks to a dragonborn paladin of Bahamut and the healing magic of the Erathian Keverel. Something greater than Remy was at work here . . . and he feared that Biri-Daar's dark assessment of his mission was correct. Why had the demon's eye been keyed to look for him? What was it he carried?

Remy was brave but not a fool. He did not want to die as a pawn in another man's game.

He looked around. Every race that made a home in the Dragondown was here, selling everything that could be grown, made, or built—by hands or magic.

"Have an apple," Iriani said, tossing him one. Remy caught it and bit into it.

It was beginning to seem as if they were commanding him to come along, and that feeling made Remy resist even though he was starting to think accompanying them to Karga Kul was the best way forward. He didn't want to be forced into it, though. "I'll stay with you," he said, meaning *until I figure out what's going on.* "If you can lend me the money for a horse."

"No lending necessary," said Biri-Daar. She was eating what looked like an entire pig's leg and had a new pair of katars thrust in her belt. "We'll sell these things off," she added, jingling the pouch containing the dead gnolls' trinkets, "and you can buy a horse with your share."

First they found a jeweler who would take the ring, armband, and earring. It was simply done, and when Kithri's bartering skills faltered, the presence of Biri-Daar ensured a fair bargain. Then they wound their way deeper into the market, toward the shadowed older districts where layers of buildings were built upon each other, leaning in to block out the sun as the streets narrowed to alleys that approached the market keep from furtive angles. It was where magic was dealt and the spiretop drakes were as likely to be carrying messages as stealing coins from the counters of market stalls.

Iriani had done business with a broker of potions and talismans there before. They found him smoking a pipe outside his shop, frowning up as if the shadows of the buildings' upper stories over his head contained some bit of occult wisdom just beyond his understanding. "Roji," Iriani greeted him.

He turned to notice Iriani and winked. "What have you found in your peregrinations across this fine land of ours, my elf friend?"

On the way there, Biri-Daar had handed off the jawbone and demon's eye to Iriani. She stood close as the half-elf suggested they go inside and chat. "Not every bit of business needs to take place where everyone can see."

"Fine," Roji said. He knocked his pipe out and pulled back the curtain across his doorway. "But most of you have to stay outside. None of us will be able to breathe if you all come in. The dragonborn is too big, the halfling will steal everything she can see. I don't like holy men. So the ranger and the boy can come in."

Iriani grinned. "It's settled, then. Remy? Lucan? After you."

The three of them followed Roji into his shop. They sat on cushions around a low table. "What do you have?" Roji asked. "And why so worried about who might see? This is Crow Fork. Nothing will happen to you here."

"Something might happen to us as soon as we leave," Iriani said. "We would prefer to be sure."

"Sure," Roji chuckled. "What is sure? Let me see what you've brought."

He looked over the jawbone, tapping on each of the teeth. "Interesting," he said. "Not the kind of thing I usually traffic in, but I know what I can do with it. Was that it?"

"No," Iriani said. "This piece is a bit different." He handed Roji the demon's eye and watched as the merchant figured out what it was.

With a sharp breath, Roji set it down. "Gods," he said. "Why didn't you destroy it?"

"No way to be sure what would happen," Lucan said. "We know you can make something out of it, and Iriani said we could trust you not to let it find its way back to the wrong hands."

"Where did you find it?"

"Around the neck of a cacklefiend a day's ride east," Iriani said.

"And who put it there?"

"I haven't tried to find out. You may if you choose. What we want is to get rid of it and make sure it stays gone." Iriani leaned forward over the table. "Roji, I know you know what to do with things like this."

"You also know that whatever I do with it, its builder will know it was I who did it," Roji said.

"I have blinded it temporarily," Iriani said. "Act quickly and escape consequence. That's your way in any case, is it not?"

Roji didn't look inclined to laugh. "What gives you the right to ask this of me?"

"No right. But you can turn it into a mirror, can't you?"

A mirror? Remy didn't know what he meant. He had very little idea of what the conversation was about. Why didn't they just sell what they had to sell and get out of this cramped little space with its shelves of skulls and beakers, its racks of wands and staves imbued with various enchantments . . .

"A mirror," Roji repeated. "That might be useful." Thinking it over, he said, "I'll take it. But you might as well know that this isn't the only eye looking for him." He nodded in Remy's direction.

A cold knot formed in Remy's stomach. "How—"

"Hush," Roji said. "It's there for anyone to see. You've got something that people want, and some of its magic has bled onto you. Anyone on this street would be able to see it. Iriani, this one is going to cause you trouble."

"I believe that opinion has been expressed," Lucan said coolly. "But it appears to be of no concern to those whose opinions matter."

"There is much about his errand that we do not yet understand. Even so, Biri-Daar and Keverel feel—and I agree—that something beyond chance was at work when we ran across the boy in the wastes." Iriani looked at Remy. "Show him what you carry," he said.

Instinctively Remy shook his head. "No."

"I'm not saying give it to him, Remy. Show it to him. He'll tell us something we need to know."

"You can count on that," Roji said. "Even though you ought to be paying me both for taking the demon's eye and looking at whatever the boy has. Now come, boy. Show it."

Remy placed the box on the table but kept his hands close to it. Roji leaned over it and looked closely at the sigils on the lid. He waved a hand over it, his fingers making the familiar sign of a magic-detecting spell. "We already know it's magic," Lucan said.

"I know what you say you know," Roji said without looking at him. "I'm trying to figure out what you don't know you don't know, if you know what I mean . . . . Ah. Remy, do me a favor and touch the box."

Remy did. "Why?"

"One of the sigils on it, unless I'm mistaken, is an alarm. Whenever the box leaves your possession, someone somewhere knows about it." He made another pass over the box and the sigils glowed a soft red. "That one there," Iriani said, pointing at a corner of the box.

"I know," Roji said. "This box has a powerful maker, to invoke her."

"Invoke who?" Remy asked.

Roji and Iriani looked at each other. Then Iriani glanced over at Remy. "Tiamat," he said. "I had thought so before, but now am sure. We will need to tell Biri-Daar of this." Iriani rapped his knuckles on the table, the old elf invocation of good luck. "Remy, Lucan, I think Roji and I should finish our transaction in private."

Five minutes after Lucan and Remy rejoined the rest of the group in the magicians' alley, Iriani emerged and led them back toward the main gate. Remy had not said a word the entire time. Tiamat? How would the Dragon Queen be involved? What had Philomen gotten him into? When they were clear of the magicians' alley and out under the sun again, Iriani said, "That went about as well as could be expected. Roji is going to destroy the eye and create something from it."

He tapped Remy on the shoulder. "He also told me that young Remy here is a target for some kind of attention from the Abyss. And that some of the sigils on the box lid are invocations of Tiamat. But you knew that already, didn't you, Biri-Daar?"

"I suspected, yes," Biri-Daar said.

"Why didn't you tell me?" Remy asked.

"I will echo Remy's question. From all of us," Kithri said.

"There are many signs that mean one thing at one time and place and another when the time and place are different," Biri-Daar said. "I suspected but was not certain. Now that Roji has confirmed what I suspected, I am thinking that our path is clear."

Iriani looked thoughtful. "I am thinking that his original errand and ours might be related. Does anyone concur?"

"I am thinking that young Remy ought to stay here and work for his bread while we go off and finish what we have started," Lucan growled.

"You have made this clear," said Biri-Daar, in a tone that closed down that angle of conversation. "And now we have decided that Remy must come with us because if we let him go and his errand comes into conflict with ours, we will be fortunate if we have a chance to correct that error."

"We have decided?" Remy asked. "I haven't decided anything." The group looked back at him. No one spoke. "You make me sound a bit like a prisoner," Remy said, meaning it to come out as a joke but realizing as he said it that it hadn't.

"You are a bit like a prisoner," Kithri said before anyone else could say it in a more diplomatic way. "But we're giving you a full share and letting you buy a horse, so you've got it better than most prisoners. Might as well enjoy it."

The main stable of Crow Fork Market was built against the southwest corner of the wall and ran for more than a hundred yards along the inside of the western wall. The corner end of the building housed travelers' horses and the opposite end horses for sale. In between were the main sliding doors, through which the potential buyer of a horse entered into a tack and grooming area. At the back of it was a large drain that caught Remy's attention.

"We're in the middle of the desert. Where does the drain go?" he asked.

The stabler introduced himself as Wylegh. "There's an underground river," he said. "Where it comes out, no man knows. Or at least I don't. But the council has paid for sewers to be cut down to the caves where it flows. One of them runs from the main keep under here and on to those caves."

"Natural sciences are so interesting," Iriani said with a roll of his eyes. "Shall we get on with the horse-trading now?"

"Agreed. Although we can all do with a bit less sarcasm," Biri-Daar said. The horse merchant waddled back down the row of stalls, stopping at a barred door that marked the farthest end of the building from the corner of the wall. Shafts of light came down through narrow skylights, doing little to brighten the gloom in that part of the stable.

"Pick one you'd like to have a look at and we'll take it out in the yard," he said, tapping on the door. A soft scraping noise came from back near the front entrance and the merchant chuckled. "They're restless today."

Lucan and Iriani exchanged a glance. Remy caught it. Something elf, he thought. What were they noticing? Iriani touched the corner of his eye and looked back the way they'd come. Lucan dropped a hand to the hilt of his sword. Remy paused until they caught up with him. "What?" he asked.

Both of them shook their heads. "Not sure yet," Iriani said quietly. "But something here is not as it seems."

"Remy!" called Biri-Daar. "There are two here that aren't outrageously overpriced and might survive a week on the road. I'll let you choose which one."

Remy headed deeper into the shadowed interior of the stable. "I don't know much about horses," he said.

"Then bring the elves. You can trust them."

"Elves?" Lucan said. "There's only one elf here."

"You're both elves as far as I'm concerned," Biri-Daar said. "Especially in the way you bicker over nothing. Come look at these two horses."

It was just at the last moment, when the grate was completely off the stable drain, that Kithri noticed. "Lucan!" she cried out.

But the hobgoblins who had levered the drain cover off and were pouring up into the stable weren't after Lucan. They fanned out into an arc with Remy at its center. He drew his sword and waited for one of them to make the first move. They came up so fast out of the drain that at first none of the party noticed that not all of them were hobgoblins; then Iriani reached out a hand and balled it into a fist. "Back to hell, imp," he said.

In the second rank of advancing creatures, the farthest on the left went up in a pillar of flame. Horses all through the stable reared and shrieked.

"No fire!" screamed the stabler. "No fire, you'll burn us all!"

Biri-Daar turned and with the flat of her sword leveled him. He crumpled under a tack bench. "Betrayer. You deserve to burn," she said, and with the return swing of the sword cut down the closest of the hobgoblins.

There were so many of them it was hard to keep track in the darkness until one or more was already attacking; they moved in groups, blending into a collective impression of pitted blades, bared fangs, and eye-watering stench. Remy got a stable door at his back and found Kithri next to him. "Worse than the sewers they come out of," she said, wrinkling her nose. Remy barked a short surprised laugh. Then he struck where she did, hoping the halfling could see what he couldn't.

Iriani solved part of the light problem by blasting a torso-sized hole through the roof and letting sunlight in. The hobgoblins skirted the light, pressing their attacks from the shadows. Keverel contributed to the stable's illumination by pronouncing the name of his god, which created a glow around the imps that flanked the hobgoblins, keeping out of the way until they could strike with the advantage of surprise.

One such glow appeared just above and behind Remy's head. He ducked instinctively and the imp's tail stinger stabbed past his ear into the stable door.

Kithri was nearly as fast as the imp. In the split second it took the tiny devil to release its stinger from the wood, she cut its tail off and with a second stroke pinned it to the doorframe by its hand. The imp shrieked and vanished, but its invisibility was no protection with the twin streams of ichor running from its hand and the stump of its tail. Remy finished it and pivoted around to deflect a spear thrust from a hobgoblin. His return stroke sent it spinning away, to meet the head of Keverel's mace. In the light the hobgoblins were not so bold. They attacked, but cautiously, as if content to keep the party where they were, pinned in the stable.

And then it became apparent why, as a larger shape loomed behind the hobgoblins, forcing its way up through the sewer opening that was barely large enough to admit it. "Troglodyte," Keverel said grimly. "The Underdark must be close to the surface here."

The troglodyte, larger than Biri-Daar, finished forcing its way through the drain and lumbered toward them between the rows of whinnying horses that bucked and kicked at their enclosures as it passed. Quickly Remy took stock before it arrived. The imps were gone, and most of the hobgoblins had fled or were staying out of the way. Some of those that remained fell victim to the troglodyte, which struck out at them with its great stone club on its way toward Biri-Daar and Lucan, who stood to meet it. Kithri, Iriani, and Remy killed off the rest of the hobgoblins from distance while Keverel limped along the wall, wounded in the thigh.

The troglodyte mauler raised its club and brought it down against Biri-Daar's shield. The dragonborn staggered under the force of the blow, and the troglodyte pressed its temporary advantage, striking again and reaching with its free hand to claw Biri-Daar's shield away. Lucan ducked in from the side under its looping backswing, striking at its hamstrings.

Kithri scampered up the support beams and crabwalked along the timbers, trying to get a position above the troglodyte while Remy joined the front line, striking low as Lucan had. The troglodyte roared and shifted off its wounded leg, a wild swing from its club shattering the doorframe of the closest stable. It swung again, off balance; Biri-Daar parried its stroke and Lucan drove his sword into its side. Kithri, seeing opportunity, leaped from the ceiling corner and landed on its shoulder. As her feet touched on its shoulders, she lanced the troglodyte's eyes with twin daggers and leaped away again.

It spun, swinging blindly and missing everything but more timbers. Biri-Daar hacked its right arm mostly off.

Remy struck again at the back of its wounded leg. The troglodyte toppled over, its club crashing to the floor next to it. Lucan struck the death blow, opening its throat as it struggled to rise.

In a fury, he was standing over the groggy and terrified stabler Wylegh before the troglodyte had finished dying. "You've got some fast talking to do if you want to save your life, friend," he said, his bloodied sword hovering over Wylegh's face. "We walk in at your invitation, and the minute we get out of the light there are hobgoblins everywhere. You make a deal with them? Who paid you? What did they want?"

Biri-Daar and Iriani squatted on either side of Wylegh, adding to his fear. Against the other wall of stables, Keverel and Kithri collaborated on ministering to the cleric's wounds, Keverel whispering healing charms and Kithri sticking on plain old bandages.

"They wanted him," Wylegh babbled. He was pointing at Remy, who stood a little off to the side and behind the three interrogators. "That's all they said. Him, the messenger."

"Who said?" Lucan asked quietly, leaning his sword point a little closer.

"Imps. Imps. They made a deal, they made promises, but it wasn't just that, once they had me they wouldn't let go—"

"Fool," Biri-Daar said. "That's the only kind of man who makes a deal with anything that comes out of the Abyss."

"Easy for you to say," Wylegh said, glaring hard at her. "You dragonborn have got a bit of the Abyss in you, I reckon."

She stood over him for a long moment, so still that Remy was sure her next move would be a downward stroke to end Wylegh's life. Yet when she did move, it was to turn her back on him. "Remy, select a horse. Wylegh, tell me how much the horse costs. We will pay you. Then we will make sure that everyone in the market knows what you have done."

There was a pause. "That's a death sentence," Wylegh whispered.

"Hardly," Iriani said. "You'll just have to put on your traveling clothes and take one of your horses out on the road. Shouldn't be too hard. After all, that's how you got here, no?"

They left Wylegh there while Remy, with Lucan's aid, selected a horse. It was a fine, large gelding, dappled gray and remarkably calm given everything that had just happened outside its stable door. "How much?" Biri-Daar asked.

"Take it," Wylegh said. He hadn't moved from the floor near the tack bench where she had first knocked him over. "Just take it."

"I pay for what I take," she said. "Name a fair price."

Wylegh said nothing.

"Lucan," Biri-Daar said. "What is that horse worth?"

"What's it worth, or what would he charge for it?"

"What's it worth?"

"Eighty, ninety," Lucan said. "That's being a bit generous."

"Generosity never goes unrewarded in the end," Biri-Daar said. She produced a pouch and counted out the money onto the tack bench. "Traveling money for you," she said. "We'll be by for our horses first thing in the morning."

They took rooms for the night in a public house adjoining the keep, where the Council of Crow Fork itself guaranteed their safety and posted guards at doors and windows. "We have been fortunate," Biri-Daar said. "First, that we have come through these betrayals with so little suffering. Second, that Iriani is known to the council and could get us a hearing before them.

"And there might yet be a third bit of fortune," she finished. "Remy, for the third time. What is it you carry?"

"I told you I don't know," Remy said. "The vizier forbade me to look at it. I'm guessing he put some kind of protection on it to make sure I wouldn't."

"I am going to show you a few things that Roji showed me," Iriani said as he made a gesture over the box. The characters carved into its lid gave off a brief, pale glow. "You guess correctly," Iriani said. "There are several different charms on it. One so it can be found in the event . . ." He glanced up at Remy. "In the event that the courier doesn't finish his errand. Others to prevent scrying its contents or physically opening it. It's thoroughly trapped and ensorcelled, this box. Whoever is sending it—also whoever is receiving it—thinks it's very important."

"And someone involved in the creation of the box and the protection of its contents," Biri-Daar added, "has added an appeal to Tiamat's protection."

Turning back to the rest of the group, he said, "I should have seen this before. It was there to see, but I didn't know

what to look for. After talking to Roji and seeing imps . . ."
He trailed off.

"What about the imps?" Remy asked.

"They tend to appear as emissaries between certain underworld beings and certain corrupt mortals," Keverel said. "Certain forces are looking for you, or for what you carry. They are mostly looking along the Toradan Road, or we would have seen much stiffer resistance so far."

"Here's my guess," Iriani said. "There are two factions in Toradan. One is waiting for whatever Remy has because they want to use it the way it was intended to be used. The other is trying to prevent it from getting there because they want to use it as leverage for some other goal. Which is which and who is who, that we might find out more about."

"Either way," Lucan added with a tap on Remy's shoulder, "there's not much interest in keeping you alive."

"Put another way," Biri-Daar said, "Philomen is involved with demons. He may not know it, but that is the case. And if Tiamat's protection has been solicited . . ." She trailed off, lost in thought.

"What?" Iriani prompted. "Dragonish business, no doubt, but are we going to be seeing drakes in the skies on the way to Karga Kul?"

"No, not that," Biri-Daar said. "But I fear what might await us at the Bridge of Iban Ja."

She would say no more on the subject, and after a short meal taken mostly in silence, the party retired each to his or her own thoughts. Remy's head spun as he lay on the straw mattress. Imps? Tiamat? What was he carrying? Suddenly he wanted very much to go home and forget he had ever met the vizier of Avankil. The Quayside life was for him . . .

Yet when he dreamed, it was of places he had never yet seen in waking life.

———— ❖ ————

"The market is supposed to be a sanctuary," Keverel said with some sorrow the next morning. They were sitting around the central oasis. Once it had been a spring in the desert. After centuries of development, it was a rectangular pool, with stone steps built into all four sides so visitors could step down and fill their canteens while merchants and travelers haggled in the surrounding plaza. It reminded Remy of one of the courtyards of Avankil, where noblewomen under parasols gossiped while flanked by tiefling bodyguards, which were the current fashion in the city. Along one side of the oasis plaza, the keep loomed, extending to the market's north wall. The other three sides were lined with permanent houses and trading posts maintained by the Dragondown's established mercantile clans, interspersed with other clearinghouses of families from as far north as the Nentir Vale. In the plaza, Crow Fork Market had the aspect of a city coming to be. A hundred feet in any direction— save for into the keep itself—it looked like a bazaar again.

The spring itself was clear and cold and deep, water welling into it from a series of underwater caves. Incursions from those watery catacombs were not unknown, and the keep kept a detachment of guards on watch around the pool at all times.

"I wish I had come here sooner," Keverel went on. "Here I can feel the spirit of Erathis moving, creating civilization from the wilderness. But I fear the market's days as an oasis in the wastes are over."

"They've been over since before I was born, Keverel," Kithri said. "Any halfling could tell you that. Every month we get merchants coming to us because they'd rather risk the river than take their chances being overrun by hobgoblins at Crow Fork. You just never knew it because you've never been here."

"It's a problem for another time," Biri-Daar said. "Today we start moving again."

They replenished their stores and made a trip through an armorer's stall before returning to Wylegh's stable to take their horses. Lucan was annoyed at having to move on without taking advantage of Crow Fork Market's many opportunities to hoodwink drunken traveling gamblers. "What's the rush? We handled that filth easily enough. We can handle it again."

They walked inside the stable, past council guards posted at the door. Wylegh had disappeared, no one knew where; his duties were temporarily in the hands of one of the keep's grooms. Remy looked around, remembering the previous day's encounter. The hobgoblins were gone, as was the troglodyte. Part of the stable was collapsed from the troglodyte's mad swinging of its club, and streaks of gore stained the timbers here and there. Remy was struck by the idea that in a small way he had left his mark in Crow Fork Market. He had become a part of its history.

"That's exactly the point," Biri-Daar said to Lucan. "That was a test. Someone is after what we're carrying. Whatever force that is, it was willing to sacrifice these to find out our strength." She looked down into the open drain, the stones at its edge chipped and cracked by the troglodyte's passage. "The next test will be sterner."

"Then you should go and make sure that there is no one left to offer such a test," came a voice from behind them.

Remy turned with the rest of the party. A brawny and bearded man, wearing the insignia of the keep council, met their gaze. "Biri-Daar of the Knights of Kul," he said. "You I know, and Iriani too. Your other companions I do not. I am Zegur of the Crow Fork Council. Your presence here has caused some difficulties."

"Zegur," Biri-Daar said with a slight bow. "Whatever difficulties accompanied us were not our doing. The market's enemies are many."

"True," Zegur said. "I would ask you to reduce their number, as you did yesterday."

He stepped to the edge of the drain and looked down. Then he produced a rolled sheet of vellum from a case at his belt. "This is a map of the highest level of the sewers," he said. "I would ask that you go in and determine where the hobgoblins and their imp companions entered."

"We are on a pressing errand to Karga Kul," Biri-Daar said.

"Wylegh the stabler has been questioned," Zegur said. "He admits that the ambush was targeted at one of your group. I do not care who or for what reason. I care only that Crow Fork Market was breached. Since that breach occurred as a result of your presence, fairness demands that you seal it again."

"Crawling in the sewers?" Kithri said. "Not me. I'll go underground if I have to, but I refuse sewage. Refuse it."

"All we'll find down there is a bad smell and boring creatures with too many teeth and not a bit of loot worth carrying off," Lucan said.

Keverel was nodding. "Without the flippancy, I agree. We should move on."

Zegur remained unmoved. "The council anticipated your reluctance. You will be paid. If you refuse, your horses will be seized to cover the damage to the stable and the disruption to commerce." He folded his arms and waited.

Biri-Daar took her time answering, and when she did, her anger was barely checked. "The Knights of Kul have ridden to the defense of this market, and many of our number lie buried in the desert beyond its gates. Even so, you would treat us in this manner?"

"I protect Crow Fork Market," Zegur said. "Those who bring threats to the market, they must also be certain those threats leave with them. I would be a poor steward if I did not find out where your troglodyte pursuer came from. You owe the market that much."

"We owe the market—" Iriani began. Biri-Daar raised a hand to silence him.

"We will go," she said. "But it will go hard with you if this delay does harm to our greater mission. Know this before you insist."

Zegur shifted his weight and nodded toward the drain. "I must insist."

Biri-Daar turned her back on him. "This is likely an enormous waste of precious time," she said. "Let us do it as quickly as it may be done."

One by one they dropped into the drain, landing on a smooth stone floor. As Zegur had said, the passage they found was no longer used as a sewer. Directly below the stable drain, a vertical pipe drained the stable's waste down and away. To either side of them stretched dry and flat passage. By torchlight they clustered around Keverel as he unfolded the map. "Let's go this way, toward the wall," he said, pointing to the left. "The other direction siphons into sewers that are in use. Not even hobgoblins would swim for long in that."

"We'd fit right in with the rest of the sewage after the way Zegur treated us," Lucan complained.

"No matter," Biri-Daar said. "He was correct. If we brought a threat to this place, it is our responsibility to end that threat."

Moving quickly, they followed the passage. Iriani lit the tip of his wand and illuminated each side passage they encountered. All were too small for a troglodyte to have traversed. Soon they came to what must have been the edge of the market, and there they found a rough hole torn in the passage wall. By Iriani's light, they saw that a short tunnel had been excavated from the passage to a natural cave. "Now we will have our answer," Biri-Daar said as she plunged in.

The floor of the cave was ancient silt, and heavily tracked. The hobgoblins and troglodyte had clearly come this way. "Enough," Keverel said. "Let Zegur send sappers down to collapse this, and let us be on our way."

"If it was dug out once, it may be dug out again," Biri-Daar answered. "We must find the outlet and tell Zegur where to watch."

"Sometimes I wish you were a bit less of a paladin," Kithri said.

"Sometimes I wish you were a bit less of a thief. Now let's go."

The cave was broad and winding, easy enough for all of them to stand up in. Here and there were remnants of long-forgotten camps and graves. They kicked through these to see what might be learned or looted, but found nothing. The cave descended slightly, and water began to seep from the walls. "Carefully now," Keverel breathed. His holy symbol had begun to glow.

Emerging into a rough oval chamber, they saw a flash of movement. One of Kithri's knives flashed in the magical light as she threw it, but it clanged among the rocks on the far side. "After it," Biri-Daar commanded, and they picked up their pace. "If it is a sentry, we must not let it get out a warning."

Kithri and Lucan were the fastest of them, especially in the darkness. They were across the chamber and out of sight before the other four had gotten halfway over the broken floor. Remy stuck close to Iriani, just behind Biri-Daar with Keverel right behind them. Ahead of them the chamber narrowed to a passage whose walls Remy could touch simultaneously with extended hands. "Tight fit for a troglodyte," Iriani commented.

"It couldn't have come any other way," Biri-Daar said.

Shouts sounded from ahead of them, and the clash of steel. They ran as best they could over the slippery rocks, coming into a large flattened chamber just as a thrown spear deflected from high on the wall to their right. Remy saw Kithri dodging and feinting between two hobgoblins, their axes striking pieces of the rocks away in showers of sparks. He closed on one of them and ran it through as it raised its axe for another stroke. The axe flew from its hands and struck him on the shoulder, numbing his sword arm. He cried out and the other hobgoblin lunged toward him—then slipped and skidded as Kithri deftly slashed the tendons at the back of its knee. As it hit the ground, she was on it, cutting its throat.

"Where's Lucan?" Biri-Daar called. Remy worked his sword from the dead hobgoblin with his left hand and hefted it. He wondered how well he would be able to fight. Waves of pain radiated from the point of his shoulder.

"Gone sinister?" Keverel asked, coming up next to him.

Remy didn't understand the word, but he tapped the sword hilt against his right arm. "I can't feel it," he said, although already sensation was returning to his fingers. "But I think I'm all right."

"Good thing. There might be more ahead."

Quickly they looked through the room, finding nothing but three other dead hobgoblins. The others had gone ahead in pursuit of Lucan. Remy and Keverel followed, and a short distance ahead found the rest of the party gathered around yet another dead hobgoblin. "A commander," Biri-Daar said as they approached. "See the brands on its cheek."

In the dim light Remy could see what looked like simple runes on the dead hobgoblin's skin, the pale scar standing out against the bristly hair that covered most of the creature's cheeks and jaw. "I hate to say it, but Zegur might be right," Iriani said. "If there's a commander down here, one of the local warlords is planning something."

Feeling was returning to Remy's arm, and a bone-deep ache settled into his shoulder where the head of the axe had struck. He worked his fingers to get the blood moving and limber up the arm again. He thought he'd be able to use it if more of the hobgoblins appeared. In another half-hour, they emerged in a slot canyon in the wastes. Once a river had flowed there, but its sole remnant was a ribbon of sand on the canyon floor, churned by the booted feet of hobgoblins and their beasts and littered by their garbage.

"Now we know," Lucan said after they had looked around to make sure they weren't walking into yet another ambush. "Who's going to report back to our charming host, Zegur?"

"I'll go," Kithri said. "It wasn't so bad after all."

They climbed out of the canyon and got their bearings. Crow Fork Market was away to the southwest. "We are not far from the road to the Bridge of Iban Ja," Biri-Daar said. "Remy and I will go toward the road. Everyone else return to Crow Fork Market quickly. Report to Zegur, but do not wait; if he will not see you right away, give the report to one of his secretaries. Gather the horses and supplies. Meet us before sundown."

"At least we won't have to hurry," Lucan grumbled.

"Come on, Lucan," Keverel said after a brief whispered consultation with Biri-Daar. "We have spent enough time as it is, and time is dear."

Leaving Biri-Daar and Remy, the rest of the party wound their way back down into the canyon and disappeared into the caves. "Let us walk," Biri-Daar said to Remy. "They will be back sooner than we think. The road is this way."

They walked west through the wastes, almost immediately drawing the attention of carrion birds that drafted in sweeping arcs above them. "You would think they knew something," Remy said.

"Carrion-eaters are forever optimistic," Biri-Daar said. "And why not? Creatures are always dying."

After that they walked in silence until they reached the road. It cut north and south, as straight as its makers could lay the stones. Remy and Biri-Daar found shade and sat where they could see the road and any approaching traveler could see them. After a while, Remy gave voice to the question that had been rattling around in his head since the canyon. "Why did you want me to stay?"

"You have a decision to make," Biri-Daar said. "And I imagined you would want to ask another few questions before making it."

"Here's my first question: You could have refused Zegur, but you didn't. Why not?"

"Because despite his base motives, what he said was true. I could not leave Crow Fork without putting right what problems our presence had caused."

"Even though it delayed your . . ." Remy thought about how to continue. "What is it you're doing in Karga Kul, anyway?"

"Saving the city from being overrun by demons." Biri-Daar spoke matter-of-factly.

"Demons?" Remy repeated. "Then why are we worried about hobgoblins?"

"Bahamut demands much of his followers," Biri-Daar said. "My pledge to him, and to the Knights of Kul, is not conditional. Crow Fork Market in its way is as important as any of the cities and settlements in the Dragondown. Each of them is a pocket of light striving against the darkness that pervades this world. I would be abandoning my oaths and all that I believe if I did not do my part to ensure its survival."

She saw the look on his face and smiled—an unsettling expression on a dragonborn. "That might be too abstract. Put another way, how do you know the demons and hobgoblins aren't working together? Remember the demon's eye, and the imps we killed in the stable. Everything is connected here, Remy. And you are connected to it as well, because of what you carry."

"What do you think it is?"

Biri-Daar shrugged. "I have no idea. But if demons are after it, I would very much like to know, and I do not think it would be wise to let it—or you—wander off into the wastes. That is why I think it's important that you come to

Karga Kul and let the Mage Trust examine it. When the rest of our party arrives, you must make your final decision. I will say no more about it."

She was true to her word, not speaking for the next two hours. Remy turned every possibility over in his mind, weighing his obligation against everything he had seen and learned since leaving Avankil. He was being hunted. Now he believed that. The sun tracked across the sky, and Biri-Daar silently offered him a drink of water. Remy thought of the Dragondown, the marvels that might await him if he went to Karga Kul—and the wrath of the vizier, who would certainly kill him if he did not go to Toradan.

Unless the vizier had been trying to kill him all along.

I could just leave the box in the sand, he thought at one point. Bury it, or throw it into a canyon. Let someone else find it. Let the hobgoblins have it.

But Biri-Daar's resolute devotion to her code gave him pause. Could he really do that, not knowing what the box contained?

In the end, when the four riding figures appeared in the distance leading two other horses, Remy realized that he knew two things. One was that Philomen had put his life in danger. The other was that Biri-Daar and the rest of them had saved it.

"North or south?" Biri-Daar asked him when they had met the rest of the party and all six of them were in the saddle and waiting on the road.

Remy took a deep breath. "North," he said.

BOOK II
THE BRIDGE

They rode north on a road sometimes covered by sweeping drifts of sand. Remy looked over his shoulder, riding second to last with only Keverel behind him. The road seemed endless in both directions, and he felt as if he was leaving behind something of his former self the farther he rode into the unknown reaches of the Dragondown Coast. The world was his to take.

"Pretty clear which roads find travelers and which don't, eh?" Lucan said. "Here we go into the real wilderness."

"At least we'll get out of this damned desert," Iriani said.

Kithri waved toward the Serrata. "In the foothills, before we start the climb up into those," she said, "the country is beautiful."

"What about after?" Remy asked.

"After? You mean on the Crow Road?" Kithri shook her head. "Never been. Never wanted to go. But," she sighed, "here I am, going. You can thank Biri-Daar for that."

"There is no collar around your neck," Biri-Daar said without looking back.

Kithri rolled her eyes. Around them, the flatness of Crow Fork was giving way to a more broken country. Monoliths of ancient rock stood angled against each other, product of no mortal's work. The ground, flat enough to bowl on back near Crow Fork, was heaved and cross-hatched with small gullies. The road cut through some of them and wound along the edges of others. The sand that maddened travelers on the road to Toradan disappeared and clumps of hardy scrub sprouted at the bases of rocks and in the shelter of gullies. Around them the landscape came to hard-bitten life.

And ahead of them, far ahead, the highest peaks of the Draco Serrata gleamed white in the morning sun.

"I thought the Crow Road was some kind of demon-infested gauntlet of horrors," Remy said. "This isn't terrible-looking country."

Keverel made a sign in the air before touching his heart and his forehead. "Do not joke about it."

"We're not on the Crow Road yet," Lucan said. "This is the road that leads to the Crow Road. It comes to an end at Iban Ja's bridge. Once we cross that, then we're on the Crow Road."

"Who's Iban Ja?" Remy asked. That was the third or fourth time someone had mentioned the name. "And why is it his bridge?"

The series of great wars between the dragonborn kingdom of Arkhosia and Bael Turath, that of the tieflings, brought down both empires in the end, but amid the blood and suffering shone acts of impossible heroism. Travelers knew these stories and traded them over mugs of ale and the picked-over bones of supper. Remy, who had traveled little and paid less attention to the events of the world beyond Avankil's walls and docks, had yet to hear those stories. His five companions looked to each other with slight smiles at his naivete; by acclamation Iriani was chosen to tell the story.

"Why me?" he asked.

Kithri pointed to each of the party in turn. "Biri-Daar has no sense of romance and would only fume about the tieflings. Lucan is the only elf in the world who can't sing, and he wouldn't be fair because the story involves both Melora and Corellon. Keverel is a cleric and you should never have a cleric tell your stories. I know too many different versions of the story and am not honest enough to be trusted. Remy doesn't know any versions of the story and is probably too honest to tell it well even if he did. That leaves you, Iriani, even though you have elf blood in you as well."

"I'll tell the story as it came to me," Iriani said.

Kithri nodded. "So start telling. It's a long way to the bridge."

The Solstice War between Arkhosia and Bael Turath was not its own war at all, but a change in plans. Yet it was called its own war because of the periods of quiet on either side of it, and because it decisively changed everything that came after. Both combatants were exhausted and winter was on the way; they fell back to their lines, entrenched, and got down to the business of preparing themselves for spring, when snow would retreat from the mountain passes and the gods would give their signals for the great war to begin again.

Then a midwinter thaw changed everything.

Later, the survivors would blame a dispute among the gods Melora, Corellon, and the Raven Queen. The Queen, it was said, was angry that the fighting had stopped so soon because the battlefields were so very good to her black-feathered subjects. But she loved winter too, and was torn between the pleas of the ravens and the immutable paths of the sun and stars.

"Melora," she said. "The wilderness is yours to command and to love. What of this great bridge the Arkhosians have built across the Gorge of Noon?"

"The Arkhosians are builders," Melora said. "I cannot interfere with their nature any more than a beaver's." In truth, though, her heart stormed at the thought of the bridge.

"But surely the gorge's majesty would be restored by the destruction of the bridge," the Raven Queen purred. "Surely you could bring this about. The Arkhosians and the forces of Bael Turath are camped not twenty miles apart, in the lower vales of the Serrata with the bridge between them. Neither force wants to move farther away lest the other claim the bridge and the only passage over the gorge for fifty leagues in either direction.

"In these lower vales, winter is not so bad," she went on. "But it is still deep in snow, and the passes choke in avalanches. Here is what I need from you."

Melora's temper was as wild as the wilderness and seas that she commanded on the earth. She knew what the Raven Queen was doing when she leaned in a little too close and spoke with a husk in her voice. She knew what the Queen was offering and what she was asking in return.

And wild, untamed Melora thought it a workable bargain.

"All I ask of you," the Raven Queen said, whispering into Melora's ear as her heart leaped and tossed like the storm-driven surf, "is that you ask a little favor of Corellon . . ."

Corellon who could sing stones into life! Corellon who lent power to the singer's voice and the artist's eye, the mage's spells and the sculptor's chisel!

Corellon, who when the seasons were divided at the beginning of the world begged for spring and received it because along with it came the knowledge that everything must ultimately die, that the green abundance of spring is the flare of a candle cupped against the everlasting wind and dark of death. This knowledge is the fuel of art, of thoughts of beauty, of all sorceries light and dark. Corellon is the patron of those who know they will die but are determined that they will bloom and learn and love first.

It is said that Corellon lives in a castle whose rations and dimensions haunt the dreams of artists, adorned with tapestries telling stories the troubadors can never find tongue to repeat. Vine-haired and stone-toothed, Melora strode through the arches of this castle and found Corellon, eyes closed, listening to the music made by dust motes dancing in sunlight.

"How would you like to push the Raven Queen a little?" she asked. Corellon's eyes opened. Melora scattered the motes and their music jangled into chaos. "How would you like to have a little spring in her winter?"

"If she has sent you, there is more to this offer than what you're telling," Corellon answered. "And I can smell her on you, which makes it a simple matter to guess what is motivating your wild little heart."

"To each her reasons," Melora said. "Spring in the high country, just for a week. Think of it! What new life might grow, what stories might the peoples of the world tell of your strength in the face of the Raven Queen's deepest winter?"

"And why is she willing?" Corellon asked.

"She is a good queen to her subjects, who belong to me as well," Melora said. "The ravens are hungry."

"Well," Corellon said. Already he had begun to think of the songs that might be sung. "What the Queen offered you, will you offer me?" he asked, archly, as the sculptures around them began to dance.

That the gods have human desires is known to every child—else why should they have given those desires to us? Ah, the wilderness is fickle!

A southwest wind curled over the passes at sunrise the next day, bringing with it smells of the lower territories where winter was forbidden. For nine days it blew. At the end of the third, each army sent scouts up the passes toward the gorge. Avalanches drove them back.

At the end of the sixth day, each army sent scouts again. They returned, most of them, reporting that the way would be clear if the freakish thaw held for another three days.

And hold for three days it did.

On the morning of the tenth day, the armies marched. On the morning of the twelfth day, they stood on either side of the bridge. By noon of the twelfth day, the bridge ran knee-deep with the blood of human and tiefling, dragonborn and dwarf. The fighting on the bridge went on into the night as both sides mustered sorcerous lights to guide their armies lest they wake up in the morning and find the other side possessing the bridge.

Centuries before, the bridge had been the Arkhosians' mightiest work of engineering, a monument to the vision of their emperors and the building genius of the dwarves who lived in the caves along the gorge. It was a thousand feet long and wide enough for twenty men to walk across abreast, with buttresses curving down into the walls of the gorge hundreds of feet below. It was large enough that all manner of creatures had taken up residence in its stone eaves and crevices, its drains and arches. The tiefling shock troops of Bael Turath had long since slaughtered the Noon Gorge dwarves, keeping only those as slaves who might teach the Turathian architects the secrets of stone that dwarves seemed to be born with—yet the secrets of the bridge over the gorge remained known only to one man, because only that one man had performed the magics that bound its stones together. The bridge, too, had been a symbol of peace between Arkhosia and Bael

Turath . . . or perhaps it had only come to seem such during a pause between two wars. When it did not carry soldiers, it carried caravans—and then in times of war, soldiers carried back as spoils what the merchants had once carried as goods.

The greatest wizard of the Arkhosians was Iban Ja, confidant to emperors, Seer of Infinitudes, and magical overseer of the dwarf engineers who had built the bridge. He watched the battle from a cliffside perch on the Arkhosian side of the gorge, participating as the battle demanded and commanding the ranks of Arkhosian wizards who found their way across the bridge with the armed soldiery. Iban Ja was a thousand years old, the stories went. Iban Ja had never been born, but made from the bodies of ten great wizards who gave their lives knowing that they would be part of the greatest wizard ever to walk the earth, the other stories went. None of them were true and all of them spoke the truth of the Arkhosians' regard for him.

He looked down as dawn broke on the thirteenth day and saw the best of the Arkhosian troops, the mighty dragonborn warriors known as the Knights of Kul. A hundred selected from ten thousand, they were the finest foot soldiers in the known world. Any one of them could cut their way through ten men and be laughed at if they got a scratch in the fight.

In the darkness, the Knights had established a foothold on the Turathian side of the bridge. In the hours before dawn they had fought their way to solid ground on the other side of the bridge, laying waste to the Turathian opposition.

And as the sun shone from a bed of clouds in the eastern sky, Iban Ja found himself seeing a fresh new telling of a very old story.

The Knights drove forward, supported by sword and foot of the regular Arkhosian expeditionary force. Behind them, support units set up defensive positions along the ledges of the approach canyon to protect the way back to the bridge. Already that morning the Knights were five hundred yards up the canyon road that, in another hundred miles, would lead to Crow Fork and the market—where, it was said, some of the surviving Noon Gorge dwarves were building labyrinthine dungeons at the request of the market's council. The Turathian forces were shattered and in full retreat.

But below the bridge, from the mouths of caves drilled out of the living rock so long-dead Noon Gorge dwarves could build the bridge's arched buttresses, came Turathian sappers. Some of them were human. Some were tiefling. And some, saw Iban Ja, were cambion. It was not the first time he had seen cambion on the other side of a battlefield. He imagined it would not be the last. Yet seeing them there, at the footings of the bridge, Iban Ja felt as if something vital had escaped him and could never be reclaimed.

Clouds covered the sun and wind howled down the gorge from the north. The Raven Queen's affections turned elsewhere as she saw that her favorites would be fed.

Iban Ja spoke instructions to a stone that carried his voice to every wizard who fought under his command. They turned as one and directed their attacks toward the sappers in the caves, besieging them with magical energies designed to kill the living without damaging the stone underpinnings of the bridge. At that moment, the Turathians played their last card.

On the walls of the gorge above the bridge, stones began to move. They shifted, spread wings, reared fanged heads on long necks, uncoiled tails tipped with hooked stingers. Ridden by cambion hellswords, these fell wyverns swooped down from the heights to tear into the ranks of Arkhosian wizards. The wizards fought back, but the distraction proved critical. Cambion magi worked magics upon the bodies of their tiefling servants while Iban Ja devoted all of his powers to destroying the wyverns. Incinerated, arrow-shot, lightning-struck, they fell from the sky to die on the stones of the bridge or in the depths of the churning river far below.

And as Iban Ja and the Arkhosian wizards returned their attention to the cambion magi, a great shudder ran through the stones of the bridge. Cambion magic drew the ghosts of dead dwarves from the stones and their spectral picks crashed into the most vulnerable seams, where buttress met cliffside and Arkhosian engineering met the ageless genius of nature.

Iban Ja called down a raven that wheeled over the battlefield. "It is your Queen that has done this, is it not?" he demanded.

The raven squawked but consented to speak. "Is this not an unnatural spring?" it answered. "And does not the wilderness rebel against the works of mortals? Beware your blame, wizard. Look you to yourself."

It cast itself back into the air over the bridge as the last words left its mouth, and the great buttresses on the

Turathian side of the gorge slipped, cracked, and fell with a sound like an earthquake into the misty depths of the Gorge of Noon. The span sagged, leaned, split two-thirds of the way across and carried Arkhosian support troops and the bodies of the fallen after the broken buttresses. Unsupported, the remainder of the span jutted creaking out into empty space for a moment longer than Iban Ja thought he could endure—then with a sound like a peal of thunder the entire span broke off and fell end over end into the gorge. The bodies of Iban Ja's wizard corps fell with it. Those few who managed to fly, and managed to survive the barrage of tiefling arrows, returned to the Arkhosian side to watch in horror as the final part of Bael Turath's great trap sprang.

From every cave, every notch, every sheltered space below a fallen rock poured tiefling and human, cambion and lesser devil. Like ants they poured blackly over the rocks, overwhelming the Arkhosian troops and closing like a flood around the island formed by the Knights of Kul. Rallying to a defensive posture, the Knights saw the collapse of the bridge. Instantly they knew what had happened. In the falling of the stones they saw their deaths, and with useless clarity they understood that even the most seasoned of soldiers can fall victim to the thrill of battle.

It began to snow. The raven that had answered Iban Ja's questions wheeled over the broken stub of the bridge.

He killed it with a flick of his fingers. The Raven Queen's fury would follow him beyond his grave, but Iban Ja did not care for her regard. He rose into the skies over the gorge, flicking aside arrows from the other side, summoning and mastering the wild energies of the storm that blew down the gorge from the great peaks of the Draco Serrata. He did not expect to live through the next hour, but Iban Ja had done a great deal of living; he was interested now in doing a little dying for the empire whose service had dominated his life.

The storm's winds blew around him, and Iban Ja breathed them in. He found the elemental language of their strength, taught himself to speak it, and commanded the winds to his service.

On the other side of the gorge, the Knights fought their desperate holding action. They saw Iban Ja suspended over the depths and believed without question that he would come to their rescue. Never before had the Knights needed rescue. Perhaps they never would again. Iban Ja commanded the armies on the Arkhosian side of the gorge to rally and prepare. "This will be my last command," he said. "In the name of every dwarf that carved you, every Arkhosian who died when you fell, every ghost whose unquiet cry shivered your stone, I say to this bridge: Know me. I am Iban Ja. And with the power of the winter wind, I command you rise."

Lightning crackled through the driving snow. The rumbling of a thousand stones echoed up along the walls of the gorge in counterpoint to the thunder and the howling of the wind. Iban Ja became the center of a whirlwind, the snow spinning so tightly and so densely around him that it appeared to the astonished soldiers as if he had spun himself a cocoon of snow and wind. Below them, blocks of stone rose from the depths of the gorge, the Noon's waters pouring from them as they came once again to the level of the roads on either side.

No single mortal could rebuild the bridge whose building had taken the work and lives of thousands. Yet such was the power of Iban Ja that he himself, as his body was swept away by his icy whirlwind, brought stones out of the depths and held them there. By force of will and magic, by strength of belief and essence, the stone rose and leveled and hung in space as the cocoon of snow spun apart and revealed that Iban Ja's body had vanished. Across the gorge stretched a hopscotch pattern of stone blocks, snowswept and icy. On one side, the armies of Bael Turath threatened to overwhelm the Knights of Kul; on the other, the massed forces of Arkhosia stood waiting the order to charge.

The horn of Arkhosia's generals blew, its note clear and piercing through the canyon winds. Arkhosia's armies charged. The hordes of Turathian tieflings rose to meet them. The sky filled with arrows and spears, magical energies and the black wings of wyvern and raven. On stones held up by the magical will of Iban Ja, the Solstice War of Arkhosia and Bael Turath came to its awful climax.

The day's ride had brought the party to a saddle between two peaks along the first row of mountains, with the foothills behind them and the higher ranges of the Serrata ahead. "How much of that is true?" Remy asked when they were settled around the night's fire.

"All of it," Iriani said.

"The gods sport with mortals that way?"

"And with one another," Kithri chuckled.

"Some of them do," Keverel said. "Some of them do not."

"Oh yes, Erathis would never do something like that," Lucan said. "Or Bahamut, that pompous old lizard. He's the most prudish of the gods. They see him at their god-feasts and wait until he leaves so the real fun can begin."

Biri-Daar had been silent all day, while Iriani told the story and then while they set up their camp and took care of the horses. Still without saying a word, she caught Lucan a hard backhanded slap to the side of the head. The blow knocked him sprawling, but he rolled and came up with a knife in one hand and his sword in the other. Biri-Daar didn't look up.

"I don't care for blasphemy," she said.

"And I don't care for paladins thinking they have the right to put their hands on me," Lucan said. He leveled the sword at Biri-Daar. She put a piece of jerked meat in her mouth, chewed it carefully, and swallowed. All the while Lucan's sword hand stayed rock-still and his eyes never left her.

Biri-Daar took a drink of water, then said, "I apologize, then. But were things to happen the same way again, I don't believe I would do anything differently."

The two of them looked at each other. Some of the tension drained from the moment. Remy realized he had been holding his breath. He exhaled, slowly, not wanting to call attention to how nervous he had been.

"Didn't someone buy . . . Lucan. It was you, wasn't it, who bought the spirits back at the market? Share them around," Kithri said. "It's going to be a hard enough trip up the Crow Road without the two of you killing each other the whole way." She made an insistent beckoning motion. "Come on. Don't stand around waving your sword when you're not going to use it. Kill something tomorrow. Tonight, let's have a drink."

She kept talking, and eventually Lucan pulled the bottle out of his saddlebag. It went around the fire and the mood lightened as the sky darkened. "Who won, anyway?" Remy said in the middle of a conversation about the kinds of fish that could be caught in the estuary of Karga Kul.

"Who won what?" Iriani asked.

"The battle. The Solstice War."

"Arkhosia, I think," Iriani said. But right away Biri-Daar contradicted him.

"At the time, it looked that way," she said quietly. "But it is not always clear who has won a battle when the crows are still picking the bones of the dead."

Kithri started singing a vulgar song about a tiefling whorehouse, just to change the mood. Everyone laughed except Biri-Daar. By the time the moon was directly overhead and they knew they had to sleep, Lucan's mood had swung all the way around. "I'll watch first," he offered. Nobody argued.

❖

In the morning Remy woke first, to find Lucan still sitting exactly as he had been when Remy fell asleep. "You took two watches?" he asked.

"One long one," Lucan said with a slight shake of his head. "The peace does my mind good. And elves don't need sleep the way you do."

Remy stretched and poked at the coals of the fire. "Then you can take all of the watches," he said.

"I didn't say we didn't need rest," Lucan said. "Just that we don't sleep the way humans do."

"How do you rest, then?"

"You might call it a kind of meditation," Lucan said. "To those who don't do it, it's difficult to explain." Fog sat in the valleys between their campsite and the rise into the next range. Remy could just see the road on the other side, winding its way up and to the north. They had been traveling west and northwest for the last day or so.

"How long before we get to the bridge?" he asked.

Lucan shrugged. "I've never seen it. Only heard stories. And the only times I've been to Karga Kul, I've taken ship from Furia."

"Furia," Remy repeated. It was the fifth of the grandiosely named Five Cities of the Gulf, the southern bookend to Saak-Opole in the north with Karga Kul, Avankil, and Toradan in the Gulf's interior. Of them, only Avankil and Karga Kul were real cities; the others might once have been greater, but had become only glorified towns. Still, Remy was smitten with the idea of it. One day, he resolved, I will go to Furia. I will see all five, and those beyond the Gulf.

"I can see what you're thinking," Lucan said. "The world's a marvelous place, for certain. On the other hand, the world can also make you very dead very fast in a very large number of different ways. So keep the stars out of your eyes, boy. Learn."

Remy nodded as he flipped twigs into the fire. He blew on them until they flared and caught. "I have learned," he said. "Already."

Lucan cracked a smile, a rarity for him as far as Remy could tell. "I think you have. There's always more, though. Don't forget that. You've got a good spark in you," he added, standing up and stretching. "You might go a long way if you live through this first trip." The elf cracked his knuckles and went to see to the horses. Often, Remy had observed, he did this before the others awoke. The storied elf affinity for animals and the natural world was strong in Lucan; Remy was starting to think that it made him unfit for the company of the speaking races.

"What's Furia like?" he asked.

"I think it's my favorite of the Five," Lucan said. "Although I hate cities, or any settlements, really. So that's something like asking me what my favorite aspect of Orcus is."

The name of the demonic prince took some of the gleam out of the morning. "Odd comparison," Remy said.

Lucan grinned again as he looked at one of the horses' teeth. "They told you never to use his name, am I right? That he might hear and be angry that you weren't being reverent enough? I've heard that as well. The truth is, Remy, Orcus doesn't care what anyone says about him. His human minions might, or might pretend to so Orcus will take notice of them and transform them into one of his hierophants.

But if someone told you that Orcus would come and eat you because of something you said, they were just trying to scare you. Who was it, your mother?"

"It's been a long time since I saw my mother," Remy said.

"Me too," Lucan said. His smile faded. "So who was it?"

"Philomen," Remy said.

"The vizier?"

"Once I was taking a sealed scroll from his chambers to a ship waiting to sail for . . . I think it was Karga Kul," Remy recalled. "He told me to run as fast as I could, to stop for nothing. I said that the only thing that would make me run faster was if Orcus was chasing me. He said . . .

"You don't want to joke about that. That Orcus isn't a fit topic for humorous conversation. He said he's far too real, and far too . . . I don't know."

"Sounds sensible to me," Lucan said. "But only if you believe that certain topics cannot be joked about. I don't believe that. Want a bit of advice? You shouldn't either. Laughter is one of the few things we have that will always be strong against the darkness. You're going to die, right?"

Remy didn't say anything. He wasn't sure it was a question that required an answer. Instead of answering, he added larger sticks to the fire. It was nearly the last of the firewood they had brought from Crow Fork Market; fortunately they wouldn't have much trouble finding it in the country ahead. Remy could see pine forests growing up the flanks of the mountains. He could smell them as well, as the rising sun burned off the fog and brought out the scents of the foothills.

"Right?" Lucan prompted.

"Right."

"Right. And if you're going to die, and you know you can't prevent it, you might as well laugh at it."

"How old are you, Lucan?" Remy asked. He heard stirring. The others were awakening, kicking at their blankets and hearing the sound of the fire as it licked up around the fresh fuel.

Lucan shrugged, moving on to the next horse. It was Remy's, and he paid close attention to what Lucan did. Here was something else he could learn, since he didn't figure Lucan would be around forever to do it for him. Teeth, ears, eyes, hooves . . . Remy watched.

"I'm not sure," Lucan said. "I celebrate my birthday on the spring solstice."

"Do you have some idea?"

"Seventy, eighty. No matter. I've got some years yet to live."

"Famous last words," Kithri interjected. She scuffed a spot in the coals for a comically battered metal teapot. Setting it in the ashes, she scooped dried herbs into a spoon of metal mesh and set it on the rim of the mug she was never without. She had brought a loaf of bread to the fire too, setting it on a rock to warm.

"Possibly, Kithri," Lucan said. "Good morning to you. How old are you, since we're interested in each other's natal moments?"

"Forty-four," she said. "Remy?"

"Nineteen," he said.

"I can tell you right now you're by far the youngest of us," Keverel said. "I have thirty-six years and can guarantee that both Iriani and Biri-Daar are older."

"And what that means," Iriani said as he broke off a piece of bread, "is that you should go get water."

Remy did, a bit annoyed but also satisfied that he was being taken into the group. He was past being grateful but not past appreciating the way Biri-Daar and the rest had brought him along and made him a part of their group.

Part of that, of course, probably had to do with the mysterious enchanted box that swung against his hip as he walked. If they had just wanted to take it, they could have killed Remy easily enough. He was no longer worried about that. He was, however, still conscious that however much they might gesture toward making him a part of the group, they were still more or less forcing him to come along. Now that he had a horse, he could have turned around and headed for Toradan, but . . .

He looked around, remembering. Scorpions, kobolds, the cacklefiend . . . they were after him, no doubt about it, which meant they were after what he had. He drew the water, filling everyone's skins at a freshet that ran down into a narrow gully and disappeared into the valley. Returning with them strung together across his shoulders, he put a question together in his mind and asked it of the first person he saw. "Keverel," he said. "Should I just open the box?"

The cleric was just standing up after his morning prayers. "What?"

"The box I'm carrying. Why not just open it? If it's going to draw pursuit either way, wouldn't we be better off knowing what's in it?" Remy took it out and tapped the latch with a fingernail. The characters carved in its lid glowed dimly and a buzzing sounded in Remy's ears.

With both hands held out in front of him, Keverel said, "Don't."

"Why not?" Remy felt the latch under his thumbnail. Two of his other fingers pressed against waxen seals worked into the seam under the box's lid.

"Remy, none of us know what will happen if you do that. You might well not survive it. Do you think Philomen put those seals on it so they would tickle you if you opened it?"

"You'll die, boy," another voice said, just off to Remy's right.

Reflexively he looked in that direction; as he did, Keverel stepped forward and ripped the box from his hands. Remy reached after it and Biri-Daar, who had appeared at his right to distract him, pinned his arms. She held him fast, and after an initial struggle Remy relaxed. "Are you going to stay settled if I let you go?" she asked.

He nodded. "I will."

Biri-Daar released him. "Remy," Keverel said. Remy noticed that the rest of the group was watching. "Either we should open this or you should give it to one of us for a while."

"Open it, then," he said, knowing they wouldn't. "Open it."

Keverel looked at the box, then around. "In favor?"

Only Kithri raised a hand.

Looking back at Remy, Keverel said, "Settled. We're not going to open it. What we are going to do is deal with whatever appears to take it from you. Then, when we get to Karga Kul, we will seek the help of the Mage Trust in either opening the box, destroying it, or figuring out another course of action." He looked at the rest. "Yes?"

A round of nods. Keverel looked back to Remy. "It is probable," he went on, "that every time this box leaves your hands, that draws the vizier's attention. It is also probable that whatever draws the vizier's attention draws other attention as well."

"What he's saying in his excruciatingly diplomatic way," Lucan interrupted, "is exactly what Roji told you back at Crow Fork Market. Every time you make one of us take the box away from you, you endanger all of our lives. By Melora, it is about time you understood that." He stalked back toward the fire, then stopped halfway there. "We didn't save your life for you to cost us ours!" he called.

Keverel walked up to Remy and held out the box. "I wouldn't have put it that way," the cleric said. "Now that it has been said, however, I do not repudiate what Lucan said. Our lives are not yours to toy with because you're having second thoughts about accepting your package. Take it."

Remy did.

"Now hold it. Do not open it. Do not complain about it. Show it to no one else until we arrive at Karga Kul. Understood?"

"I understand," Remy said. "Sorry."

"We want no apologies," Biri-Daar said as she walked by him carrying the waterskins he'd dropped when she grabbed his arms. "We want—we need—to be able to rely on you."

They broke camp and saddled up to ride without saying anything else. It was a quiet day after that, down into the valley and on along the road as it rose toward the next range of the Serrata . . . until they saw the first of the orcs.

Remy spotted it first, leaning out from an overlook on the steep slope that broke up from the road to their right. Lucan was riding next to him. Without pointing, he said, "Lucan. Orc on the mountain, up to the right."

In one smooth move, Lucan unslung his bow, nocked an arrow, and fired. The snap of the bowstring got the rest of the party's attention; they came ready, hands on hilts. At their last river crossing, Remy had picked up a pouch full of lemon-sized stones. He shook his sling loose and fitted a stone into it, looking up the slopes on either side of the road as Lucan's arrow found its mark. The orc sentry crumpled out of sight. For a moment none of them said anything; they held still, putting every sense to work finding out whether there were any more.

"Should we go make sure?" Kithri said quietly.

Lucan shook his head. "No need."

"I believe him," Biri-Daar said. "We go on, but carefully. There is never only one orc."

Never only one, Remy thought. That was the first one he had ever seen.

"And where there are orcs, there are usually hobgoblins giving their orders," Biri-Daar added.

The followers of Gruumsh had been the material of stories to scare the children of Avankil since Remy had been old enough for his elders to want to frighten him. He had always known they were real, but until seeing that one Remy had never expected to see an orc in the flesh. He certainly hadn't seen it for long.

And now he was learning that they were serving the hobgoblins. It was as if all of the fables Remy had heard as a child were coming to life around him.

"Wouldn't be surprised to see ogres before it's all over," Kithri said.

The horses' hooves clipped along the ancient stones. They looked up and saw nothing except scrubby pine trees and hawks riding the updrafts along the faces of the mountains that rose up around them. Occasionally a lizard skipped between rocks. Every motion wore at their nerves a little more. "Bring them," Lucan repeated every so often. "Bring them. Anything to kill the suspense."

About an hour after the first sighting, they saw smoke in the sky ahead. An hour later, the road rose next to a tumbling creek until they crested a ridge and discovered the source. There had once been a farmstead there; three or four thatched outbuildings arranged around a central home with stone walls and a beam roof. They could tell it was a beam roof because the charred stumps of some of the beams still angled up from the top edge of the walls. The outbuildings were collapsed into smoking rubble. In the yard just outside the doorway lay a body, facedown. Not far away lay a dog, eviscerated, its limbs cut off and flung away. They approached and Keverel said, "Gnawed the bones. Not just of the dog."

"Who lives out here?" Kithri said. "Might as well beg the passing orcs to stop for lunch. Until the ogres eat them in turn."

"A bit of respect for the dead," Biri-Daar said.

They looked around to see if there were survivors, but found none. "Not a terrible place," Lucan said. "Fish in the river, deer in the valleys. Enough sun for a garden. I would settle down here. Right at the edge of where the mountains rise up." Tears stood in the elf's eyes. "Biri-Daar, I realize that our errand is of terrible import, but if there is an afternoon to spend killing orcs I would consider it a boon."

Iriani looked out across the clearing, across the road to where the ridge curled and rose farther into a maze of notched canyons. "An afternoon well spent," he said.

From inside the house, where she had gone to ensure there were no survivors, Biri-Daar emerged. "At times, one must put aside an errand to spend an afternoon in charity."

The orcs' track wasn't hard to follow. It led across the meandering river at a broad ford less than a mile along the road from the sacked homestead. From there it climbed at an angle away from the road, following an old landslide scar up to an overhung ledge where a pair of orcs stood cracking bloody bones in their teeth. Lucan dropped one of them with an arrow and Remy the other with a slung stone. Immediately Kithri appeared from the scrub at the side of the ledge to make sure both were dead. At a hand signal from her, the rest of the party made their way to the ledge. The overhung hollow opened into a cave. Without hesitation they fell into the order of battle that had already become their unspoken habit. Biri-Daar and Keverel led, flanked by Lucan and Remy, with Kithri and Iriani immediately behind. They stormed down the main passage, kicking aside heaps of stinking refuse and making it all the way to the first split before they encountered resistance.

Surging out from the pitch-dark depths of both branches, the orcs swarmed them. As soon as it happened, their order of battle meant nothing. Orcs were everywhere, trampling over their dead to overwhelm the invaders. They were subhuman, savage beasts living in filth, destroying all that was beautiful. All of Remy's childhood stories came to life; he cut them down as fast as they got within range of his sword, and still there were more. Light blazed along the ceilings of the passages, revealing broken-off stalactites and the teeming forms of the orcs. Keverel had brought the light, and in the sudden illumination Iriani could see where all of his comrades were. Remy saw him step off to one side, putting himself against the wall; Remy went with him, anticipating that the wizard would be planning something magical and would need protection to complete it.

He was right. As soon as he got there, he deflected challenges from a cluster of orcs and then the branch passageway exploded in a crackle of fire that incinerated every orc in sight. The fire vanished and the rush of air drew the air from Remy's lungs.

In the other passage, Biri-Daar and Lucan were hewing their way through the remaining orcs. The rest of the party joined them and together they punched into the chamber at the heart of the orcs' lair . . . just as the surviving orcs scattered and a pair of ogres appeared, flanking a larger orc with ritualized scars surrounding the open socket of the eye he had sacrificed to his god. "Eye of Gruumsh," Lucan said. "You, orc! Elf here!"

As clumsy a ploy as it was, it worked perfectly. The god of the elves, Corellon, had gouged the eye from the orc patron Gruumsh. The orcs who mimicked that wound nurtured a hatred of elves and all things elven.

The Eye of Gruumsh said something in Orcish and the ogres lumbered forward, both to protect it and to destroy the elf interloper. Biri-Daar met one of them head on, stepping inside the looping swing of its morningstar and opening its guts with a hooked thrust. The other ogre swatted Lucan down to his knees and the Eye of Gruumsh sprang closer for the kill, its battle cry nearly drowning out the dying roars of the gutted ogre. It had its spear raised, its mouth open, its one good eye wide in triumph—until Kithri's thrown knife flashed across the chamber and struck at an angle up through the roof of its mouth.

Its cry trailed off and the spear thrust drove through Lucan's shoulder instead of his ribs, the spear head snapping off on the stone floor. Staggering, the Eye of Gruumsh took another blow as a second knife snapped into the hollow of its throat under the jaw. It dropped straight down, still gripping the haft of the broken spear.

Remy and Biri-Daar pressed the remaining ogre. If there were any more orcs about, they had fled into the deeper recesses of the cave. The ogre fought with a fire-hardened wooden club, broken blades hammered into its head. Knowing it was outnumbered, the ogre backed toward an opening in the cave, forcing them to approach it from the front. Its club made a heavy *whoosh* with every swing, each powerful enough to splinter a row of skulls and fan their brains out across the nearest wall.

Even an ogre's strength has limits. Biri-Daar, fearless with the strength of her god, pressed near the limit of the club's range. She timed the swing and the backswing—once, twice. On the third, she stepped inside and jammed her sword up under the ogre's armpit. The ogre clamped the wounded arm around the dragonborn paladin, crushing her to it in a suffocating embrace. The club dropped; with its free hand, the ogre tore Biri-Daar's sword free of its flesh and threw it away.

Then Keverel was there, smashing his mace into the arm that held Biri-Daar. With him came Remy, his blade flicking out in search of the vulnerable gaps in the ogre's hide armor. Iriani protected the rear, destroying the occasional straggling orc as it appeared.

Last, and most lethally, came Kithri, dancing between the ogre's legs to open the artery on the inside of its thigh. She was fast, and the ogre was terribly wounded—still it was fast for its size, catching her with a spastic kick that smashed her into the wall. She cried out and rolled away as the mortally wounded ogre toppled against the wall above her and slid down, its wounded leg unable to hold its weight and its lifeblood spilling in a thick fall from shoulder and thigh. Remy stepped in again, thrusting deep into the pit of its stomach. It flailed at him, missing, and Biri-Daar fell away from it, fighting free of its grasp as it slid down the wall and died.

Before it had drawn its last breath, Remy vaulted the body and kneeled next to Kithri. Her face was wild with pain, her teeth bared and gritted. When he picked her up to carry her back to Keverel, she cried out again. "Hush," Lucan said heartlessly, whatever native tact he possessed temporarily driven out by his own wound. "You'll draw whatever else lives back in these caves."

Kithri might have said many things. Instead she took his advice, clamping her mouth shut even when Remy laid her down on the hard stone next to Lucan. She did manage to glare at him; he winked in return.

While Keverel did what he could to heal them both, Biri-Daar called Remy over. "We need to follow these two passages as far as we can, to make sure we got them all," she said. "There have been no young, which means this is a raiding party. Probably they only planned to stay here a few weeks, until they had despoiled the area. If we had gotten here a few days earlier . . ." She trailed off and Remy instantly knew what she was thinking.

If they had not stopped to save him, they would have found the orcs before they destroyed the homestead back in the ridge clearing. Saving his life had cost the lives of anyone there.

"It's a fool's choice," Iriani said softly. He too could see where Biri-Daar's thoughts had gone. "When you can tell the future, paladin of Bahamut, then you may reprimand yourself for telling it incorrectly."

Biri-Daar looked at him, then around at the carnage. "Let us search and make sure this place is cleansed of its filth," she said.

"And do bring back whatever you find that is both light and valuable," Lucan added. He caught his breath as Keverel sank a needle into the meat of his shoulder. "Hurry, before this murderous cleric puts an end to me."

"We should have such fortune," Kithri muttered. Her voice sounded odd to Remy but he put the thought out of his mind. Biri-Daar had ordered him to clear out the back tunnels, and clear out the back tunnels he would. Keverel knew his business.

Remy found nothing in the rear tunnels, even when assisted by a cantrip of Iriani's that set a pleasant light glowing from the buckle of his belt. Trash, bones, filth. Nothing else. He returned the way he had come, carefully, and found both Lucan and Kithri sitting up. "Time to go," Iriani said.

"This is an awful place," Lucan groused. "Odor enough to kill you dead, orcs and ogres nearly enough to kill you all over again . . ."

". . . And nothing to show for it," Kithri finished for him.

"Perhaps it is just that the two most larcenous members of our group did not participate in the search," Biri-Daar suggested without looking at either of them. She was working with a row of damaged scales on her arm, picking loose the bits that would not heal.

Everyone else in the cave looked at one another to be sure that the paladin had in fact told a joke. They were never sure.

It was true that their search had yielded very little that was valuable, and of that virtually nothing that was light. The only thing of any value was an enormous mirror framed in what looked like silver. Iriani had found it leaning up against a dead end in one of the side tunnels. He could detect no magic in it. "Break off the frame and let's take it with us," Kithri said.

Everyone ignored her. Some of them did take the chance to regard the progress of their beards. Of the three who had to shave, none had since leaving Crow Fork Market. "Soon we'll all look like dwarves," Iriani said upon seeing himself. "Dwarves who have spent time on the rack."

When they emerged into daylight again and found their horses cropping the brush at the edge of the river, less than two hours had passed since Remy and Lucan had cut down the two orcs snacking on the ledge. The sun was dropping toward the western peaks. "We've wasted the afternoon on this," Keverel said. "None of us wants to camp so close to that nest, I would guess."

"You would guess correctly," Biri-Daar said. "But few of us would wish to go much farther."

"Then over the next pass," Lucan said.

Kithri spat from her horse. "This pass, that pass. What difference does it make?"

"Over the next pass is into the final climb toward Iban Ja's bridge," Lucan said. "I don't think we'll find any orcs or ogres up there."

"Why not?" Remy asked.

"The cambions and hobgoblins scare them away. Or slaughter them," Iriani said.

Nodding, Lucan added, "That's if the sorrowsworn don't get them first."

"Sorrowsworn?" Remy had never heard the name. Or term.

"Perhaps you will have the good fortune not to find out," Iriani said. Nobody would say anything else about it. They rode on, and camped beyond the next pass, alighting from their horses just as the last of the sun vanished behind the mountains, its dying rays slanting up into the sky.

As it turned out, they did not reach Iban Ja's bridge until the second day after they cleaned out the lair of orcs. Biri-Daar was reluctant to push the pace while Kithri and Lucan were recovering from their wounds. When they did come to the bridge, Remy realized that everything he had heard about it—and by that time he had heard quite a lot—had utterly failed to prepare him for the reality of seeing it for himself.

They had just stopped for lunch at the head of a slot canyon through which the road angled down, following the canyon floor. Already Remy could hear a distant roar, but despite what Biri-Daar and Lucan said, he could not believe that was the sound of a tributary river to the Blackfall, rumbling from the bottom of a gorge said to be a thousand feet deep. "What is it really?" he asked with an uncertain smile. They shook their heads and said if he didn't believe them, he would just have to see for himself.

Which now he was.

The road ended in a tumble of scree that fell a few dozen yards to the lip of the gorge itself. Remy couldn't see its bottom from where they stood. Around them reared up impassable walls of stone, with the narrowest of ledges on the left side of the scree.

And ahead of them, hanging impossibly in the empty air, was the Bridge of Iban Ja. Remy tried to count the stones, but could not. Some of them were larger than the house where he had last taken a meal in Avankil. Some were no larger than a man. Gathered together, they were a mosaic impression of a bridge, the gaps between them sometimes narrow enough for a halfling to tiptoe across and sometimes wide enough that no sane mortal would endeavor the jump without wings. Bits of cloth on sticks fluttered from cracks in some of the rocks, the guideposts of long-past travelers. All of the stones moved slightly, rocking in the winds that howled through the Gorge of Noon as if they floated on the surface of a gentled ocean, or a wide and flat stretch of river. Snow clung to some of them, and drifted in sculpted shapes across the flat edges of others.

"Well," Kithri said, "now we've seen it. Biri-Daar, what did you say the other way across this gorge was?"

"It involves traveling fifty leagues off the road to a ford," Biri-Daar said. "We have no time. I have crossed Iban Ja's bridge before. It held me. It will hold you."

"And by this point, crossing it is no longer a matter of choice," Keverel chimed in.

"Is that so," Kithri began. She saw Keverel pointing back up the road, turned to see what he was indicating, and saw—as Remy did at that exact moment—the band of tieflings standing in the road behind them. As they watched, the band of perhaps a dozen was fortified with ten times as many hobgoblin marauders.

Remy had seen fewer tieflings than dragonborn. The dragonborn in Avankil had their clan hall, and conducted business when they had business to conduct. The city's tieflings, perhaps sensitive to the permanent stain on their heritage, kept to themselves when they could. When they dealt with non-tieflings, their bravado and short tempers resulted in vexed interactions. Everyone Remy had ever known, from Quayside toughs to Philomen the vizier himself, had warned him to steer clear of tieflings.

Now here he was, his back to a pathway of rocks floating in midair, facing a large number of exactly those creatures he had been told his entire life to avoid. Remy touched the box hanging at his side and wondered what it might have contributed to this turn of events. He imagined that, if they survived the next hour, Lucan and the others might have similar questions.

"It seems that some of these tieflings still believe they fight for Bael Turath," Lucan observed.

"And that we, somehow, wear the colors of Arkhosia," Kithri added. "Well, we do have a dragonborn with us."

"It gets worse," Lucan said.

"I can hardly see how," Kithri said.

"I can," Iriani said. "Out there on the bridge, see that? That is a cambion magus."

Something about his tone struck up a quiet, creeping fear in Remy's mind. Iriani, who had faced down everything they had seen thus far without batting an eye, now paused. "Devil's offspring," Iriani said. "You must not speak to it. These magi have the gift of deceit. They would talk any of you right off the bridge."

"You're assuming any of us are going on the bridge," Kithri said. She was up on a rock at the very edge of the cliff, looking down into the gorge. "If," she added, "you can call it a bridge. Whoever named it, I'm guessing, had never laid eyes on it."

"I read once that Iban Ja's ghost lives inside one of the stones," Keverel said. "One wonders whether he would be an ally or foe."

More tieflings and hobgoblins spilled from crevices in the canyon walls. "Time to find out," Biri-Daar said. "Unless we'd rather fight our way through them and go back to Toradan."

"I think I would rather do that," Kithri said. "But I also think you were making a bad attempt at a joke."

"And I think that your sense of humor is not nearly as

well-developed as you assume," Biri-Daar said. "Iriani. Let us go and rid the world of a cambion."

She leaped to the first block and crossed it in three steps. Iriani followed. As they stepped across the next gap, the hobgoblins gathered at the end of the road charged with a roar. Behind them, the tieflings cocked crossbows and fired, getting the range to the nearest part of the bridge. Kithri danced down the rock face to the edge of the scree, flicking a stream of daggers at the mass of hobgoblins before she made a running jump toward the first stone of Iban Ja's bridge. She landed at the stone's edge and tumbled, springing to her feet. Right behind her came Lucan, nocking and firing arrows with uncanny elf grace as he picked his way backward down the scree before firing off a last shot and turning to skip across the void to the stone.

Shoulder to shoulder, Remy and Keverel backed their way toward the edge of the cliff, skirting the rim of the scree slope to the place Kithri had selected for her leap. "My ancestors were citizens of Bael Turath," the cleric said. "We were one of the few families who refused to take part in the diabolical pact that created these tieflings. I do believe they would hold that against me if they knew."

"Maybe we shouldn't tell them," Remy said.

The leaders of the hobgoblin charge reached them, four abreast; among them came tieflings as well, bearing the cruelly carved blades of their kind. "We should go," Keverel said. "Remy."

"What?" Remy said, thinking the cleric was talking to him. He glanced to his left and saw that Keverel had spoken over his mace, which glowed briefly with a pale light before Keverel deflected the first tiefling's swing and stove in its skull with a blow of his own. At the contact, Remy felt a surge of strength; his sword grew light in his hands; he flicked aside two wild attacks, pivoting between the pair of tieflings to hamstring one and sink the blade half-deep in the other's back.

A blow rang across the back of his helmet and Remy's eyes swam. He heard the whistle of an arrow passing close and the gargled scream of an enemy trying to breathe into punctured lungs. The blows of Keverel's mace, steady as the tolling of a bell, marked the time as they fought a slow retreat to the edge of the cliff, with Lucan and Kithri killing from distance while Biri-Daar and Iriani made their way ever closer to the cambion magus at the midpoint of the bridge.

"Go," Keverel said when they reached the edge. "You first."

Remy didn't argue. It was in the cleric's nature to send others first. He jumped, clearing the gap easily, and landed on his feet. Keverel was right behind him. As soon as they turned back to the cliff edge, the hobgoblins started to follow. Not all of them made the jump; some caught the edge of the stone and then slipped to fall screaming into the misty depths of the gorge. Others slipped or were pushed off the cliff face by the press of their charging comrades. The tiefling crossbowmen, abandoning the idea of Iban Ja's bridge altogether, had started working their way up the sides of the canyon wall in search of shooting positions. One of them reached a ledge thirty feet or so above Kithri's former perch. It was taking aim when Lucan noticed and picked it off.

"That won't be the last one," he said. "We're going to need to get out into the middle before too many more of them get up there."

From stone to stone they leaped. The larger ones moved not at all at the impact of mortal foot, but landing on the smaller ones was precarious because they dipped and tilted from the fresh weight. Remy quickly discovered that the old bits of cloth and their stakes were a reliable guide to a safe passage using stones of sufficient size, and he thanked all of the gods—not just Pelor—for the life and work of the unknown traveler who had set them there. "Hold them here for a moment," Keverel panted as they gained an especially large block set at an angle to the rest, so that anyone wishing to make the leap onto it had to land on one corner. Remy and Keverel waited for Kithri and Lucan to make the jump with them. Together the four held back five times that number of hobgoblins.

"Where do they all come from?" Kithri wondered aloud.

Lucan loosed an arrow at something only he had seen, back toward the lip of the gorge. "The halls of the dwarves that lived in the gorge, I'd guess. It was one of the places their ancestors lived after they drove the dwarves out." He nocked and fired another arrow. "Cambion back there, too."

"Still?" Kithri skipped off to one side for a better perspective.

"No, was," Lucan said. "But don't be surprised if there are more of them spotted in among the tieflings here."

Behind them, Biri-Daar and Iriani were within fifty feet of the cambion magus. Landing after her most recent leap, the dragonborn faced the cambion magus and clashed her sword and shield together. "Make way and live, devil," she said. "Or remain and die. It's all the same to me."

The cambion spread his arms in a welcoming gesture. "After the battle," he said, "I will find your head at the bottom of the gorge. I will place it next to my hearth and I will make it speak those words again and again."

Hellfire arced between the magus's hands. Iriani landed alongside Biri-Daar on the first stone of the bridge as flames curled out of Biri-Daar's nostrils. The thrill of battle burned through her. With an enemy before her, she knew who she was. Together they strode to the next gap and cleared it in a long step. They paused, waiting for the stone under their feet to stop rocking. Three stones remained between them and the cambion.

"Quickly there!" Lucan called over his shoulder. Crossbow bolts were beginning to fall around them as the tieflings found the range. They were forced to give up their position, which meant giving up that entire block all at once; the moment they stepped back, hobgoblins leaped across and pursued them to the next gap. It turned into a sprint punctuated by reckless leaps across greater and greater gaps. Kithri slowed their pursuers down somewhat with a scattering of caltrops in their wake. A half-dozen hobgoblins pulled up with punctured feet, bogging down those that came behind until they were shoved out of the way.

That gained them a full stone of distance, with two gaps. They turned and poured arrows, sling stones, and throwing knives into the front rank of their pursuers, slowing but not stopping them.

Then out of the caves that lined the gorge, where once the tieflings of Bael Turath had undermined the great bridge, came the black wafting shapes of sorrowsworn.

"I was afraid of this," Iriani said. He and Biri-Daar were two jumps from the cambion magus. He had spent the trip drenching the two of them in every protective magic he could think of while they said their prayers to Corellon and Bahamut that the devil's Abyssal magics would not overcome them.

Now the sorrowsworn—three of them, surrounded by the flickering midnight torrent of what could only be shadowravens—meant that he was going to have to divide his attentions. With a sweeping gesture, Iriani erected a magical barrier that would slow the sorrowsworn. At the same time he looked back toward where his four companions were slowing the pursuit of the tieflings. "Sorrowsworn!" he cried out. "Keverel!"

The cleric turned and saw the sorrowsworn. Immediately he dropped his shield to brandish his holy symbol of Erathis in their direction. "You slivers of death, fragments of the Shadowfell itself," he intoned. "You haunters of battlefields, reapers of souls. You will not take those under the protection of Erathis!"

At the god's name, the rising sorrowsworn slowed. The brilliance of Keverel's holy light held them back . . . but the shadowravens swarmed around the stones, looking for a way in.

"Biri-Daar, finish this!" the cleric called. If the sorrow-sworn got close, their trickery would get inside the mind of whoever they seized on first. They fed on despair and relished the final thoughts of the suicides they created. In the midst of a battle, one moment of distraction caused by uncertainty or remembered failure could be decisive. The sorrowsworn could not approach too near, but they could reach out and find one who might be prey to their wiles.

In the same way wordly fire burned wood, the cambion's magian fire was fueled by the soul. It raised its staff and Biri-Daar's mouth opened in a scream as she felt the soulscorch burn through her. By her side, Iriani did the same—and both of them, strengthened by their gods and by the wordly powers of the cleric Keverel, survived the soulscorch and kept on. Iriani blew across his palm, and a film of ice appeared on the block where the cambion magus stood. It slipped, reaching out to break its fall and melt the ice with a fiery discharge. Steam masked it for a moment as the ice boiled away; when the gorge's winds blew the steam away, Biri-Daar stood before it.

It struck at her with fire. She struck back with steel. Again fire blazed from the cambion, washing over the dragonborn to leave her charred and smoking—and again she answered with a sword stroke, cracking its staff in two. The discharge of the staff's hellish energy enveloped them both in a swirl of fire; when it faded, Biri-Daar opened her mouth and spat out a long tongue of her own fire.

"You guessed wrong, devil," she said, and struck the cambion magus down to its knees. Then she struck it again, bringing her sword down across its back and crushing it to the ancient stone of the bridge. The cambion magus lay still. Its blood spread black in the cracks of the stone. Biri-Daar knelt to send it on its way.

"Bahamut watches me as I prove myself worthy," she growled, flames licking from her mouth. "Your masters turn their backs. Take that knowledge with you when you stand at hell's gates and beg admission."

She stood and clashed sword and shield once more. "Tieflings of the gorge, your magus is dead!"

A cry went up among the tieflings, yet still they pressed forward, driven by the hobgoblins behind and among them. Biri-Daar saw this and for the first time since Remy had known her, he saw uncertainty on her face. It lasted only a moment, and disappeared in a gout of fire as she threw her head back and roared. "To me!" she cried. "To the other side!"

From stone to stone came the other four as Iriani held off the sorrowsworn, who were too fearsome an adversary to fight directly should they get near enough to use their life-stealing scythes. The Raven Queen, thought Iriani, still had an interest in this bridge even after all those years, the centuries since the fall of Arkhosia. Iriani's power was a river like the Blackfall, turbulent, channeled only by the deep canyon walls of his will. And while he arrested the sorrowsworn's deadly march, Iriani lost sight of the cambion magus after he saw Biri-Daar cut it down. He took it for granted that the magus was dead and that the tieflings would flee in disarray. One moment of uncertainty, of inattention. An old story, told again and again and never the less true for all of its repetitions.

O wizard you have failed your companions, you have failed yourself, you have turned your back on the adversary while he still plots against you.

The dying cambion magus harbored hopes of finding an afterlife in the Nine Hells that exceeded what it had found in the mortal realms. It had killed many and for years kept the bridge from being reborn as a path of commerce that might have united the cities of the Dragondown. Now, as the life drained from it and the black blood of its body spilled over the sides of the rock where it lay, disappearing into spray long before it found the roiling waters of the Noon a thousand feet below. The cambion magus knew that if it died there, the mortal interlopers would roll its body off the rock, to smash against the rocks or be torn to bits in the rapids. That was all right. He would stand before his infernal masters and claim that his deeds on the mortal plane merited rank and servants in the infernal realms.

Fool.

His final bit of proof would be this half-elf wizard who even now stood within arm's reach, resolutely defying the charge of the sorrowsworn and the shadowravens who flocked about them.

Fools die and you are a fool, first. You will die, and then because of you, all of your companions.

The cambion's mouth was dry. It had to speak the charm three times before making all of the sounds correctly. And then it knew that as the last syllable left its mouth that this final spell would kill it. There was no regret in this knowledge. The spell would kill another as well.

The shadowravens boiled in a cloud around the stones of Iban Ja's bridge, unable to approach because of Iriani's protective charm and the energies of Erathis and Bahamut projected through Keverel and the paladin Biri-Daar. The six adventurers had slaughtered tieflings beyond counting, and the cambion magus charged with holding the bridge lay dying; the far side was nearly gained.

Then Iriani looked down, toward the sorrowsworn, and his charms faltered. "No," he said. He began to turn, his face a terrible mask of helpless realization and terror, but before he ever saw the magus again, the wizard Iriani immolated in a pillar of soulfire. It burst from the twin seats of the soul in head and heart, annihilating Iriani's body in the time it took for his comrades to feel the heat. The cambion magus died knowing it had succeeded; Iriani died knowing he had been close, so close to delivering his comrades through to the next stage of their errand. As quickly as the blast of soulscorching fire appeared, it blazed out, leaving Iriani's body unmarked but lifeless, to topple sideways onto the edge of the rock. The body rested there for a moment. Maybe it was the wind that took it in the end, or the heavy tread of a man or elf or hobgoblin fighting for its life that rocked the stone just enough. Or perhaps the last escaping breath of an elf wizard named Iriani, native to the forests that blanket the mountains that give rise to the Whitefall on its course toward Karga Kul and the ocean, was enough to settle the body so that it tipped, bit by bit, over the edge. And fell.

The cambion magus was dead and smiling. And the shadowraven swarm began to press closer.

"Break!" screamed Biri-Daar. "To the far side! Run!"

They ran, pursued by the last of the tieflings, slashing their way through shadowravens that cut them terribly with undead beak and talon. For the rest of his life Remy would remember the shadowraven talon that slashed along his forehead seeking his eyes. Through the spatter of his own blood he saw his sword cut through it, saw the blade tear the shadowraven into tatters of shadow that blew away in the winds of the gorge. They ran and leaped from stone to stone, finding the other side together, fighting the last of the tieflings as they scrambled up the ruined giant's playground of fallen and tilted stone blocks that remained of that side of Iban Ja's bridge.

When they were across, the tieflings and hobgoblins fell back. Not just to the next stone away from the surviving portion of the bridge. They fell back stone by stone until they reached the exact center of the gorge. There they raised their swords and spears, clashing them on shield and roaring a song of victory.

"Did they win?" Lucan panted. "I didn't think they won."

"We're here," Biri-Daar. "But Iriani is not."

"I saw him fall," Remy said.

Kithri was nodding. "Me too. He was already dead."

Looking out over the mass of hobgoblins and tieflings, Biri-Daar said, "So should we be. The shadowravens do not follow, the sorrowsworn retreat to their lair. The rest come only halfway. Why?"

Lucan was looking at the road that stretched ahead of them, from the lip of the gorge into a misty and forested middle distance. "I have a guess," he said.

Behind them, the tieflings sang. Biri-Daar looked at them with hate plain on her face. When they had caught their breath, though, she led them away and would say no more about their passage across the Bridge of Iban Ja.

Not even when Kithri tried to provoke her. "You weren't quite yourself out there, paladin," she said lightly after they had walked a few hours into the woods. "Shouting, demonstrating . . ."

"It got those tieflings into a frenzy, that's certain," Lucan added.

Biri-Daar raised a hand, palm out toward them. "Do not try to bait me. If Iriani's death is on my head, I will know it. I will repent it. Keverel, I would speak with you a moment."

The cleric followed her a little way apart from the group. The rest of them walked in a loose group. They had no horses, no packs; they would be living from what they could forage until the next settlement, and none of them knew where that settlement might be. "When I passed through here some years ago," Lucan said, "there was a trading post near where the Crow Road emerged from these woods."

"Bring on the dancing girls," Kithri said with as much sarcasm as she could muster.

"Your tongue is somewhat dulled of late," Lucan said. "I fear for your health."

"I fear for yours if you don't hold your tongue," she snapped.

Remy saw the stresses pulling at the group. He said nothing. It was not yet his role to have something to say. He walked. They all walked, in small groups that shifted and broke and reformed as they rose away from the Gorge of Noon into the highland forest on its eastern rim. None of them had much to say because each of them had much to think. Iriani, dying, weighed on their minds.

"These woods are touched," Lucan said sometime later, when dusk was nearly total and they had resigned themselves to a night of sleeping rough.

"Feywild?" Keverel said softly.

Lucan nodded, looking around. "They will show themselves when they wish to," he said.

Which was just at the moment of full dark, when Remy could no longer see a trace of color in the woods around him or on his own clothes. "Travelers," came a voice from the trees to their left. "It is forbidden to traverse this part of the road without the permission of the Lord of the Wood."

Lucan answered first. "I can see you, elf. And you can see me. Come out and let us talk like civilized beings."

"You know you don't belong here," the elf said, appearing at the side of the road. "The stink of the city is in your clothes."

"I belong where I choose to go," Lucan said.

"No. You may choose to go anywhere. But you may not choose whether the people already there decide you belong." The elf winked at them, sporting cruelty in his smile. "Same for your half-breed who didn't make it this far. It's the curse of mixed blood, I'm afraid."

There might have been blows exchanged then. On both sides hands fell to sword hilts and eyes locked, gauging defenses and reflexes and—most importantly—intent. More elves appeared from the trees.

Then another figure on horseback spoke, and everyone else present realized that he had been there for the entire exchange even though none of them had heard him approach. "Easy, Leini. They've lost a friend," he said. "They shouldn't have to endure your baiting after that."

"This is none of your business, Paelias," the elf Leini said.

"I believe it is. These travelers, who have spent their day fighting the tieflings and killing off the cambion magus of the old bridge, deserve better than your hostility." Paelias turned to Biri-Daar. "You may stay until your companions have healed enough to go on. But we want no traffic with the wars of the outside, or the hatreds of this world. You survived the bridge; for that we offer you respect, and a meal, and a dry place to spend the night. Please don't ask for more. Even if," he finished, glancing at the sharp-tongued Leini, "he provokes you."

He dropped from his horse to the ground, executing a bow and flourish in the same motion. "Paelias is my name, as perhaps you have overheard," he said. "This is Leini and these are his associates. They live in these woods and I have traveled, which means that my manners are superior to theirs and that I am more handsome, despite our common heritage. Leini and his kin live in these woods and dispose of the tieflings who stray within its boundaries, but—as your elf companion noted back down the road—there is a bit of the Fey in this forest as well. It is my home, at least when I am not somewhere else . . . and you would not be shocked, I think, to know that other eladrin reside here."

Greetings were exchanged. Leini and his companions were barely civil, but they did not challenge Paelias directly. "Follow us," said Paelias. "Even elves with Leini's manners would not refuse hospitality to tiefling-killing strangers."

"And cambion magus-killing," Kithri said.

"Very good," Paelias said. He winked and even Remy could see that in his eyes was something of the color of starlight. "For that we might even be able to find some wine."

Eladrin, Remy thought. If he had always thought of orcs as creatures of story more than life, he had been certain that eladrin were figments of storytelling imagination. They were said to be celestial knights, walkers of the planes, emissaries of divine powers, kin to the elves though not entirely elf. Yet here was one, tall and magnificent, pouring him a goblet of wine around a fire that warded off the chill of the highland woods. "One needs these wood-dweller elves to kill off the demonic riffraff," Paelias was saying. "They aren't much for company, though. I watched part of your engagement at the bridge today. You might be much better company."

"You watched . . ." Biri-Daar broke off and nodded to herself.

"That's why they didn't follow us," Kithri said.

"Well, it wasn't just me. The tieflings know that any elf in these woods will hunt them down and send them back across the bridge without their skins." Paelias drank. "But enough about these woods. What's the news from across the gorge?"

He looked at Remy. "You're a young one. Where do you come from and how did you get tangled up with this motley band?"

Remy told the story, leaving out the details of what he carried and who had sent him. Paelias watched him as he spoke, and listened carefully, and by the time he had told the story Remy was sure that Paelias knew not just that Remy had lied but what he had lied about and why. There was something in the demeanor of an eladrin—or this eladrin, anyway. The star elves, as they were called in Remy's child-hood fables, were mighty figures, passing where they wished among different planes and able to see through the deceits of mortal and immortal alike.

"A fine tale," Paelias said. "And you, paladin: What has Karga Kul for you—except a homecoming?"

Biri-Daar frowned. "How would you know where I was hatched?"

"All dragonborn wear a bit of their birth shell somewhere on their bodies," Paelias answered. He drank again. "But as far as I have heard, it is only the dragonborn of Karga Kul—the descendants of the mighty Knights of Kul—who dangle their bits of shell in the air as a remembrance of the Bridge of Iban Ja."

Remy saw the dangling earring in Biri-Daar's right ear. He had never paid attention to it before, but now Paelias's words had opened up an entirely new understanding of the dragonborn paladin and her demeanor out on the bridge.

"You have heard accurately," Biri-Daar said. "Many stray bits of lore have stuck to the inside of your head, Paelias."

"Not all of it is stray," the star elf answered. "I practice the magical arts, and as you can see, I am eladrin and therefore not entirely welcome among these elves." Paelias walked a coin across his fingers and back before flipping it into the air, where it disappeared. "The Feywild is a little too much of sameness for me. Here, in the mortal world . . . I find the change exciting, the living and dying, the way that every being here knows of its mortality. Karga Kul . . ." Paelias mused. "I have never seen the cities of the Dragondown Coast, although there are cities across the ocean where my name might still be remembered.

"But you are tired and I am keeping you up for my own amusement. You must sleep, and grieve in what ways your traditions demand on the first night of a loss. In the morning we will talk further of Karga Kul. And," he finished with another wink in Remy's direction, "of messengers rescued in the desert."

In the morning Remy woke feeling more refreshed than he would have thought possible. The forest air, the clean bed . . . the longer he was apart from civilization, he thought, the more he desired its trappings. Perhaps the adventurer's life was not for him. Coming out of the cabin where Paelias had decreed they be put up for the night, Remy passed a group of elves gambling with what looked like ancient arrowheads as chips. He nodded to be polite, but expected no response and got none. Across the cleared center of the camp, he saw Paelias sitting with the rest of the group.

"You slept late," Kithri said. "The rest of us have already been to Karga Kul and back."

"Only in our minds, only in our minds," Keverel said.

With a snap of his fingers, Paelias said, "That's what planning is, going somewhere in your mind so when you get your body there you can get it out again." He shook his head. "Karga Kul. Strange place."

"You said last night you had never been there," Biri-Daar reminded him.

"And you were kind enough to observe last night that I have much in the way of lore stuck to the inside of my head," Paelias answered with a smile. "We are both correct. I would, however, like to see Karga Kul. What say you?"

"Let's talk it over," Kithri said.

Lucan and Paelias exchanged a glance. "Excuse us," Lucan said.

Nodding and retreating, Paelias said, "Of course. I will be at our meeting place by the road. Yea or nay, inform me there."

———◆———

The first vote was three to two against. Remy, Lucan, and Kithri didn't trust the eladrin. "And why should we?" Kithri asked. "He appears, wants to know our story, wants to come along at the drop of a hat . . . if you ask me, this is some trick because of Remy."

"Because of me?" Remy repeated. He was confused.

"What you carry," Lucan amended. "I agree. At least I agree that this is a possibility we must consider. Why would anyone want to come along with us when we're probably all going to go off and die?"

"We're not going to go off and die," Biri-Daar said. "We have a sacred trust and we will fulfill it."

"Except if we go off and die. Like Iriani."

"Iriani," Keverel said quietly, "is precisely why we could use someone like Paelias. The god provides."

Other eladrin had ringed them in while they conversed; already Remy could tell them from the elves. The Feywild clung to them even in this world, as if they brought a bit of it with them whatever plane or region their bodies occupied. One of them stepped forward and spoke. "We do not endorse Paelias's desire," she said. "He is flighty and foolish and possesses powers whose extent and purpose he does not know."

"Sounds like the rest of us," Kithri said.

"Once before, Paelias left this wood in search of adventure," the eladrin said after staring Kithri into silence. "When he returned, it was twenty years before he would speak of what had happened."

"And what had happened?" Lucan asked.

"He got a number of his companions killed," the eladrin said. "Because, as I have said, he is flighty and foolish. If you would take him with you, you must know this. We found it our duty to tell you."

"Does anyone around here have anything good to say about him?" Kithri asked.

With a shrug, the eladrin answered, "Perhaps. But you will find no one here who would trust Paelias with his life."

They traded with the elves before leaving, and the elves cheated them mercilessly, reserving their most ruthless bargains for Lucan. He had his eye on a pair of boots since his had been badly torn in the bridge fighting. "Oh, these boots are powerful," the elf cobbler said. "You will move silent as a cat and your enemies will think you are a shadow."

Lucan bought them, cursing the cobbler and the entire race of elves as he paid the exorbitant price. "This is more than your share of what we've won thus far. It puts you in debt to us," Biri-Daar observed.

"Oh, fear not," Lucan said, putting on the new boots. "I'll work for my keep."

Five horses and tack for the long trek ahead of them, plus replacements for gear that had worn out or been broken on the trek so far—oil, torches, flint and steel, fresh waterskins—took all the gold they had. They rode away from the elf encampment feeling cheated and still feeling the cloud of Iriani's death. Paelias, seeing them approach the road, spurred his mount to meet them. "Let me guess," he said. "They told stories about me and then swindled you at market."

"You were watching," Kithri said.

"No," Paelias said. "That is what they do. The elves of these woods don't like me because I come from the Feywild and they don't like the Feywild. The other eladrin don't like me because I like this world a little too much. Probably you voted among yourselves that you don't want me along. That's fine. I will ride with you for a while. You can't stop me unless you want to fight, and if we fight it will end badly for all of us. So. Let us ride. Yes?"

The five survivors of the battle on Iban Ja's bridge looked at each other. "All right. Yes," Biri-Daar said after a long moment. "You may ride with us for a while."

BOOK III
THE CROW ROAD

They emerged from the elves' forest the next morning. The country around them was still wooded, but more sparsely. Sunlight reached the ground there, and the air was heavy with the scents of alpine summer. "Now we're on the Crow Road," Lucan said. He pointed up to the trees that lined the road, and Remy saw them: crows standing sentinel, one in the top branches of each tree.

Mindful of the story he had heard about how Iban Ja's bridge had gotten the way it was, he asked, "Are those crows or ravens?"

Lucan laughed. "Most people can't tell the difference. These are crows. But you'll see ravens along the way. You'll see just about everything if you travel the Crow Road from one end to the other."

"And what is at the other end?"

"Well, that depends. Either you get off before the end and work your way through the Lightless Marsh to . . .

this sounds strange, but there's a place where the Lightless Marsh isn't lightless anymore. That's the best way I can explain it. You get to that place, and you realize that you have somehow re-emerged into the world from wherever you were before. Which, if you're traveling the Crow Road, is everywhere. And anywhere."

"And if you don't get off? If you see the Crow Road through all the way to its end?" Remy pressed.

"Well," said Lucan slowly, "then you reach the Inverted Keep."

"The Inverted Keep?" Paelias looked amazed. "Really? I understood that to be a legend."

"Most people in the Dragondown would say the same about Iban Ja's bridge," Lucan said. "But they are both real."

"Most of them would also say it about the Crow Road," Keverel added.

Paelias nodded and scanned the treetops for more crows. "True enough. Yet here we are."

"Is it called the Crow Road because crows sit in the trees?" Remy asked. "They do that everywhere."

"It's called the Crow Road . . ." Kithri started, then stopped. She looked at Lucan.

"What?" he said.

"You tell the story," Kithri said. "If you don't, you'll just complain about how one of us does it wrong."

In the years before Arkhosia and Bael Turath put their stamp on the world, a great and now forgotten empire arose in the highlands between the Blackfall and Whitefall rivers. So long ago did it rise and fall that even most of its ruins are destroyed and gone, and its languages and arts, its deeds both villainous and glorious, are lost. All that remains of this vanished empire is the Crow Road.

Ancient records of Bael Turath and Arkhosia speak of it and describe it exactly as it appears to the adventurer of today: a road whose stones no frost can heave, which even buried under mudslides centuries old looks as if it was built yesterday when dug out again. It is a road to outlast the ages.

And on it the traveler will experience things that exist on no other road.

The story is that the nameless empire contained a great builder, who wished not only to build roads across the face of the mortal world, but between the planes and other realms as well. The folklore of this people—this is one of very few things known about them—held that crows and ravens had commerce with all of the realms. Therefore, after the builder surveyed his route but before he lay the first stone, he brewed a great enchantment using all of the magical might his empire's wizards could muster . . . and he taught the crows how to understand human speech.

Then he learned their secrets. "I have given you a gift, crows," he said. "Now in return you may tell me the secret of your ability to perceive and travel to all realms, whether astral or abyssal, elemental or fey."

But the crows were crows, and would not tell. Have you ever tried to convince a crow to do anything? To this day, when you speak in the vicinity of a crow, or a raven, be careful. Say only what you would not fear to have repeated in front of your enemies.

Great grew the builder's fury. Eventually he reasoned that if he could not get the answers from the crows while they were alive, he would learn it from what happened when they were dead. A bounty went out through the empire, and dead crows began arriving at the castle where the builder had his plans. At first they arrived a few at a time, brought by the bored children of local farmers. Then, when word spread that the builder paid the bounty he promised, crows started to arrive by the saddlebag-full, and then in sacks large enough that mules brought them to the builder's door. He paid, and paid, and paid. Soon the crows had learned to stay away, but they had also learned why, and from that moment forward the crows were sworn enemies of the builder and of his road.

He had one more card yet to play, however. When he brought his crews out to the edge of the elves' dark wood and dug the first stretch of the road's bed, he laid the body of a crow under every tenth stone.

Now the crows hated the road and the builder, but the road was also a crows' burial ground and they flocked to it because—though they might be larcenous, fickle, and cruel—crows honor their dead. The road stretched mile after mile, and every man or dwarf, halfling or elf—every mortal being that died building the road was buried under its stones. Walking it, the builder decreed, would be a voyage that paralleled the path between worlds.

Of course he was quite mad by this time, and grew madder as the road went on. The builder ordered exotic beasts of the Shadowfell and Elemental Chaos, the Feywild and the Abyss, all of the planes. He ordered them brought to the road and there he killed them and buried them beneath its freshly laid stones. And each of those deaths permeated the stones, and brought a bit of the other realms to the road.

Over it all watched the crows, since the builder had so many that he still buried one under every tenth stone.

At last the road reached its juncture with an even older road that led along the path of the Whitefall. He could have stopped there, but the builder had dead crows yet, and a few of the strangest unnameable creatures the magical hunters of other planes could bring him. He built onward, and buried his last crow under the final stone of the road, at the edge of a bluff overlooking a bend in the Whitefall. There he thought he could rest, and there he built himself a keep that would be his last building, where he could grow old looking out over the road he had built.

"So that's the Inverted Keep, isn't it?" Remy asked.

Lucan nodded. "That's what the story says."

"How did it get inverted? What happened to the builder?"

"Those are other stories," Lucan said. "I'm tired of telling stories. Let's ride, and let's look out for what the crows get up to along this road."

"Sounds like the crows are the least of our problems," Kithri said.

"Some of them are shadowravens," Lucan said.

Kithri nodded. "See?"

"But there are no sorrowsworn around because no great battle has ever been fought on the Crow Road. No general has ever kept an army together along its path."

"Why would a general have wanted to come this way?" Biri-Daar wondered. "Between here and Karga Kul there is nothing."

Lucan took a drink to wet his throat after the story. When he was done he said, "Who other than generals knows why generals do anything?"

Keverel leaned over toward Remy. "This, you see, is why none of us became soldiers."

For the rest of the day they rode. Remy turned over in his mind the idea that Biri-Daar was a descendant of the Knights of Kul. How was it possible to know things like that? Iban Ja was a name in a story. Even the archivists of Arkhosia were unsure when he had lived, which meant they were unsure when the bridge had fallen.

What history might lie behind Keverel, or Kithri?

What, Remy wondered, *might lie behind me?*

He knew little about his own family. His mother Melendra had died five years before, when he was fourteen and by the laws of Avankil a man. Since then he had slept at the docks, usually on ships that had been abandoned or whose captains had died onshore. It took the Avankil authorities quite a while to track down and auction off those ships. In the meantime they served very well as a protected place to sleep for the urchin youth of the city. Remy had avoided the gangs by spending just enough time at the keep for the gang leaders not to trust him, but also to decide not to kill him . . . which he could have made difficult because a year after his mother died was when he had bought his first sword.

Of his father he knew nothing but stories. His mother had told him that his father was a sailor on one of the fast ships that escorted valuable cargoes on the cross-Gulf run between Furia and Saak-Opole. This route often ran afoul of pirates at the Kraken's Gate, part of the archipelago at the mouth of the Dragondown Gulf. To hear Remy's mother tell it, his father had fought through the pirates a dozen times and more, and had seen things in the waters beyond the Kraken's Gate that he lacked the words to describe. Physically, she said, Remy resembled his father more and more as he grew older. He wondered what she would say now that he was grown. He wondered whether his father was alive, squinting into this same sunset from the deck of a ship in the Gulf—or dead, his bones long since sunk into the seabottom muck far away from the light, deeper than even the sahuagin will venture . . .

"Remy."

He looked up into the concerned face of Lucan. "You were far away for a minute there," Lucan said.

"History," Remy said. "I was thinking about history."

Lucan whistled. In the trees, crows ruffled their feathers at the sound. "They will talk to me a little because I know some of their language," he said. "Crows don't like it when you assume that they will learn your speech and you don't have to learn theirs."

"Is that right," Remy said. He wasn't sure whether Lucan was joking or not.

Lucan raised his arm and whistled a complicated pattern. Out of the setting sun fell a crow. It landed on his forearm and cocked its head at him. "See?" he said to Remy.

"I see you can call it," Remy said. "I haven't seen that it can talk."

"Awk," the crow said. "Talk."

Lucan clucked at it. "Slow, slow. No need to rush." He looked up at Remy. "It has been a very long time since they received their gift. Most of them never use it and it comes back slowly when they try."

"Time," the crow said.

With a wink at Remy, Lucan said, "Time, right. Plenty of time."

"No time," the crow said.

"Why not?" Remy asked it.

"No time to talk," the crow said. It flapped over to Remy and landed on his shoulder. Leaning in close to his ear, it said, "Found you. They found you. Time to watch you die."

He would learn later that some of those who had died building the Crow Road returned as spectral undead, yearning for their bodies to live again—or, failing that, to at least be buried with the ceremonies of their gods. There were undead in Avankil, of course. Bodies rose from the slack waters under the piers, or dug their way out of the rubbish heaps where murderers disposed of their victims. Ghosts haunted the lower corridors of the keep and the places near the walls where the specters of soldiers remembered invaders long since gone to their own rewards. The Crow Road, though, built on death, gave rise to undeath with every step.

They turned after the crow spoke and saw behind them the insubstantial shapes of wraiths and specters. They did not pursue; they shepherded. "We're being walked ahead to meet something," Paelias said. "I wonder what."

"I'd rather not find out," Kithri said. She rubbed at her forehead over her right eye. Remy had noticed her making that gesture frequently these past few days. He wondered if she was still suffering the effects of the ogre's kick back in the orc lair. Lucan seemed to have recovered, but the Eye of Gruumsh's spear point had passed only through meat; his joint and bones were unhurt, and Keverel had sewn his wounds up so well that Lucan was already complaining that the scars would be too small to impress the barmaids of Karga Kul.

The crow still sat on Remy's shoulder. "Ever get the feeling that you had a crow on your shoulder so the enemy knows who to aim at?" Paelias said loudly.

Feathers rustled in the surrounding trees, and out of the deepening darkness came more crows, to festoon the party and the horses. "Wrong again," croaked the crow on Remy's shoulder. They kept a stead pace, moving forward, always forward, even though the time for camp had long since come. Remy's eyes jittered back and forth from fatigue. He couldn't focus on anything for long.

"Found me, you said," he said to the crow.

"Awk," the crow said. "Aye."

"How come they don't attack, then?"

"Because of us," the crow said. Its voice grew clearer the more it was used.

"How droll," Lucan said. "It tells us it's time to watch us die, then says that we are not dying because of it."

"Perhaps you have failed to attune yourself to the crow sense of humor," said Biri-Daar. She was riding out in front of the rest of them, scouting to make sure the mass of undead behind them had not somehow raised reinforcements ahead.

"Are you suggesting that a crow has more of a sense of humor than I do?" Lucan said.

"If she wasn't, I will," Kithri said.

The crow on Remy's shoulder followed this back-and-forth with cocked head. "Awk," it said at the end.

"Really, they're not attacking us because of you?" Remy asked it.

"Really."

"Why are you doing this?"

"The elf, awk," the crow said. "Speaks our language. Few Tenfingers care. Awk."

"Who would like to apologize first?" Lucan said smugly.

"What I want to know," Kithri said, "is why the wraiths back there are afraid of a bunch of crows."

Paelias chuckled. "This is the Crow Road, isn't it?"

The crows on their shoulders and on the pommels of their saddles *awk*ed.

All night they rode, until the horses' heads drooped and their riders were slumped forward over the horses' manes. Even some of the crows rode silently, heads tucked under one wing. Remy remembered little of that night except the occasional flutter next to his ear as his first crow passenger shifted in its sleep.

The sun rose directly ahead, bringing them out of sleep with sandy eyes and frayed nerves, not to mention bruised backsides. The crows were gone. When they looked behind them, so were the wraiths. "Well," Paelias said. "If that's the appetizer, I wonder what the main course will be?"

Biri-Daar yawned, showing teeth that seemed to go all the way down her throat. "That will be funny exactly until we find out."

"Remember that the builder of this road poured more and more of his madness into it as he went, and his madness grew more and more consuming," Keverel commented. "It could well be that the crows will not want to confront whatever comes tonight."

"Then perhaps we should sleep during the day," Kithri said. "As much as I hate to suggest it."

They could all tell how much she hated to suggest it by how her eyes stayed half-lidded and her head lolled a little while she spoke.

"Not a terrible idea," Biri-Daar pronounced after some consideration. They rode off the road and found a sheltered spot in a dell over which the branches of trees had knit into a canopy. There they staked out the horses, attended to their immediate needs, and slept.

"Awk," said a crow. Remy awoke and saw it staring into his eye. He flinched. Then he realized that if the crow had intended harm, the harm would already have come. Shadows were deepening under the trees; in the gaps through their branches he could see both orange and blue in the sky.

"Right," he said, sitting up. "Time to go. Thank you."

The crow *awk*ed and flew away into the trees.

Remy went around the camp waking everyone up. Even Lucan and Paelias, who did not sleep, muttered and blinked and had a hard climb back to wakefulness from their quiet meditative state. "It's a twilight world out here. Up here. On this road." Paelias stretched and cracked his neck. "One can only wonder what awaits us around the next bend."

"An unholy abomination that will catch those words and shove them down your throat, sideways," Kithri growled.

"Oh halfling, do excuse me," he said. "I do not mean my humor to offend little people with headaches."

She spun, knife in hand. "Stop!" Biri-Daar commanded. She stepped between them. "Sheathe the knife, Kithri. And Paelias, if you must speak, perhaps not all of your speech could be dedicated to aggravating those who must ride with you."

The eladrin appeared to consider this. "Perhaps," he allowed. He swung up into the saddle and went out onto the road to await the rest of them.

———◆———

Perhaps inspired by Paelias's example, Remy found himself trying to pick a fight later that day, when they had stopped for water and Kithri started her sparring with Paelias again. Remy listened to it as long as he could, Paelias coolly provoking her and Kithri gladly being provoked to complain about the unfairness of the larger party members to her—the horses were too large, the portions of the meals poorly considered, the tasks given her were demeaning and mundane . . . finally Remy had had enough. He had a few things he needed to say, too. "What's unfair is that I keep on fighting with you and keeping the enemies from your backs, and then the minute you have a chance to gather your thoughts you get suspicious again. When does the fighting count for something?" Remy was going to have trouble stopping himself, he knew. He always did once he started to let his feelings run. "And how do I know I can trust you? You keep me along because I have this box, maybe, and maybe you know what to do with it and you're just waiting for the moment to do it and then I'm going to get a knife in the back. How do I know that's not going to happen?"

None of his companions could answer . . . except Paelias. "Simplest of questions," he said. "You don't know. None of you do. Remy, you could be waiting to kill us all. Biri-Daar could be waiting to do something unspeakable to Remy at the correct moment. And I," he added with a dramatic gesture, "might be scheming to do you all in. We can't know. Shall we kill each other now, or shall we assume that we are working toward a common goal for the moment?"

No one spoke.

"Perfect," Paelias said. "Then we should ride. It's a long way to the Inverted Keep, and this Crow Road has us all at each other's throats. Remember that."

Several uneventful days passed, enlivened only by bickering. Then, one afternoon, Biri-Daar dropped back from her customary position at the front of the group. When she was next to Remy, she said, "So. I have told you part of why we must go to Karga Kul. Would you like to hear the rest?"

Looking straight ahead, Remy nodded. "Yes, I would," he said.

Karga Kul! Where demons fear to tread . . .

When the Crow Road was built, Karga Kul was there. When Arkhosia and Bael Turath destroyed each other in blood and sorcery and the smoke of sacked cities, Karga Kul was there. Its scholars claim seven cities have risen on the great cliff where the Whitefall meets the sea, and seven times seven languages have been spoken in the halls of its keep, and seven times seven times seven rooms are built below the lowest level in a dungeon from whose furthest corners one can step, incredibly, *up* into the Underdark.

And in one of those seven times seven times seven rooms is a door that leads nowhere on the mortal plane. This door is bound in iron, its hinges ruined with acid, molten lead poured into the cracks and the magical sigils of seven civilizations inscribed into the lead.

Over all of this, forming an unbreakable barrier, is the eldritch Seal of Karga Kul.

If any man or woman knows who put the seal on that door, the story has never been told, or it has been lost over the centuries. What is known is that on the other side waits Doresain, the Exarch of the Demon Prince Orcus. For a century of centuries he has waited for that door to open. His demonic allies and underlings wait with him: the apelike barlgura, insectoid mezzodemon, avian vrock and great pincered glabrezu, six-armed marilith with the serpent's tail. The Abyssal chamber where Doresain held his watch was lit by the infernal glare of the immolith, and the hulks of goristro muscled smaller demons out of the way along the walls.

Somewhere in the world, it was said, secret cults worshiped Orcus. The most dedicated of these cults spawned powerful death priests, anointed by Orcus himself and given power over men's dreams. These cults work to open gateways between the Abyss and the mortal realms; their methods are assassination, infiltration, seduction . . . rarely do they show themselves. Karga Kul is their greatest prize, and the one they have never gained. Other armies have marched on Karga Kul, and broken on its walls. Never has the seal been broken, and never have the demons of the Abyss been unleashed to ravage the city from the inside, and, with it destroyed, spill into the mortal world.

Periodically the seal grows weak, and must be reinscribed. The quill that may inscribe the seal is kept far away, in a location known only to the Knights of Kul, the dragonborn elite given the Duty of Moidan's Quill after the great victory at the Bridge of Iban Ja . . .

"That's you, isn't it?" Remy said.

Biri-Daar nodded. "Me, and my ancestors stretching back perhaps a hundred generations. I am given a most sacred trust."

"We have the quill now?"

"No." Biri-Daar looked out over the Crow Road, where shapes danced in the gloaming as the sun fell into the mountains behind them and the sky darkened through violet and toward black in the distance ahead. "Moidan's Quill was first held by Bahamut himself. He inscribed the symbols that hold the Abyss bottled in the bowels of the dungeons below Karga Kul. Never have the dragonborn guardians of the quill failed to present it when the seal grew faint and needed reinscription. I will not be the first."

Remy worked out in his head what he was already assuming to be the truth. "It's in the Inverted Keep."

"Yes," Biri-Daar said. "It's in the Inverted Keep."

"How did the Inverted Keep get . . . inverted?" Remy asked. Also he wanted to ask what were those shapes dancing at the edge of the darkness ahead of them, but they were far enough not to worry about just yet . . . and in any case could be just illusions born of the road's bizarre origins . . . and the story Biri-Daar told was too fascinating. Remy couldn't imagine listening to anything else . . .

There was a jerk around his waist, and Remy flew off his horse and hit the ground hard. The impact jarred something loose in his shoulder, and also in his mind. He had been ensorcelled! Something . . .

The thing wrapped around his waist was a vine. Remy dug his heels into the earth and found his knife. He slashed at the vine until it snapped, and fell backward against the embankment of the Crow Road.

Suddenly the earth around him was alive with the vines— no, they were roots. And one of the great old trees at the edge of the road was moving. "Treant!" shouted Lucan. "A blackroot!"

Treants, those legendary guardians of the forests, were as vulnerable as other kinds of life to the undead transformations that occurred along the Crow Road. This one moved with the sound of crackling bark and the whisper of long-dead leaves that did not fall from its branches. The roots binding Remy dragged him toward it. "Behind it," he called out as the rest of the group leaped off their horses. "There's something behind it!"

From either side of the treant, sword wraiths appeared, their blades catching the moonlight. Remy struggled to draw his own sword but his arm was bound fast. All he could do was saw with his knife at the roots that drew him ever closer to the treant's great fists, which would pound him into a bloody paste in the undergrowth.

If the sword wraiths didn't kill him first.

Keverel was the first to reach him. Forbidden by his oaths to use bladed weapons, he lent his weight to Remy's struggle against the roots, while raising his holy symbol high with one hand and calling out. "Back, spawn of the Shadowfell! By Erathis, you shall not have this boy!"

The wraiths paused and flitted smoothly away from Keverel, keeping Remy between them and the cleric. "We will have either him or what he carries, holy man," one of them said. "Or perhaps both."

"And perhaps we bring you along as well. The Shadowfell has delights for the mortal who denies himself worldly pleasures," the other added. One of Lucan's arrows passed right through it, wisps of black the only sign of its passage until it thunked into the trunk of the treant. Rumbling, the undead tree spirit took a step toward Remy.

Paelias landed next to Remy, sword drawn and ready to engage the wraiths. "You surely draw a lot of attention, youngling," the eladrin said. His sword flicked out and was parried by one of the wraiths. "Lucan! Even the odds, mind?"

From the wraiths' side, Lucan attacked, driving one of them into the other. Both glided out of his reach, but Paelias was watching the shadows and was ready when the first emerged from the shadowglide. His sword struck home, bringing a miserable screech from the wraith, whose return stroke caught only Paelias's blade. Pressing his advantage, the eladrin struck again, and with a trailing scream the swordwraith vanished. Lucan awaited the other's return from its shadowglide, looking hard for any trace of moongleam on its blade.

Biri-Daar thudded to the ground next to Keverel as the blackroot treant took another slow, implacable step forward. "I am loath to do this," she said.

Landing next to her with flint and steel in one hand and an oil-soaked torch in the other, Kithri said, "If you let it squash Remy, it will probably go away."

"Life is never that easy," Biri-Daar said. She took a running step and leaped, new twin katars from Crow Fork Market reversed in her hands to use as improvised climbing axes. Below her, Kithri ignited her torch.

Lucan and Paelias backed slowly toward each other, keeping Remy and Keverel in the corner of their fields of vision. "You didn't accidentally hit both of them?" Lucan asked.

Paelias shook his head. "Just the one. Might have killed it. Or whatever it is you do to finish a wraith."

Then the second swordwraith appeared, all the way on the other side of Keverel, emerging from the shadows cast when Kithri lit her torch. She reared back and threw it at a knot of branches halfway up the treant's trunk, on the side opposite where Biri-Daar slowly worked her way up to the suggestion of a face in the dead branches of its crown. It swatted at her but could not dislodge her, and the torch caught its bark on fire. Immediately the treant devoted all of its attention to putting out the flames; using the distraction, Biri-Daar reached the base of the crown, where its ears would have been if the treant had been human. Instead of ears it featured a knotted hole on either side, with a multitude of tiny branches sprouting like whiskers above and around it.

On the ground, the swordwraith's blade flashed out to strike an unwary Kithri, who was striking flint over another torch—but with a clang, Keverel flung out his mace at the last moment, deflecting the blow. His protective blessing wavered and the swordwraith turned on him, slashing open his mail shirt and the flesh underneath.

Her torch lit, Kithri swung it around and swept it through the denser shadow of the swordwraith's head. The flame bloomed up and down its body and its screech pierced the night, spurred to a higher pitch when a leaping Paelias landed next to the prone Keverel and dispatched it with a stroke of his sword.

All of them looked up at Biri-Daar then, as she drew a deep breath and put her beaked mouth to the blackroot treant's ear.

She did not want to use fire. She did not want to burn the forest or destroy the spirits that lived therein. But she did very much want this blackroot treant to find death, to return to the soil that had given it life. All of that time spent with elves and rangers had made her too sensitive, no doubt—but whatever the cause, when Biri-Daar unleashed her dragonbreath into the knothole at the side of the blackroot's head, she did so with more pity than anger.

Flames flared out through the great rotting holes of its eyes and mouth, roaring along with the agonized roar the blackroot made. Blindly it grasped at Biri-Daar, found her, flung her away into the trees—but too late, as the flames caught the dead leaves of its crown and exploded into a great mushroom of fire. The roots holding Remy spasmed, twisted, and fell limp. Kithri sawed them away from his legs with a knife. "Lucan! Paelias! Find Biri-Daar!" she yelled over the sound of the flames.

In the last moments of its undeath, the blackroot staggered back toward the forest where its roots had first found sustenance. Then, Remy saw, it caught itself, jerking back from the edge of the forest in a shower of embers. Turning, losing its balance as the life burned out of its long-dead heartwood, the blackroot took one great step—over him, over the moaning Keverel, over Kithri—onto the Crow Road. And when it had gotten both feet on the road, it fell, its roots and branches dying by inches, curling and blackening as the flames found every inch of what centuries before had been one of the noblest beings of the world.

"Did you see that?" Lucan said wonderingly. "It moved out of the trees."

Kneeling over Keverel, Kithri said, "Lucan, don't be an idiot. It was undead. It didn't know where it was going."

"You believe what you believe," Lucan said. He looked over at Paelias, whose chiseled face bore the same expression of disbelief as his own. Both of them looked at Remy.

"I think I saw it too," Remy said. "It stopped and turned around, didn't it?"

"Go find Biri-Daar!" Kithri screamed. "Go!"

They went, not wanting to argue, even though they were fairly sure that Biri-Daar was all right. She had survived far worse than a short flight through tree branches.

And they were very sure that they had seen that night something that none of them might ever see again: an undead creature remembering, at the moment of its death, something of its long-gone living self.

Neither Lucan nor Paelias said anything about this as Biri-Daar limped out of the darkness before they had gotten a hundred paces away from the road. They fell into step with her, waiting to see if she needed help. She waved them away. "Sore is all," she said. "I am tempted to believe that the other trees . . . treants, perhaps, but perhaps just trees . . . I am tempted to believe that they looked after me a little."

"I believe it," Lucan said. "After what I saw that blackroot do, I can believe anything."

That night they were able to sleep a little, in the lee of a grassy knoll far enough from the road that the crows wouldn't follow them all the way. "How much farther are we on this road?" Paelias asked. "Which of you have traveled it all the way?"

"All the way? None of us," Lucan said. "I have been on part of it."

"I too. As far as the Crow's Foot at the Tomb Fork," Biri-Daar said.

Paelias looked around. "Just the two of you," he said. "And neither as far as this Inverted Keep. Interesting. Well,

I'll take the first watch and perhaps in the morning one of the crows will bring us a map."

In the morning, while they brewed tea and toasted bread, Remy said, "Would the crows do that? I mean guide us." Keverel was slicing jerked meat. He paused and looked at Lucan.

"Interesting," he said. "Would they?"

Lucan chuckled. "My guess is that I have no idea. I'll give it a try."

They waited as Lucan walked closer to the road and whistled out to the crows. Two of them flapped down into a dead tree closer to him. Remy watched as the crows bobbed their heads at Lucan. He pointed down the road, made a circular motion in the direction of the sun. After a few minutes, the crows flew back to their stations at the tops of the nearest trees. Lucan walked back toward the camp and the crows began to caw.

"They're just sentries," he said. "They're descended, or say they are, from the crows buried along this part of the road, which according to them originally came from a clan that lived on the edge of the elves' forest near the Gorge of Noon. Who knows whether it's true.

"But they also said that they thought it was five more days to the Crow's Foot, and a day after that to the Inverted Keep. I'm not sure how clear their ideas are about how far we can go in a day."

"Not far enough," Kithri sighed. "Is there water on the way?"

"Odd you should mention that. The crows said that the

last day or so of the trek would be through a swamp." Lucan squatted by the fire and poured tea. "They don't like the swamp. They wouldn't say why, but it was clear they didn't like the swamp at all."

"Well, I love swamps," Paelias said brightly.

Keverel snorted. "Gods," Kithri said. "You made the cleric laugh. Either this will be a great day or we will all die."

Saddled up and back on the road, they watched the crows watch them for that day and the next. The Crow Road leveled out and traversed a broad landscape of naked granite and clear water, punctuated occasionally by twisted pines festooned with observant crows. "So," Remy said when they had ridden the entire day without incident. "I'm starting to feel unusual because nothing has happened."

"You mean nobody besieging us because they want your box?" Kithri said.

"Or undead spirits wanting to drag us down below the stones, to transform us into ghouls and wights." Keverel smiled thinly. There had been too much of that in the reality of their days for it to carry much humor.

"When we get to the Inverted Keep, what are we going to find?" Remy asked.

"I don't know." Biri-Daar looked at the clouds gathering to the northeast. "I've never seen it except from the other side of the Whitefall. And I have never spoken to anyone who has been in the Keep and returned."

"What *do* you know?" Paelias. "Every time someone asks you something, O dragonborn leader, you tell us what you don't know."

"What do I know?" Biri-Daar repeated. "I know that the Inverted Keep hangs hundreds of feet in the air over the Whitefall, and that the way into it involves a way underground through the tomb of the Road-builder. I know that he transformed himself in some way, and presides over the Keep as he has done for centuries. I know that . . ." She faltered.

They rode in silence until she was ready to speak again.

"I know that there is a dragonborn there. One of my ancestors," Biri-Daar said quietly. "I know that one of the Guardians of the Quill is there. That . . ." Again she trailed off and again she mastered herself. "That will not be so once we have come and gone."

None of them knew what to say. Remy watched the dragonborn who had led them this far, and he understood more about how and why she did what she did.

"I will find Moidan's Quill, and bring it out, and we will take the quill to Karga Kul," Biri-Daar said. She said it to the sky but meant them to hear it. "The Mage Trust of Karga Kul will use the quill to reinscribe the seal and replenish its power. There are too few points of light in the world," Biri-Daar went on, and her voice broke. "Karga Kul is one of them. It is also my home though I have not been there in many years. I would not have it drown in the chaos of the Abyss."

If someone had asked him to list five things he thought he would never see, Remy would have put seeing a dragonborn cry high on the list. And he would have put tears from Biri-Daar at the top of any list. The paladin cried silently and without motion, riding forward with no change in her pace or expression. "It occurs to me," Lucan said, "that if all of us chose to bear the sins of our ancestors, we would surely be suicides."

"I fear that I can disagree. My ancestors have pledged themselves to Erathis for as long as there are records in Toradan," Keverel said.

"Surely we don't have to remind the good cleric that holy men sin," Kithri said. "If we do have to remind him, I know some songs."

"I don't think so," Keverel said, but once Kithri got started with a song, there was no stopping her.

◆━━━◆━━━◆

Here I am, Remy thought periodically over the next few days of riding. *I am with a group of strangers on a quest that means little to me. Why did they insist I come with them? Why didn't they leave me at the market?*

The box that had caused all the trouble was a foot long, give or take, and perhaps three inches wide and two deep. Its clasp was pewter and the seam between its lid and the box was invisible—unless magical attention was directed at it. The seam had glowed right along with the sigils on its lid when Iriani had first investigated the box. Remy wondered again what would happen if he opened it. It had been some time since anyone or anything had tried to take it from him.

What did Philomen want? Was Biri-Daar right that the vizier was untrustworthy, that he had sent Remy out into the wastes to die? Biri-Daar's theory was that Philomen needed the object Remy carried to disappear because other forces in Avankil wanted it. Or that Remy was never intended to survive the trip to Toradan, and that after his death some agent of the vizier's would have found his body and recovered the box.

No one in the group seemed to have any patience for the idea that Remy had been intended to deliver the box to Toradan.

"Who were you supposed to speak to there?" Biri-Daar asked on their fourth day. The Crow Road switchbacked down a steep slope for as far as they could see in front of them before disappearing into what looked like a lowland jungle. They weren't in the lowlands yet, but before they got to the Whitefall there would be a good deal of marsh to traverse. Biri-Daar remembered that much of her previous passage along the road.

"I was given a place," Remy said. "The vizier told me that when I arrived at Toradan, I should find the Monastery of the Cliff and speak to the abbot. But he never told me the abbot's name."

"The Monastery of the Cliff," Biri-Daar echoed. "What would those monks want with a package from the vizier of Avankil?" She clucked her tongue, something that Remy had learned meant she was mulling a problem with no obvious solution. "You were sent out into the desert to die, Remy," she said shortly. "That is clear to you now, isn't it?"

"I know it's clear to you," Remy said. "That's why I came along. But I still don't understand . . . I don't know anything. What does any of this Karga Kul business have to do with me?"

"The Abyss pursues you. And demons threaten Karga Kul," Biri-Daar said quietly. "Do you want to stake your life on that being a coincidence? I would sooner cut my own throat than deliver an unknown, magically guarded item to the monks on the cliff."

"Why?"

"It has been long years since those monks kept their holy orders," Biri-Daar said.

They rode in silence for some time after that. Eventually Remy worked up his nerve and said, "Biri-Daar. This is a personal quest for you."

The dragonborn nodded.

"Almost an obsession."

Biri-Daar made no response.

"Perhaps your obsession is making it seem like my errand has something to do with your quest," Remy said. "I don't see it."

"Would you like to turn around and go home now, Remy?" Biri-Daar asked.

Yes, Remy wanted to say. *I would like to turn around and go home and forget that any of this ever happened . . . .*

Except that wasn't true. All his life he had dreamed of adventure. He had looked at the ships docked in Quayside and imagined going all the places they had gone . . . all the places his father had gone. Remy had insatiably devoured every tale of heroism and magic, of questing and exploration, that he could find. He had learned to read solely so he could follow the stories told in the one book his mother had—her great-uncle's memoirs about his time at sea in the waters far beyond the Dragondown Coast, waters beset with floating ice or great mats of living vines that grew up from the depths to ensnare and destroy unwary mariners . . .

He had memorized the names of every city and town on the coast and determined to visit each and every one, swearing to himself that he would make his name in the world and leave behind stories that other men would write.

"No," he said to Biri-Daar. "I don't want to go home."

"Wise," said the paladin.

"We both know I can't go home anyway. It's not wise to accept that which cannot be changed."

"Perhaps not," Biri-Daar said. "But it is certainly unwise not to. You are good company, Remy. And you have the makings of a fine warrior, it seems to me. But you are with us because . . . I must be honest here. You are with us because I trust nothing that has any taint of the vizier," Biri-Daar said. "And that includes you."

The Crow Road wound like a snake through swamp and jungle after descending along the flanks of the last northeastern range of the Draco Serrata. The earth itself turned first to mud and then seemingly to a slippery tangle of root and rotten leaf, as if they walked on a pad of floating plant matter under which there was nothing but dark water all the way to the center of the earth. That was what it felt like when the skies lowered, and through the midday semidarkness they tried to keep to the road, feeling its algae-slicked stones under their feet until inevitably they stepped off and began to slide into the depthless muck. Biri-Daar nearly roped them all together, but at the last minute thought better of it; the threat was a little too real that they might all be reeled downward like a stringer of fish.

"Hey, Lucan, what do the crows have to say?" Kithri asked on their second day out of the mountains. The entire world was the drip, drip of water in the overhanging trees and the softly terrifying sounds of creatures unseen moving in the shadows.

"These are the Raven Queen's watchers here," Lucan said, looking up into the tangled canopy. Remy couldn't even see the birds he was seeing, and even if he could have seen them, he wasn't entirely sure about the differences between crows and ravens. "They are less willing to speak to me. The Queen, they think, is unhappy with our errand."

"Why would that old bitch care about what we do?" Paelias spat off the road into still black water. "She'll get her share of dead whether we ever see Karga Kul or not."

"The Raven Queen has never concerned herself with getting enough," Biri-Daar said. "For her, the only enough is everything. Every life we save is an affront to her."

"Then let's make sure we do enough killing to keep her happy before we start saving all those lives," Kithri said, so brightly her voice was almost a chirp.

"The ravens say one thing," Lucan added. "Ahead, the dead things buried under the road are not always dead." He paused, listening. "And the live things are in commerce with the dead."

Keverel, in a humorless mood, made a warding gesture. "Must the crows speak in riddles?"

The ravens cawed back and forth to each other. "*Ravens* speak the way ravens speak," Lucan said with a shrug. "You don't have to listen. They also said that in another mile or so, we were going to have to learn to swim. Then they laughed."

In another mile or so, the Crow Road subsided below still black water. It was still visible, as a ribbon of open water winding between impenetrable walls of jungle swamp on either side, but as far ahead as they could see it did not re-emerge from the water. The horses stopped at the water and would not go forward no matter how hard they were spurred or dragged. They dug in their hooves, eyes wild and rolling, until the party gave up and stood apart from their mounts at the water's edge.

"So the crows tell jokes as well as riddles," Keverel said.

"Ravens," Lucan corrected him again. "But the same is true of crows."

They stood watching each other and looking out over the water for a long moment. "Does anyone know how to charm a horse?" Paelias asked. No one laughed.

"The horses know better," Lucan said. "Too bad we don't."

"The only way is forward," Biri-Daar said. "If the horses will not go, we will go without them. Salvage as much of your gear as you can."

They loaded themselves with what they could carry, then drew lots to see who would go out into the water first. Paelias won, or lost. "Cleric," he said. "Bless me."

Keverel did, calling the power of Erathis to protect the eladrin. "Now we will find out what power Erathis has," Paelias said, and he took a step into the water. It was ankle deep. He took another. "I can still feel the road," he said. He stepped farther out. After ten paces he was knee-deep. After ten paces more, still knee-deep.

"All right," Biri-Daar said. "Anything that can't get wet, stow it high. We walk until we have to swim, and then we'll see what happens."

"Easy for you to say," Kithri said. But she stepped into the water right after Paelias, and swallowed her pride when she needed to be lifted onto Biri-Daar's shoulders as the water grew slowly but inexorably deeper.

They slogged through for the rest of the day, usually in knee- to thigh-deep water but every so often holding swords and packs over their heads as they negotiated stretches where the water deepened to their necks. Once they had to swim for a stretch. All of them expected at any moment to be snatched under the water by something formless and horrible. Keverel, Biri-Daar, and Paelias kept up a steady stream of whispered and gestured charms, to disclose the presence of malevolent creatures and to ward them away when and if their presence was discovered. It was only a matter of time. They knew it was only a matter of time.

In late afternoon shadows, the water held at thigh level. "Biri-Daar," Keverel said. "We can't do this all night. We're going to need to camp. It'll be dark soon and I don't relish trying to build a treehouse in the dark with the local wildlife coming out to greet us."

Biri-Daar stopped. "Agreed," she said after a look around. "Lucan. What's your feeling about the trees around here?"

"Most of them are dead. There are a few blackroots farther back off the road," Lucan said. "If we keep fires burning, I don't think they'll come too close, but none of these trees are going to like fire very much. That means they don't like you very much, Biri-Daar. But if one of them is going to let us stay, it will be one of these old willows. They soak up so much water that you can't hardly burn them if you drop them into a volcano." With a wink, he added, "And they're just a bit more friendly than most of the trees you'll find back here."

"Do they talk?" Remy asked.

"Not exactly," Lucan said. "But I can tell what they feel. Some of them remember this marsh before the Crow Road was built. They don't like what it has become. One of those will let us hammock for the night."

"Well, which one? Let's find it," Kithri said. Her usually invulnerable good cheer had been much tested by the amount of carrying and assistance she'd needed during the day. Pride was a difficult thing.

Lucan pointed ahead of them and to the left. "See the willow there? It's willing."

They sloshed toward it, keeping on the road until the last minute, when they had to leave the relatively stable footing of the stones for the treacherous swamp bottom. It was twenty yards perhaps to the long-hanging branches of the willow. As they made their way forward, the water started to boil around them, and Remy knew that the feeling he'd had all day—the feeling of being observed, awaited, hunted—had been justified.

They came out of the water all at once, yuan-ti malisons in a double circle around them, eyes gleaming black. "I should have known we wouldn't get through a place like this without finding them," Keverel said grimly. "Wherever there is poisoned water and dark magic, there will be yuan-ti."

They started moving closer together, deciding whether to move for the safety of the tree or open space of the sunken roadbed. "Something in the trees, there," Lucan said.

Keverel glanced over where Lucan had pointed. "Abomination," he said. They could see its coils draped over a low branch of a live oak. Its only humanoid features were four arms and a head that had aspects of both man and snake.

Before he got his shield up, a spear hit Remy square in the pit of the stomach. Without his mail coat it would have punched straight through his vitals and he would have died before he could count to fifty. With his mail coat, the impact still punched the wind from Remy's lungs and the strength from his legs. He went down, gasping in water and choking it back out. Hands caught one arm and in his hair, hauling him back to his feet. "Stay up!" Keverel shouted in his ear. Remy clutched at the cleric, gathering his balance. Another spear rang off Keverel's shield.

"To me! The willow!" Biri-Daar's voice rose over the sounds of the battle, and twining through it all, the rattle and hiss of the yuan-ti. It was a sound nearly like speech, so that Remy's mind looked for words in it, but never quite found them. Hypnotic and dangerous to hear, the hiss of the yuan-ti was every bit as dangerous as the poison in their fangs or the blades in their clawed hands.

Paelias sent a blast of magical energy spreading out across the surface of the water, singeing the yuan-ti and gathering them a moment to get into a defensive position. More spears arced in, but they had shields ready. Lucan even flicked one aside with his sword. Above them, the incanter whispered, its almost-words buzzing in their heads, distracting them, keeping them off balance. Remy started to get his breath back, but something was wrong and he couldn't tell what.

Lucan looked around as they knit themselves into a circle. Blades out, backs in. "Where's Keverel?" he shouted.

Of the cleric there was no sign.

Paelias swore and dived underwater before any of them could stop him . . . and with a whistle and hiss, the incanter in the tree uncoiled and dropped down, disappearing with barely a ripple after him. A moment later the water exploded into foam near the base of the tree. Simultaneously the rest of the yuan-ti reappeared, closing in with spears and nets. Kithri, already neck-deep, said, "Try not to step on me."

"What?" Remy said.

Without repeating herself, the halfling took a deep breath and ducked under.

That left Lucan, Biri-Daar, and Remy. Three swords against two dozen yuan-ti. "We fight," Biri-Daar said. "They cannot gain what you have, Remy. If we must kill ten of them for each of us, or twenty, then that is what we must do."

One of the yuan-ti, more aggressive than the rest, probed with its spear. Biri-Daar caught the barbed spearhead in one of the curls of her blade and jerked the malison off balance, close enough that both Remy and Lucan ran it through without having to take more than a step.

The others, seizing the opportunity, surged forward—but at that moment Keverel stood up out of the water, blood running from claw marks across his face and neck. In the crook of his arm dangled the lifeless form of the yuan-ti incanter. "There!" he cried, and brought his mace down on the incanter's head. The blow forced one of its eyes out to dangle on the surface of the water. A concerted hissing whistle arose from the rest of the yuan-ti.

Paelias appeared, and he and Keverel backed toward the circle. "Where's the halfling?" Keverel asked. He let the incanter's body go. It sank out of sight.

"She went looking for you," Remy said. He was still seeing double sometimes, and feeling weak in his hands and knees. "Too long ago."

As if they were actors in a play, two of the yuan-ti between the circle of warriors and the inviting branches of the willow threw back their heads with a gargling hiss and sank into the water. Behind them, Kithri appeared, scampering up the hanging willow branches. Nearby yuan-ti stabbed their spears at her, but she quickly moved higher, out of reach. "Let's go!" she cried. "How much of a path do you need?"

"Now you know," Remy said.

Keeping the circle, they forced their way through a thicket of spearpoints, catching and killing any yuan-ti that drew too close, making a tortoiseshell of their shields when the yuan-ti drew back their arms to throw spears instead of thrust them. Little by little, they fought their way toward the safe haven of the tree.

"Where did you go?" Remy asked Keverel.

"Slipped," the cleric said. "Paelias found me at the same time the incanter did. I couldn't see, but they could. I think it bit him. Have to see to him when this is over."

"See that you do see to me, holy man," Paelias said. As he spoke he slowed the advance of the yuan-ti with a sheet of ice across the water. They started in breaking it apart with the butts of their spears.

It didn't look like any of them were going to be seeing to anything when the yuan-ti were through. There were too many of them, even without the incanter. And there was nowhere to stand. Still they fought their way to the trunk of the willow and got their backs to it as the yuan-ti closed in. Kithri picked some of them off with throwing knives that snapped out of her hands faster than any of them could see in the failing light, but more arose from the water . . . and still more were coming through the jungle canopy.

Remy had been afraid but now was not. If he was going to die, he was going to die among comrades who had plucked him from the wastes and begun to teach him what it was to be a man, to fight for something worth fighting for. He would fight until he could fight no longer . . . as he had the thought he struck down into the water to his right, burying the point of his sword in the open mouth of a malison poised to strike at his thigh.

"Up into the tree," Biri-Daar ordered. Lucan caught a branch and swung himself up, taking a glancing slash across his leg and returning with a blow that struck out one of the yuan-ti's slitted eyes.

A net sailed from the shadows, its weights clattering against the willow trunk and its weave tangling the sword arms of Biri-Daar and Lucan straddling the tree branch above her. More nets spun in to catch at Paelias's limbs and web the spaces between the branches and the water. Remy cut at them, but they were coming in faster than he could handle them.

Help arrived then, from a most unexpected quarter; a blizzard of short arrows swept across the yuan-ti from an angle back in the direction of the sunken road. Whistles echoed across the water as small shapes appeared in the trees, coming from nowhere to ambush the yuan-ti. Their closing circle suddenly became a sandwiched line. Remy worked furiously to free Biri-Daar and Paelias from the net cords that tangled them. Lucan was already free. From higher in the tree, Kithri shocked them all by whistling just as their shadowy rescuers had.

"Halflings!" Kithri cried out. "The Whitefall halflings!"

They struck out from the trunk of the tree, forcing the yuan-ti back into the teeth of the halflings' barrage. Remy flinched as the arrows of the unseen halfling archers hissed by uncomfortably close. He sunk lower in the water—and saw that the sigils on the package from Philomen were glowing brightly through its wrappings. Anything under the water could see it.

And something did. Erupting from the swamp-bottom muck, two undead corruptions reached out for him. Their mouths fell open, spilling water and weeds and teeth. The sound they made seemed intended to be words but Remy could not parse them. He struck at one, his sword slowed at first by the water; still the blow landed and the creature's arm snapped off just above the elbow with a crack of rotten bone. He swung around, staggering against invisible roots, and barely deflected a swiping claw. With a shock of recognition he realized what he was fighting, and just as he did Biri-Daar appeared, the righteous fires from her mouth incinerating one of the undead and her sword hacking the other back down into the muck from which it had come. "Apostate," she said, the words smoking in the dusk. "Heretic."

Dragonborn. They had once been dragonborn.

The yuan-ti were gone, driven back into the vine-draped darkness by the hail of halfling arrows. The halflings themselves were suddenly appearing everywhere, calling out to Kithri in a riverboat pidgin that Remy recognized but did not understand. The burning undead floated for a moment, the stinking water extinguishing the flames in puffs of loathsome steam. As it sank, Biri-Daar watched and spoke softly for only Remy to hear. "The builder of this road has much to answer for," she said.

Their halfling rescuers were a river tribe that raided into the Lightless Marsh whenever the mood took them, it seemed. Few of them spoke a Common that Remy could understand, and the only one among the travelers who could understand their river pidgin was, of course, Kithri—and even she laughed at their odd colloquialisms. "We Blackfall halflings are a very different bunch," she chuckled. "Intermarriage must bring some raucous festivals."

"What are they doing this far into the marshes?" Keverel asked. "There's nothing back here but abomination."

"According to them, abomination and loot go together like bread and cheese," Kithri said. She was about to go on when the leader of the halflings spoke up in Common.

"The road is as much waterway here as anything else," the halfling said, pointing back at the gap in the trees where the submerged Crow Road led on toward Tomb Fork. "So here we are. Would you prefer to dispute further, or shall we make our exit?"

"Exit sounds good to me," Lucan said. "This is no forest. This is a cesspit."

The halflings had stowed their boat in the lee of a dying cypress whose girth it would have taken six men linking arms to encircle. The boat was flat-bottomed and broad-beamed, designed to take weight over distance on quiet water. Currently it was empty of cargo save for what looked like a short pyramidal stack of muddy coffins. Remy asked if that was what they were, but everyone he asked pretended not to speak Common. The boat accepted the five adventurers' weight with no trouble and its pilot

Vokoun, at a bow tiller, waved at a half-dozen polers to get them moving.

"There are more yuan-ti than there used to be around here," the pilot said as they poled their way through the swamp. Along the sides of the raft, archers stayed at the ready. Ahead, there was light—a patch of sky. Remy felt a weight leave his chest as he saw it. They had been closer than he'd thought; how terrible it would have been to die so near the goal . . . or the next stage in the goal, at any rate. "We run the tributaries all along here," Vokoun went on, "and dip into the swamps as we hear about this or that ruin that might be worth a look. Usually whatever we find isn't worth the fight to get it, especially the closer you get to the road. But today our shaman had dreams about the roadside near the fork, so we decided to come and see what might need our attention." He turned to the group and winked. "Turned out to be you. Should have known you had a halfling with you. That's probably what the shaman was really dreaming about. Half the time he's chewed so much kaat that he can't interpret his own mind."

Vokoun paused for breath and Biri-Daar jumped in before he could get started again. "Can you take us as far as Iskar's Landing?"

"Sure, that's where we're going anyway. From here, not much choice." Vokoun spat overboard. Remy noted from the color that he was a bit of a kaat chewer himself. "But what do you want to go there for, if you're headed for Karga Kul? We can get you there. For a halfling cousin—even a Blackfall cousin—it's the least we could do."

"We are in your debt," Keverel said formally.

Vokoun laughed. "You sure are. But it's a debt we'll never collect, so why worry about it?" He spat again and looked over his shoulder at the sleeping Kithri. "She's not doing well? She's hurt?"

"She was badly hurt by an ogre some time back," Keverel said. "She is healing, but more slowly than I would like. It's the air, the bad spirits . . . for all I know, it's the crows. Whatever it is, she's not doing as well as I would have hoped. But she is tougher than the rest of us; she'll come through."

Vokoun clucked in his throat and said something in the river pidgin to the archers. Each of them made a similar cluck and a quick gesture over the sleeping Kithri. Biri-Daar and Keverel exchanged a glance. Remy watched, wondering if Keverel would add an Erathian blessing. When he did not, Remy then wondered whether it was because he didn't want to offend their hosts or because he believed that, among halflings, the halflings' beliefs carried more power. Remy knew little of gods. He had heard their names, and his oaths, when he swore them, were to Pelor, but that was because his mother had done the same. To devote one's life to the service of a god . . . it was not the life Remy would choose.

And yet he would choose—was choosing, had chosen— a life of adventure, and so had Biri-Daar and Keverel. So perhaps a life lived for a god was not such a bad life after all. Remy was thinking of that when he fell asleep to the whoosh of the poles and the slap of water against the front of the halflings' flat-bottomed boat.

In the morning, sun beat down on Iskar's Landing and Vokoun's band of river traders—or river raiders, if there was a difference—was gone. There the second terminus of the Crow Road—the Southern Fork—wound down through a cut in the highlands to a flat place at a sweeping bend in the Whitefall. The landing itself was a collection of docks and a rope-drawn ferry across to the Karga Trace, which rose through the Whitefall Highlands and led after fifty leagues to Karga Kul itself. River traffic from upstream stopped there during times of year when flooding out of the Lightless Marsh made the Whitefall too dangerous to sail; during those times, an impromptu town arose, loud with gambling, whoring, and the rest of the activities bored travelers get up to when their journeys are interrupted for weeks on end. There had been no rains in the past month, however, and the Whitefall ran easy there, deep and green in the shadowed overhang of the bluffs along its north bank.

Remy had dim memories of arriving the night before, stumbling off the halflings' boat where it beached on the bank of a Whitefall tributary stream that ran into the main river a hundred yards upstream of the landing. He had stripped off his wet clothes and wrapped himself in a slightly less wet blanket and fallen straight back to sleep near a campfire on the riverbank.

"They got out of here early," Remy said to Lucan. Someone had strung the wet clothes near the fire to dry.

"That they did," Lucan answered. "But you also slept

in. You can thank our cleric for your dry clothes. What a mother hen he is sometimes."

Remy got dressed, looking around. Keverel was nowhere in sight.

"Before they left," Lucan went on, "the halflings offered us a ride the rest of the way down the river if we make it out of the Keep."

The Keep, Remy thought. He looked upriver, half expecting to see it. Lucan saw what he was doing. "We're not that close," he said. "We'll have to head back up the Southern Fork to the main road and then to the Road-builder's Tomb. According to Vokoun, the road isn't underwater after the Crow's Foot, and the local beasties are fairly tame because they're scared of whatever's in the tomb. Sounds good to me."

"Sure," Remy said. "Except the tomb part."

"There's where you're wrong." Lucan pulled a mug out of the ashes near the fire and tested the liquid in it with a fingertip. Satisfied, he took a sip. "Tombs mean plunder, young Remy. And even our paladin won't object to us helping ourselves to whatever we find in this tomb. Not after the undead dragonborn the two of you saw back there."

"She told you about that?"

"Why wouldn't she? Biri-Daar's proud, but she's not one to hide things from us. You could live your whole life and not be part of a band whose leader cared more for your life than she does." Lucan drank again, then sneezed. "She's not much fun, but she's a leader even I can trust. And I don't trust leaders."

Keverel and Paelias came up from the riverbank, where they had been trading travelers' tales with the others passing through the landing. "The word is out that something got away from Avankil that wasn't supposed to," Paelias said quietly. None of them looked at Remy. "There are bounties. Whatever it is we're doing with Remy's package, we should do it quick or we're going to have demons like orcs have lice."

"And we need to get moving out of here now," Keverel said. "It won't be long before some of the more unsavory characters down there figure out that maybe we might be carrying what we're asking about."

Paelias looked pale and shaky, as if he had just finished vomiting. "Believe I should have something to eat," he said. "But I don't much feel like it."

Keverel took his arm and pulled his sleeve back to reveal a bandage. Pulling the bandage back, he revealed a yuan-ti bite mark, four punctures that formed an almost perfect square on the eladrin's forearm. "The poison's not going to kill you. I made sure of that. But you are going to feel a bit under the weather for a day or so yet," Keverel said.

"Wonderful news," Paelias said. Then he bent over, Keverel still holding one arm, and threw up at his own feet.

Biri-Daar and Kithri approached from the other side. "We leave now," Biri-Daar said. "Much of the morning is gone and we're not going to want to spend a night anywhere near the tomb. That means we need to get to the Crow's Foot in the Crow Road today and find a defensible place to make camp. Paelias, can you do it?"

"The real question is, does he want to do it?" Kithri asked. "Thought you were just riding along with us for a while."

"A little poison isn't going to stop me going into a tomb full of horrible monstrosities with my new companions," Paelias said. Then he threw up again.

Kithri's skepticism notwithstanding, Remy realized that at some point Paelias had become one of the group. No one had said anything about it, and he couldn't tell exactly when it might have happened, but he was one of them, with the same mission.

They broke camp quickly. Remy wanted to ask Biri-Daar why the sigils on the box had glowed so brightly. Had someone put a charm on it, to call attention to it when certain kinds of creatures were near? Was it sensitive to the presence of the undead?

Or was something within it calling out to the undead? Or to the yuan-ti?

Remy had many more questions than answers. But he wasn't going to be able to ask many of them that day, not with the pace they were going to have to set if they wanted to make the Crow's Foot with enough light to set a fire and call the watches before dark.

They made it, just. The sun was low, touching the mountaintops, when they came over a crest on the Southern Fork and saw the Crow's Foot ahead of them. The Tomb Fork led straight away to the east, along high ground. The tomb itself was obscured by the undulations of low hills, but above and beyond it they saw their destination, and each of them regarded it in silence for a moment, awed by the powerful sorceries that had made it possible.

High over the Whitefall, its towers burning in the sunset over the Draco Serrata, hung the Inverted Keep. "I fear what we will find within," Biri-Daar breathed. Remy asked her why, but she would not answer. They camped in silence, and in the morning entered the tomb of the mad sorcerer and self-proclaimed king who had built the Crow Road.

BOOK IV
THE INVERTED KEEP

The next day as they broke camp, Remy couldn't keep the questions out of his mouth any longer. He walked up to Biri-Daar and asked, "Did those . . . you know . . . Did they rise because of me? Because of what I'm carrying?"

She had been working a whetstone through the complicated curls on the back side of her blade. Without stopping, she said, "Perhaps."

He waited. When she didn't go on, he prompted her. "Should we open it? Should we know what we're getting into if we go into a tomb? If this is going to raise undead, we'll likely find our share of them in a tomb, won't we?"

"We likely will," Biri-Daar said. She paused in her sharpening and added, "But we have committed to a course. We are taking you to Karga Kul and the Mage Trust. They will know what to do. And if they do not, then I have no hope of figuring it out here. So it's best not to think of it."

Remy would have pushed the conversation further, but Biri-Daar stood. "Time to get moving."

◆───✦───◆

The Road-builder's Tomb was ringed by the last paving stones of the Crow Road, at the terminus of the grand and terrible project begun somewhere near the Gorge of Noon a thousand years and more before Remy stepped onto those stones and said, "So. We have to go down to go up?"

"Yes," Paelias said. "And then apparently up will be down."

In the center of the keyhole created by the turnaround at the end of the Crow Road lay the open entrance to the Road-builder's Tomb. "The story goes that he couldn't stand the idea that the road could end," Paelias said. "Once, I believe, there was a keyhole at the other end as well. Some say it was destroyed in the war between Arkhosia and Bael Turath. Others say it was never there at all."

"I heard that the dragonborn of Karga Kul pulled up those stones and carried them off for their clan lair in Toradan!"

They turned as one. The speaker, standing on the far end of the ridge where they had made their camp, leaned on a tall shield, his face split in a broad grin. He was tall and broad, heavily built, his skin the color of old brick. His horns curled back from his forehead, carved with symbols of clan and god. "A tiefling," Kithri said. "How about that?"

Biri-Daar took a step forward. "You provoke me, tiefling?" she asked.

"I jest, O mighty dragonborn, Biri-Daar, paladin of Bahamut." The tiefling approached and dipped his head in formal greeting. "I am Obek of Saak-Opole. My ancestors and yours, dragonborn, did battle on the Bridge of Iban Ja. Now, though, events conspire to make us allies."

"Do they?" Biri-Daar looked back at the rest of them. "What say you?"

"I am curious how a tiefling appears to bait our resident dragonborn just when we're about to go into a tomb that is, according to legend, heaped to the ceiling with treasures beyond imagining," Lucan said. "If this is a strategy, I cannot fathom its goal. Not to mention my curiosity as to how you know her name."

"The goal is simple," said Obek of Saak-Opole. "Word has spread on the river of a certain something headed to a certain place. You can always use another sword. I can use a chance to get back to Karga Kul and settle an old score there."

"You don't need us for that," Keverel said.

"No, I need her." Obek pointed at Biri-Daar. "She is known in Karga Kul, and I sought her specifically. Without her, the Mage Trust will strike me down as soon as I am within sight of the gate. With her, I at least have a chance to enter the city. That is all I ask."

"And what do you offer?" Biri-Daar asked.

Obek drew his sword. "This. You're going to need it."

"You're a fool," Paelias said, and burst out laughing. "I thought I was the only one."

Moving closer, Obek said, "You and I have nothing in

common, eladrin. You're a freebooter. I would sacrifice my life to get back inside Karga Kul. If the only way to do it is by going through that tomb and that keep . . ." He spread his arms. "No one day is a better day to die than any other."

Biri-Daar walked up to the tiefling. "In one hour we are entering the Road-builder's Tomb. You will not enter with us."

———◆———

On schedule, in an hour, they began the entry of the tomb. From the rise, Obek watched but made no move to follow.

The Road-builder's Tomb began with a broad flagstone plaza, each stone carved with a different rune. "Once I read that these stones are a code, and that whoever solved it would bring the Road-builder back to life," Keverel said.

"I've heard that he brought himself back to life," Lucan said.

Kithri looked at each of them in turn. "Any other stories?"

"I heard that he takes the guise of a tiefling and tries to come along with anyone stupid enough to want to enter his tomb," Paelias said. They all looked at him. "Why not bring him along?"

"Because, idiot," Lucan said. "He could as easily be coming after Remy's little box. How do we know otherwise? How is that he appeared at exactly this moment?"

"Suspicion makes you die younger," Paelias said.

"Unless you get murdered in your sleep because you weren't suspicious enough," Remy pointed out.

"Everyone be silent," Biri-Daar said. "The tiefling does not come with us."

The unpaved earth that formed the hole in the keyhole was overgrown with highland brush and a few stunted, wind-sculpted trees. "It's supposed to be in the center here, the exact center," Keverel said. They hacked a path into the undergrowth, stopping periodically so Keverel could get his bearings. At what he determined to be the center, they tore the brush out by the roots, first chopping the larger trees out with camp hatchets. Then, using the trunks, they levered the roots up out of the earth, leaving a pit . . . that in the middle seemed a bit deeper than it should have been, exposing a stone that was a bit too regular in edge . . .

Half an hour later they had exposed the entrance to the Road-builder's Tomb.

A simple stone stair, just wide enough to descend single file, led down into the cleared and trampled earth. Below the natural roof formed by generations of root systems, its first eight steps were exposed. Below that abbreviated space, they found a solid seven feet of earth and brush, packed by the ages into nearly stonelike hardness. "Ah, the glories of adventuring," Kithri said.

Two hours later they had cleared it out, chipping it into pieces and handing them up in a chain to toss them out onto the plaza. Kithri, by far the smallest of them, was stuck down in the hole, levering pieces loose and scooping helmets full of loose dirt and gravel. When the landing was clear, they brushed off the door and examined it.

Unlike the paving stones, the door was unadorned. It was constructed of simple bricks and mortar. Neither Paelias nor Lucan nor Kithri could find any magical traps or bindings. "Well," said Keverel when they had cleared the door, "Erathis forgive me."

The door was not designed to open. Neither was it designed to withstand repeated impacts from a steel mace. Its blocks, held together only with mortar, began to shift almost immediately. Half a dozen blows had knocked it loose enough that Biri-Daar and Remy could wedge the edges of their shields into the gap and pry it open far enough for them to enter.

Biri-Daar went first, her armor aglow with a charm Keverel placed on all steel they carried. Lucan and Remy came next, then Kithri, with Paelias and Keverel acting as rear guard. When they were just inside the door, Biri-Daar stopped and said softly, "Kithri. Quick, back to the top of the stairs. Is the tiefling still there?"

She vanished and returned a moment later, her coming and going nearly soundless. "No sign of him."

"Too bad," Lucan said. "We could have used the company."

Paelias stopped. "Didn't you just—"

"One thing you can always count on from Lucan," Kithri said, "is that he'll be contrary."

"Quiet," Biri-Daar said. They moved forward into the tomb.

The first passage was long and straight and angled slightly downward. The stone under their feet was dry, the air in their lungs musty with an odd hint of spices scattered centuries ago and never dispersed by wind or age. Light from their armor and ready blades suffused the passage with a glow bright enough to illuminate but not blind. On the smooth bedrock of the walls, the story of the building of the Crow Road unfolded in a painting that stretched from entry to a plastered-over doorway at the passage's end.

"Any sign?" Biri-Daar asked quietly.

"None I can find," Paelias said. Keverel shook his head. Kithri darted forward to look for the kind of mechanical ambush that even the most skilled magic never found. She, too, backed away without finding anything.

Biri-Daar gave the plaster an experimental tap. All of them could hear how hollow a sound it made. She hit it again with a forearm, sending a cloud of dust rolling along the floor and leaving a visible dent in the door. Lucan punched a hole through where she had hit it and he peered into the darkness on the other side. "Antechamber," he said. Then he sneezed.

Remy and Biri-Daar broke out a hole big enough to step through, covering themselves with choking dust that picked up the magical glow. The effect was of walking into a faintly luminescent fog as they passed into the antechamber and saw what lay within. Like many prominent personages who built themselves extravagant tombs, the Road-builder had wanted his to reflect his station and achievements in life. So in the antechamber were arranged the tools and materials of exploration and roadbuilding. In wall sconces, bejeweled surveyor's tools gleamed next to hanging picks and shovels of solid gold. On the ceiling, a sky map was picked out in diamonds.

Along the walls below the sconces, rows of shining silver wheelbarrows were piled high with uncut gems and chunks of ore representing debris. "Amazing," Lucan said.

"Delightful, I would say," Paelias added. He picked up an uncut ruby the size of an acorn. "Hard to believe nobody ever bothered to come find this before."

A distant boom echoed in the chamber and down the hall. All of them looked back toward the tomb entrance, which was much too far away to see directly. "Our tiefling friend?" Kithri wondered.

Another boom came, and the rumble of what sounded like a collapse. "Well," Lucan said to Biri-Daar. "I hope you're right that we can get to the Keep from inside here. Now how were we going to get out of the Keep?"

"One thing at a time," Biri-Daar said. She was still looking back to the entry passage, and she drew her sword. The rest armed themselves as well, as the guardians of the Road-builder's tomb began to pour into the antechamber.

They were long dead, the last crew to work on the Crow Road, buried with the Road-builder instead of beneath the stones of his road. Their bodies were held together by the posthumous strength of his magic—some had once been human, others dwarves, even a few tieflings and orcs among them. They thronged in the entry hall, dully responsive to their single imperative: to destroy the intruders.

And, incredibly, to rebuild the tomb. As Paelias flung a searing splash of light onto the ceiling, they saw back toward the entrance that some of the reanimated workers were already moving stones and mixing mortar from the dust of the floor and the black fluids of their own bodies. How many times had this happened before? "I revise my earlier statement," Paelias said. "Instead, I choose to find it hard to believe that anyone ever survived this to get into the Keep."

"Hold them!" Keverel cried out suddenly, as within the antechamber more walking dead emerged from the stones of the walls. He forced them back with the channeled power of Erathis, blinding and confusing them, as the rest of the party dug for their lives. They used the picks and shovels and mauls, but gold was a poor material for weapons—heavy and soft and slippery in the hands of the half-decayed guardians. A heavy sledgehammer, its striking face set with a single great emerald, went over Remy's head and rang against the wall, cracking the gem and bending the hammer's handle. Remy first struck off the hands holding the hammer, then the head of the animated corpse. But right behind it loomed a great hulking corpse of what must have been an ogre in life, swinging a pick whose head was as long as Remy was tall. Keverel was smashing his way through the others, breaking them apart and crushing the skulls to make sure.

At the antechamber's entrance, Biri-Daar and Lucan and Paelias made a wall too strong for the surge of undead to break. The corpses died again and again, some of them coming back to life beneath the marching feet of their successors only to be cut down again as soon as they could rise. It was going to be up to Remy to deal with the undead ogre.

It brought its great pick down, burying it a foot into the stone floor as Remy skipped aside and hacked at its arm. Once, twice, three times he struck as the great hulking zombie worked the pick free. On the third blow, he severed its arm just above the elbow. It swung the stump at him, spraying him with a foul black fluid. With its other hand it got the pick free and pivoted to gut him with a sideways swipe.

Remy ducked under it and dragged his blade along the underside of its wrist, cutting it to the bone. The pick flew from its hand and crashed into the other wall, crushing a smaller zombie against the row of wheelbarrows. The ogre's severed arm still clung to the pick handle. It reached for Remy, its eyes infernally alight.

And then one of them went out, its light replaced by the gentle gleam of Keverel's magic imbuing the steel haft of one of Kithri's throwing knives. A moment later, the same happened to its other eye. Remy closed, swinging his sword as if cutting down a tree. He chopped through one of its legs and danced back as it fell. Behind him he heard Biri-Daar and Lucan shouting about something but he could not turn to see what it was; as the zombie hulk hit the ground, he struck again and again at its blinded head, eventually hacking away part of its skull and brain. Tremors ran through it, subsiding into silence.

Remy turned to see that everyone else had stopped fighting as well. All visible corpses were just that—corpses. Keverel was whispering blessings over them to permanently release those that had been rising again.

Ten or twelve feet outside the antechamber door, the last stones were being fitted into a new wall closing off the hall. The Road-builder's crew were doing their jobs.

"This was a trap for wandering tomb robbers," Paelias said. "Not hardy fighting folk such as ourselves. One wonders if the Road-builder left anything a little more interesting."

"More interesting than being forced to go through the rest of the tomb and discover what joys await us in the Inverted Keep? Careful what you wish for," Kithri said. She was eyeing the ceiling, and as soon as she spoke, she began climbing one of the walls, using the edges of alcove and sconce for footholds until she was within arm's reach of the ceiling. Then out came a stubby, thick-bladed knife and she began to work it into the nearest of the star map's constellations.

"Don't," said Paelias.

Kithri couldn't believe what she was hearing. "These are diamonds, Paelias. What do you mean, 'don't'?"

"I mean don't," he said. "It is not for nothing that I chose the path of the starpact. Maps of the sky are sacred."

"I'll put something else in their place," Kithri said.

"Kithri. Look around you. Is there not enough to carry?"

The argument might have gone farther, but the ogre corpse interrupted it by coming back to life. It reared up onto its single leg, wounds still gaping, the pulpy mass of its brain sliding out through the holes in its skull left by Remy's sword. With the advantage of surprise, it struck with its remaining hand, the momentum of the blow toppling it off balance even as its open palm swatted Paelias flat against the wall.

Keverel jumped forward, his mace crashing into its head as it hit the ground again. He pounded it into silence, then spoke his blessing and release. The others were gathering around Paelias, who had fallen motionless across two of the wheelbarrows, his posture not unlike the vanquished zombie crushed by the hulk's pick. Lucan slapped lightly at his face, and Paelias's eyes slitted open. He said something in a language Remy didn't understand.

Lucan answered in the same language. Elvish, Remy realized. Lucan looked up at Keverel, who was wiping his mace clean. "His mind is scrambled," Lucan said.

The cleric squatted in front of Paelias, who focused on him with difficulty. "Paelias," Keverel said. "Do you know who I am?"

"The Erathian," Paelias said. "Keverel. Holy man."

"Yes," Keverel said. Out of Paelias's field of vision, he was doing something with his hands. Blood began to trickle from the star elf's nose. He licked it from his lips, but kept eye contact with Keverel.

"We can't stay here," Biri-Daar said. "The crew will awaken again if we are here long enough to let them."

"Perhaps not," Kithri said.

Lucan nodded. "Perhaps they have done their work once they have walled us in." From the other side of the new wall, the sounds of building echoed. The crew was completing its work.

"Do they plant the trees again?" Kithri wondered.

"Don't be stupid, Kithri," Paelias said suddenly. "They're zombies. The undead don't go out in broad daylight to plant trees, for the gods' sakes."

Everyone looked at Keverel for confirmation. He winked. Paelias looked around at each of them, wiping away the blood from his lip. "What?" he said. "What?"

"Never mind. Are you fit to go on?" Biri-Daar asked.

"If he can insult me, he's ready," Kithri said. "Let's get what we can carry and see what the rest of this hole has to offer."

"Not the star map," Paelias said.

Kithri glared at him. "Fine. Not the star map." She looked up at it with longing that would have been touching had it not been motivated entirely by greed. Then she sifted through the litter of spilled gemstones and dismembered zombies, looking for the most efficient way to fill her pockets with riches.

Remy found himself next to Keverel as they found a zigzagging descending passage from the antechamber to what they assumed must be the actual burial chamber. "What did you to do him?" he murmured, not wanting Paelias to hear.

"Some healing closes wounds on the outside of the body, some on the inside," Keverel said. "His wound was to both body and mind, at the place where they meet. Very difficult to minister to those. But Erathis is powerful. He has never deserted me in a time of need."

Biri-Daar hissed from just ahead, a signal they had learned meant shut up, potential danger. Slowing, the group drew tighter as they came to a short stair at the bottom of which was another plastered-over entrance. On the floor directly in front of it lay a trowel and a pan of long-dried plaster. Biri-Daar descended the stair and said, "Be ready for the road crew."

Weapons drawn, they looked in all directions as she slid the pan and trowel out of the way. Nothing happened. She tapped at the plaster. Nothing. "Be ready," she said again, and punched a hole in the plaster.

The doorway was timbered over as well as plastered, and took longer to break down. When they were done there was still no sign of the road crew. They stepped over the rubble of the doorway into the Road-builder's burial chamber.

It was two or three times as large, in every dimension, as the antechamber. Their light barely reached the ceiling, but it did manage to pick out a diamond star map slightly different than the previous. Remy wondered if each one reflected the sky on a particular date, and if so what the dates were. The Road-builder's death? The completion of the Crow Road? Probably he would never know. The treasures in the burial chamber were different. The antechamber had celebrated the Road-builder's tools; the burial chamber celebrated the culmination of the work. The floor was a map of the Dragondown, with the Crow Road picked out in a single poured stream of gold. The Whitefall was a string of opals, the Blackfall obsidian. The Dragondown Gulf, covering nearly a quarter of the room's floor, was worked from lapis lazuli. In the center of the room, the Road-builder's sarcophagus sat untouched. Four feet high and seemingly large enough for three men, it was inlaid in gold, jade, and mother-of-pearl with a fantastically complicated collage of different creatures. There were men and halflings, crows and wolves, legendary creatures Remy had never believed existed such as beholders and the semi-sentient molds said to creep the darkest corners of dungeons. Demons, dragons, vampires . . .

"These are all of the creatures he buried under the road," Keverel said. "His menagerie."

Lucan walked over to it and tapped on its lid. "Do we crack it?"

Remy looked to Biri-Daar, knowing what her answer would be. She would have enough respect for the dead that she would not have the sarcophagus itself violated even if they took with them everything else they could carry.

"Yes," she said.

Stunned, Remy echoed her. "Yes?"

"It has been many centuries since the Road-builder lay in this tomb," she said. "Open it."

Lucan found the seam dividing lid and case. He wedged the blade of his knife into it, working it all the way around the sarcophagus. Bits of precious stone and gold flaked onto the floor. "I'm going to need a hand here," he said when he'd circumambulated the sarcophagus. Biri-Daar, Keverel, and Remy stepped up.

On Lucan's count of three, the four of them heaved the lid up. It overbalanced, tipping on end and sliding to the floor with a deafening boom. "That ought to bring the road crew along," Kithri observed. Whatever anxiety the idea provoked in her was not enough to prevent her stooping to scoop up some of the larger fragments of gold inlay.

The inside of the sarcophagus, as Biri-Daar had suggested, was empty.

But not just empty. Instead of a floor, only black space lay at its bottom. A cold damp breath blew out of it.

"Rope," Biri-Daar said.

Among them, they had two hundred feet. "This is where we go down to go up," Lucan said.

"And then," Remy added, remembering their morning's exchange, "up will be down. Is two hundred feet enough?" he added as the rope uncoiled down into the darkness.

"Someone has to go first to find out," Keverel said. "I will."

"No, you won't," Kithri said. "I will. I'm light enough that if there isn't enough rope you can pull me back up."

"The halfling talks sense for a change," Lucan said.

Kithri climbed up onto the lip of the sarcophagus, tipped an imaginary cap at them, and rappelled away into the darkness. She looked up when all of her save her face was in shadow. "One tug means all is well. Two means leave me. If you feel two, don't believe it. What I mean is three, except I didn't have time."

"What would three mean?" Paelias asked.

"Help," she said, and lowered herself out of sight.

They had received no message from her when the road crew arrived at the door looking to clean up their mess . . . and them with it.

This was the elite, the foremen and their hand-picked laborers. They were brawny, grim, twirling their picks and mauls with flippant menace. There were dozens of them, crowding the passage from the burial chamber doorway past the first bend and beyond. "Don't think we can let them rebuild the sarcophagus lid," Paelias said, looking down at the pieces of it scattered around their feet.

"Not until we get down there," Lucan agreed.

Remy shrugged. "Or Kithri comes back up."

"Hold them," Biri-Daar said.

The words had not left her mouth before Lucan's arrows were ripping into the front ranks of the crew. As they slowed, piling the others up behind them, Remy and Biri-Daar herself met them at the doorway, holding them at the choke point where they couldn't use their numerical advantage. Keverel, a step back, held forth his holy symbol. "Erathis commands!" he boomed. "You shall not enter!"

Slowed, pained by the holy force of the god, the undead tried to press forward. "Keep them back, Keverel," Paelias said. He was leaning over the edge of the sarcophagus, the fingers of one hand resting on the rope. "We've got a tug."

"Remy, you and the eladrin go," Biri-Daar said. "Lucan too." She had her talisman of Bahamut out; its fierce glow threw the room's shadows into sharp relief and washed over the undead crew, driving them back. Remy started to argue, but Lucan shouldered his bow and caught Remy's arm.

"It's not cowardice when the chief tells you retreat," he said. "We go to the Keep. So let's go."

When they got back to the sarcophagus, Paelias was already on the rope, skipping nimbly down the seemingly bottomless shaft. "Will the rope hold all of us?" he called.

"Two, anyway," Lucan answered. "Go quickly and tug when you're at the bottom. Go!"

Paelias went. Remy and Lucan looked toward the door. Keverel and Biri-Daar appeared to be holding the road crew back. "Go," Lucan told Remy.

Remy shook his head. "You."

"Remy, I'm going to have to throw you if you get stubborn. Then your box will break and every demon in the Dragondown will be here before we can catch our breath. Do you want that?" Lucan winked. "Go."

The rope was taut in Remy's hands, and trembling as Paelias rappelled farther down below him. His scabbard tangled his legs and his shield scraped against the opposite wall of the shaft as he lowered himself away from the rim. "Go, go," Lucan said again. He looked up. "How goes it?"

"Move, Lucan!" Biri-Daar's voice rang down the shaft.

Lucan's face appeared over the rim. "Remy!" he called. "Is the rope slack under you?"

Remy braced his feet and reached down. The rope moved freely in his hand. "Yes," he called back. "But I didn't feel any tug."

"Devil take the tug," Lucan said, swinging his leg over the edge. "Going, Biri-Daar! Fall back, let's go!" As he dropped into the shaft, Lucan looked down over his shoulder. "Quickly, Remy. Quickly. Even Erathis won't hold them back forever."

Remy had climbed his share of walls. And drainpipes, rope ladders, timber pilings . . . if it was a way to get from a low place to a high place or the other way around, Remy had climbed it. But none of that had prepared him for rappelling down a rope into pitch darkness of uncertain depth with a tenuous restraint holding back an undead army above him that would, given the chance, cast his rope down into the darkness after his suddenly falling body. Above him, he saw Lucan's silhouette, and above it the rectangle of the sarcophagus rim, illuminated by the flowing energies of Erathis and Bahamut. "Biri-Daar! Keverel!" Lucan shouted. "Let's go!"

From below Remy heard a voice. Kithri, he thought, but he couldn't hear what she was saying. He called down to her, but she didn't answer. Something lethal was doubtless lying in wait for them. Remy rehearsed the ways that he could finish the descent, come down off the rope, find his feet, and be ready to fight while a desperate and cruel enemy awaited him. Would Kithri and Paelias still be alive? He hadn't heard any sounds of battle, or even the quick sounds of an ambush. No ring of steel on steel, no screams, no crash of bodies . . .

"Remy," Kithri said.

She was closer than he would have expected. Remy looked down—and realized that down was no longer down. He was on his belly, scooting backward along a narrow tunnel. What he'd thought was looking down, was looking over his shoulder. Kithri was there, beckoning him. "You need to get off that rope," she said. "I'm not sure when you move from tomb to keep, but I do know that we can't be sure how far someone would fall along the way if we got too many people on that rope. Come on."

He doubled around in the tight space and belly-crawled the rest of the way, coming out into a low, dark room that smelled as bad as any place he had ever been in his life. "Gods," he said. "What happened in here."

"Whatever used to happen in the Keep," Kithri said, "its current residents still need a sewer. Get over here." She led him across the floor to a raised ledge out of the muck, where Paelias was scraping filth from his boots. "Charming, these acts of derring-do," the eladrin muttered. "Oh, look, our boy Remy is here. Welcome to the Inverted Keep."

From the tunnel—the drain, Remy realized—that somehow, through some magic, led to the tomb of the Road-builder, there came a flare of fire. Biri-Daar's roar echoed after it. Remy started up and headed back toward the mouth of the drain, but Paelias stopped him. Lucan appeared, head and shoulders over the drain's edge before he realized what he was about to dive into. With an oath to match the environment, he pulled up short. "What have we done here?" he said.

As he skirted the edge of the sewer pit, Biri-Daar skidded out of the drain. "Keverel!" she called.

The cleric's voice sounded very far away. "Coming . . ."

A moment later he struggled into view. Blood covered the left side of his face and he moved gingerly as he swung his legs around to step down. "Took a fall," he said. "The road crew was kind enough to throw the rope down while they restored the tomb to its pristine state."

Heedless of the thigh-deep filth, Biri-Daar recrossed the sewer pit and lifted Keverel into her arms. She set the cleric down on the ledge. "Lucan," she said. "See to him."

The ranger looked over Keverel, first checking to see that the gash on his head was superficial and then working down the length of his body. "Nothing seems broken," he said, "and I think the cut on his head is just a cut on his head. What say you, holy man? Take a drink."

Keverel drank from the skin Lucan offered. He pushed himself to a sitting position against the wall and said, "My head aches and only this witch doctor of a ranger would say that nothing is wrong with the rest of me. But I'll feel better if we get out of this stench."

"Me too," Kithri agreed. "As it happens, there's a door right over here."

By the light from her knife blade, she showed them a barred iron door. "An old lock," she said, producing a set of picks folded into a leather purse. "I'll have it open before Lucan can find something else to complain about."

"I doubt that very much," Lucan said. "For example, I will complain about Keverel's ignorance of shamanistic traditions among the rangers of the Nentir Vale."

The lock popped open. "See?" Kithri said.

"See what? I complained," Lucan said.

"No, you said you were going to. I win." She smiled sweetly at him and swung the door open with a shriek of rusted hinges that must have been audible to every denizen of the Keep.

"Where does it go?" Paelias wondered.

Biri-Daar walked through into the drier and infinitely less odoriferous chamber beyond, a small landing at the foot of a stair going up. "It goes out of there," she reported. "What else do we need to know right now?"

They climbed the stairs, gradually shedding the stink of the sewer pit—and also, more ominously, shedding the light charm Keverel had maintained on the steel they wore or held. "Something about the magic of this place," he said, with a worried expression.

"Or something with you," Kithri said. "Truth, holy man. Is the cut on your head just a cut on your head?"

He nodded. "Here," Biri-Daar said, holding out a small pewter vial to him. Keverel took it with a questioning look.

"It is a healing brew, from the clan," she said. "If it can heal the burns of an acid fog or the madness of hearing a banshee—and it can, I have seen it—it can dispel whatever ails you."

Keverel drank it off, his face twisting. "Awful," he gasped.

"My people are not vintners," Biri-Daar said. Then, unexpectedly, she laughed. On they went into what appeared to have been a dungeon once. The cell doors were open and hanging crookedly on rusted or broken hinges. "The Road-builder may know we are here already," Biri-Daar said. "We must be on guard."

They peered into each empty cell as they passed. Some contained bones, and once or twice a rat flitted through their light back into the darkened corners. But nothing rose to oppose them. A torture chamber exposed to the light for the first time in centuries yielded only hanging chains and instruments long since corroded into ruin. After it, they found a stair leading up. As they climbed it, Lucan said, "We're going down right now."

"Don't talk about it." Paelias looked a bit queasy.

"Best to keep it in mind, I think," Lucan said.

"Keep it in mind all you want," the star elf replied. "Just don't talk about it."

That was when Remy sprung the trap. He felt a stone shift under his foot and instinctively he leaped forward and up to the next stair, one hand against the wall to his right, looking down between his feet for the hole or blade or poisoned needle he was sure must be there. As he landed, he heard a fading scream. He spun and saw that a pit yawned open where the two stairs below him had been. Stones at its edges were still tumbling inward. Shocked, Remy saw Kithri and Paelias above the gap, Keverel below it—and Lucan hanging by his hands from its edge, scrabbling to get a foothold on the vertical wall below.

"Biri-Daar!" Kithri screamed down into the darkness. An answering roar told them she was alive. Paelias was reaching down for Lucan when he looked up, said, "If the fall didn't kill her, it won't kill me either," and let go.

"Pelor," Remy whispered. The others were shouting down into the hole. He heard Lucan's answering voice, Biri-Daar still roaring. He heard the clash and ring of steel, and a throaty inhuman rumble like no voiced sound Remy could remember.

The next thing he knew he was jumping in himself, tearing free of Paelias's grasp and holding out his gloved hands to keep track of the walls as he fell. His mouth opened and a barbarian's yell came out. It felt good. Whatever creature was down there, it would know that Remy of Avankil was coming.

He hit the ground in a rubbish heap. Rotting garbage and discarded bits of clay, glass, wood—everything that might conceivably have been thrown away during the years of the Keep's normal existence—splattered away from him as he sank waist-deep in the slippery muck at the bottom. There was shouting, and that gurgling rumble, echoing all around him. Light flared as if Biri-Daar was using her dragonbreath just around the bend . . . but what bend? Remy couldn't tell where the walls were. He pulled one of his feet free, feeling it hang up on something hard; as he shifted his weight, looking around for Lucan and Biri-Daar, he realized that his foot was stuck beneath a long bone. "Out of the way!" someone shouted from above. Remy slogged off to his right as Paelias and Kithri hurtled out of the darkness into the filth side by side. They too fought their way off to one side as Keverel scarped down the chute and landed awkwardly on his back, nearly disappearing into the refuse before Remy and Paelias caught him and steadied him so he could get upright.

"Lucan!" Remy called. "Biri-Daar!"

Light flared again, and Remy started to understand that the room they were in curled in on itself. He put one hand on the inside wall of the curve and followed it. Ten steps later he was in sight of Biri-Daar and Lucan. And the three incredible creatures that menaced them.

They were low to the ground and reptilian at first, their skin slick and oily, their legs splayed and jointed like an alligator's. But they were larger than any alligator Remy had ever seen, and their mouths were nearly circular, gaping large enough to swallow a halfling whole. From their shoulders sprouted tentacles with clusters of serrated barbs at their tips, and—most incredible of all—a tail-stalk with a vertical row of three reddish eyes, faintly luminescent, curled over the beasts' backs, wavering back and forth to take in the newcomers.

"Otyugh," Keverel said from just behind him. "If we can see three, there are probably more." He and Paelias pivoted to form a rear guard as Remy and Kithri surged forward. One of the otyughs was wounded, its tentacles both amputated and great rents showing around its jaws. Taking advantage of their brief moment of surprise, Remy slashed its eyestalk off. The spurt of blood smelled even worse than the rotted slush underfoot. Tears filled Remy's eyes; he blinked them away and struck again as Biri-Daar hit the otyugh from her side with a reversed blow that tore huge gashes along the hollow of its jaw. In a fountain of stinking blood, the creature fell, wallowing in its death throes.

Fresh yells from behind him told Remy that Keverel and Paelias were encountering more of the otyughs. He closed in on the second facing Lucan and Biri-Daar; the third, mortally wounded by Lucan's flickering blade, waved its tentacles feebly as it died. In the uncertain light Remy could see that both Biri-Daar and Lucan were wounded. Infection would be almost certain given the environment. He hoped that Lucan's ranger lore would keep both of them from blood poisoning.

Over his shoulder he saw that Paelias and Keverel already had dispatched the fourth otyugh. Remy turned back to the sole survivor of the first three. With Biri-Daar and Lucan and Kithri, he cut it down, Lucan applying the killing stroke.

Immediately Keverel and Lucan began treating wounds. Biri-Daar and Lucan himself were scored by the tentacles' barbs. "A walking font of disease, the otyugh," Keverel said, disgust plain on his face. The worst wound was on Biri-Daar's hip and thigh, where one of the otyughs had bitten partially through her armor. The punctures left were deep and already blackening around the edges. Fever was beginning to shine in her eyes.

Lucan found a packet of dried herbs in his satchel and ground them between his fingers. He pressed a small amount into each puncture, Biri-Daar hissing as he did so. "That will hold the infection off. Or should. Let's get healing, holy man," he said.

"Until we get out of this rot, no healing will take hold," Keverel said.

"Light," Paelias said. A stone in his hand blazed up brilliantly, illuminating the dimensions of the room. It was high-ceilinged, with holes in the ceiling that must have been rubbish outfalls. "Back to the chute from the stairwell," he said. "Perhaps we can climb it."

But it was too high from the floor. Paelias played his light around, noting every cranny and shadowed corner in the spiral room. "Why this shape?" he wondered aloud. "The floor slopes down as well. It's—"

"There's probably a drain at the bottom. Long ago, when this keep was still in the ground, its builder found a way to let the garbage rot and drain into an underground river. It's the same thing they do at Crow Fork Market, no?" Lucan thought for a moment. "If we could get out that drain, we might be able to scale the side of the Keep."

"Are we dam-builders now?" Kithri asked. "We'd have to hold all this back to get through this drain. If it's there. And if it's in a place that would let us get to the outside of the Keep and climb up."

"You mean down," Lucan said.

"If only I worshiped a god," Kithri said. "Then I would be able to plead for you to be struck dead."

Since there was no way up, they decided to go down. First they had to find pieces of debris large enough that they might be able to build some kind of barrier, a coffer dam of sorts they could use to expose the drain.

If there was a drain.

And they had to work fast because the miasma of the rubbish pit was very near to overcoming all of them, most threateningly Biri-Daar. She moved sluggishly, the pollution in her blood barely held at bay by Lucan's herbs and Keverel's healing magics. "There's only so much we can do down here," Keverel said. "We need to get out soon or that fever's going to . . ." He trailed off.

"So much for your god's favor," Kithri said.

Keverel looked at her and held her gaze until she looked away. "Blasphemy isn't getting us anywhere either."

"How is it that we're wading around in rotted potato peels when no living human has eaten a meal in this castle in . . . what? Hundreds of years?" Remy looked around in consternation.

"I don't think time passes here the way it does outside," Keverel answered. "These old vegetables might have been peeled and discarded a thousand years ago."

"Next time I go adventuring, I'm staying above ground."

"We are above ground, remember? And at least it's not a sewer," Lucan joked. They found several pieces of wood all together near the mouth of the trap chute and started working them loose to take farther down near the drain. Then Paelias stopped.

"Did you hear that?" he asked.

They listened. From the chute came a whispering, scraping sound. Then a whistle.

They looked at each other. Bad enough, ran the thought through every mind. Bad enough that we should be trapped down here; now something comes down into the trap to finish us?

Then they heard a voice. "Hsst! Is that Biri-Daar the mighty dragonborn paladin down there?" After a silence, the voice came again. "Come now! I heard you speaking to each other. I threw a rope down. Climb up or starve. It's your choice, but make it soon. I'm not waiting forever."

Paelias shone his light up into the chute. The curling end of a rope lay less than four feet from its mouth. "Ah, light," came the voice. "See the rope? Let's go!"

"It's the tiefling," Keverel said. He looked at Biri-Daar.

"Yes," she said. Her eyes were dull with weariness and fever. "It's the tiefling. Climb."

Obek's saturnine visage hovered over each of them in turn as they reached the steepest part of the climb, just below the gap in the stairs. "So," he said when all six of them were back on the stairs. "Shall we move along to the tower of the keep?"

"Not until we get some explanation," Keverel said. "Begin with how you came to be here."

"I went through the Road-builder's Tomb, just as you did." Obek looked smug. He had the upper hand on them, and knew it, and looked determined to enjoy it while he could. Sitting there on the stairs as if they were all around a tavern table, he waited for their approbation.

"You fought your way through the road crew on your own," Lucan said, his voice heavy with sarcasm.

"No," Obek said. "I went straight through the tomb, not stopping to loot or fight. The Road-builder's crew only fights if you are still there when they arrive to do their work. Then

I followed your trail to this stair, where it ended. Simple. Now. To the tower?"

Biri-Daar's lidded gaze had remained on the tiefling during the exchange. Remy wondered whether her fever was subsiding now that they were out of the pit. "Obek," she said.

He stopped his needling and looked at her. Something deep and unspoken hung between them. Remy understood that he would never understand it. Human history was evidence that if humans were good at one thing, it was forgetting. Dragonborn and tiefling, it seemed, kept their histories alive . . . and in that was the danger that the past would rise up and overwhelm the present. That was what had driven Biri-Daar out on their quest to begin with, the sense that she could and must redress the failure of an ancestor.

I'll take the present, Remy thought. *It's all I can handle. Let the past and future take care of themselves.*

"You are resourceful and strong. So are the rest of us." Biri-Daar paused. "But why dare the Road-builder's Tomb so you can follow us to the perils of the Keep? There is more to this than you needing political cover to get back into Karga Kul."

The tiefling leaned forward and the smile faded from his face. When he spoke, he spoke to Biri-Daar, but his words were meant for them all. "People look at me and see a devil. They've all heard the stories about Bael Turath. Thousands of years ago this happened, and yet I am held to account for it. All tieflings are. We have been pariahs ever since. Soldiers, sailors, explorers . . . we live hard, we die young. None of it ever makes any difference." Obek's eyes glowed dimly in the near-darkness. "You want to know why I have to get back into Karga Kul? Because if I do not, and the Seal is broken, every demon that comes through the gate is going to mean a thousand tieflings killed in cold blood somewhere else because they are mistaken for the demon-haunted. Some of them will deserve it. Most of them will not."

Obek stood. "I do not wish to have that on my soul when I go to meet my gods."

"Does anyone here believe a word he is saying?" Lucan looked from one of them to the other disbelievingly. "The Road-builder's crew ignores you if you just keep moving? Surely we are not going to believe that just because he says it."

Obek returned his gaze. "You want answers, friend elf, or are you content to turn your friends against me?"

"I want answers," Biri-Daar said.

"The stories of the Road-builder's Tomb are around for certain people to hear," Obek said. "I have heard them. I could have told you of the crew if you had bothered to ask. I know a man who survived the trip through the Tomb and the Keep. The way he told it, the Road-builder let him live to spread the story . . . but took his hands so he would not loot the tomb. He told the story for his bread."

"Where did he tell this story?" Biri-Daar asked. "Not in Karga Kul. Every story of the Road-builder that has traveled there, I have heard."

"And I in Toradan," Keverel chimed in.

"Different stories travel to Saak-Opole," Obek said. "Probably all of the stories are lies, but we Northerners know better than to trust anything that comes from Avankil or Toradan, and we know that in Karga Kul is one of the thin places between our world and the Abyssal realms. Fit those two things together, and you know why I am here."

There was a long silence. Remy did not know what to do. He was far out of his depth and had no idea how any of them could ascertain the truth of Obek's tales, and tales about tales. A man without hands who had survived the Keep? Fanciful. But not impossible. What were they going to do? Remy waited, knowing that all he could do was follow the lead of Biri-Daar and Keverel, whose quest this was.

In the end, it was Keverel who spoke. "Obek of Saak-Opole," he said. "We consent to have you travel with us. But know that none of us may expect to survive to see Karga Kul. Or what may happen once we are there again."

Obek extended his right hand. "You will see," he said. "There will come a time when you look at each other and think yourselves fools for debating over this so long."

As they shook hands, Remy realized it was the first time he had ever touched a tiefling. He had seen them occasionally in Avankil, but the superstitions about the race died hard. Few in that city trusted tieflings—or dragonborn, for that matter, but the dragonborn were understood to be of a higher nature. Tieflings, the average citizen of the Dragondown believed, were still barely a step away from the Abyssal side of their heritage.

"So, you are Remy," Obek said. "What is it you carry, Remy?"

Steel sang as Lucan drew, the point of his sword snapping still an inch from the hollow under Obek's jaw. "That's the wrong question, tiefling," Lucan said.

"Draw back, ranger," Obek said. He didn't seem afraid. His hand in Remy's was callused and powerful, but Remy felt no threat.

"Answer, then."

"I overheard certain things at Iskar's Landing," Obek said. "And put them together with the rumors that rumble from the darker corners of Karga Kul and Toradan. There are those who want Philomen's errand completed, and those who would take the cargo and send it to the bottom of the Gulf." His eyes settled on Remy again.

"We do not know what Philomen's errand is," Biri-Daar pointed out. "That is why we brought Remy. We could not chance letting his package fall into the wrong hands."

"No one seems to know what the errand is," Obek said. "You have been in the wilderness for some time. I have been in the city. Rumors fly, and there are more plots afoot than anyone can count. There has been a great slaughter in the Monastery of the Cliff at Toradan, and demons cluster like flies in the older parts of Karga Kul. Whatever he has, it is a critical piece of a very important puzzle."

Paelias stepped forward and pushed Lucan's sword down. "So by gathering up our hapless Remy and his most dangerous cargo, we have put ourselves in the same danger he is in."

"Truth." Obek nodded. He turned back to Biri-Daar. "You are here for Moidan's Quill, are you not?"

There was a long pause before she answered. "Yes."

"Then you will be facing the Road-builder himself," Obek said.

"He will not be the worst we face," Biri-Daar said.

"He will be if he kills us all," Kithri said. Everyone turned to look at her. "It's true," she said. "Since we're all of a sudden so concerned with truth above all else."

Biri-Daar started climbing the stairs again. She seemed stronger. They would need her at her strongest, Remy thought. All of them climbed up and out of the lower levels of the Keep, emerging to the strangest sight any of them had ever beheld.

Over their heads, the churning ribbon of the Whitefall, the black stones of the canyon that contained it, the greens and browns and yellows of the highlands stretching away to the Draco Serrata in one direction and the coastal plains in the other. A sky of every color but blue, and the sky itself, underneath and endless, darkening directly below their feet to a midnight indigo in which they could see the faintest pinpricks of stars.

"My stomach will not accept this," Lucan said. He turned away from the vista, facing the wall of the Keep's central tower.

The rest of them looked around the courtyard, where lay the remnants of the Keep's first garrison and residents—their bones, their clothing, their boots. Kithri and Remy kicked through it, wondering if there was anything of value and wondering, too, whether these long-dead soldiers and cooks would rise to attack the living intruders. But the bones stayed dead, and yielded nothing more interesting than a ring of keys. Kithri picked them up. They were iron, and without rust.

"Interesting," Paelias said. "There's no rhyme or reason to the way things age and decay. In the refuse pit I saw an apple core that looked as if someone had bitten into it this morning. Here we have bones as dry as any found in a thousand-year-old tomb."

"It's a dead man's magic," Lucan said. "Emphasis on the man. Humans know so little of time that they have even less grasp of it after they die."

The eladrin and the elf ranger looked each other in the eye, something passing between them. "What?" Keverel asked.

"Lich," Biri-Daar said. "They are deciding between them that the Road-builder has become a lich."

"Yes," Paelias said.

Remy looked at each member of the group in turn. They were all facing one another except him and Obek. Sidling a step closer to the tiefling, he asked quietly, "What's a lich?"

"A human wizard of great power," Keverel said, "who undergoes a dark ritual to survive beyond death. If the Road-builder is a lich, we're going to need to find his phylactery, the vessel that contains his soul. We must destroy it to kill him. It will be somewhere in the Keep."

"Perhaps, perhaps not," Paelias interjected. "For all we know it's back in the tomb. It could be anywhere."

Keverel looked doubtful. "It's a rare lich that wants its phylactery too far away. But we shall find out soon enough."

Over at the wall, Biri-Daar looked out through an arrow slit, listening absently to the lich discussion. Remy had come to the wall as well, his head spinning with the inversion of earth and sky. The paladin's brief season of humor seemed to have faded. Again she was her implacably determined paladin self. "I fear the worst about the quill," she said, "and we must find it to confirm those fears or teach me that they were mistaken."

"Biri-Daar." She looked over at him. Remy was nervous to say what he was about to say, but it needed to be said. "Couldn't we leave the box here?"

"We don't know what's inside," she said.

"True," he said.

"You will carry it until the gods will that you put it down," she said. "There is no avoiding that. Accept your burden, Remy. Carry it through. The reasons will become clear to you."

He realized then that he was more like Kithri or Lucan than Keverel or Biri-Daar. The gods were real to him but distant. He spoke the name of Pelor because it had been spoken around him in his boyhood. In contrast, Erathis and Bahamut were real and present, a constant and living influence over the cleric and the dragonborn paladin.

Looking out the window at the bottomless sky below, Biri-Daar said, "There is a long way to fall."

"How far would you fall? Before you turned around and started to fall down. Real down." Kithri had appeared next to them. She looked confused. "When we came down the shaft inside the Road-builder's sarcophagus, one moment it was climbing down and the next up and down weren't the same directions. How far away . . . is there a magical field?"

Paelias, also coming over to lean against the windowsill, shook his head. "I do not know. This is an ancient magic, a kind of magic few initiates in any discipline would attempt—would know how to attempt—today."

"Back to the lich," Biri-Daar said. "O eladrin, you manipulate the conversation with surpassing skill."

Paelias rolled his eyes. "Simple truths are all I speak."

"It's time to go." Biri-Daar shifted the straps of her shield and walked from the wall to the great double doors, bound in dwarf-forged iron, that hid the mysteries of the central keep.

The great hall of the keep was quiet and cool, the only light within cast by the gap between the open doors. Once the hall would have been alive with a fire in the hearth, music from bards and jongleurs, the echoing impacts of bootheels and the click of dogs' nails, but all of those noises were lost to the past. What remained was silence. "Where will the Road-builder be?" Biri-Daar asked, talking to herself. She turned to Lucan and Keverel, who had entered behind her. "How many towers are there? I thought I counted four from the ground."

"Four at the outer corners of the walls, and then there are four in more of a diamond shape inside," Lucan answered. "I made a circuit to be sure. It looks as if there's some kind of bridge connecting the tops of all four towers."

"I'll answer your question," Obek said. "The Road-builder will be where he can see his road. That means up." He pointed to an open stairwell at the far end of the great hall. "All the way up, is my guess."

<hr/>

Up into the tower they climbed. At each landing they stopped and broke down the doors facing each other across the tattered woven rugs that were the only splash of color in the gray stone of the tower's interior. The rooms had once, perhaps, been sentry posts or firing positions for archers, storage areas or maid's quarters. They were small, furnished only with ruins, their slitted windows looking out into the dizzying inverted outside world. On the sixth landing, Biri-Daar held up a hand. "Kithri," she said. "Up one floor and back, quickly."

Kithri could move like smoke. She was back within a minute, but even that minute was long enough for the rest of them to grow edgy and over-watchful, certain that something had happened to her and that they were waiting for an onrushing doom.

Then Kithri reappeared. "Next floor opens onto a bridge," she said. "It passes over the courtyard inside the central keep to a rooftop garden. If you go the other way on the bridge, it connects all of the towers—just like Lucan thought from down below."

Biri-Daar nodded. "That garden is where the Road-builder, when he was human, was known to study and walk. Or so the stories would have it. If he has become a lich, he will be there or he will be inside the chambers that adjoin it. From here, we must act as if he will attack at any moment."

They assumed their battle order, altered with the addition of Obek, and ascended that last floor, coming out onto the open stone bridge that arched from the tower to the Road-builder's garden. "Don't look up," Biri-Daar said.

"Or down," Lucan added. Obek humored him with a dry chuckle.

Remy heeded neither injunction. He had never been afraid of heights, or of hanging upside down, and the sheer displaced wonder of the Inverted Keep kept drawing his attention. He looked down, and there were stars beyond the walls of the keep; the broken stone bridge protruding from its main portcullis gate obscured a fingernail moon, ghostly in the afternoon sky. He looked up, and there was the thunder of the Whitefall, in fierce rapids above them, canyon walls descending red and gray to the highland where the Road-builder's Tomb sat below the keyhole at the end of the Crow Road. Remy could see the ridge where they had camped, and where Obek had waited for them to go into the Tomb and then followed when they were far enough ahead that the Road-builder's crew had had the time to do their repairs.

The tiefling walked at Remy's right. He too seemed to be enjoying the view. "I wonder how far one would have to jump before down would be down again," he said, and tapped Remy with an elbow. "Eh?"

"I was wondering the same thing downstairs," Remy said. Up this high, he wasn't quite as keen to discover the answer.

Ahead of them, the bridge peaked and then began its descent toward the garden. In another hundred yards they would have their answers about the Road-builder, one way or another. Keverel whispered a blessing of strength and fortitude over them. Remy felt the strength of the cleric's belief wash through him, invigorating his limbs and focusing his mind. There would be battle and there would be victory. They started their descent to the garden.

As they approached, they began to see details. The garden was a riot of undead plant life and bizarre hybrids, fruits that looked like faces and flowers that dripped blood or gave off faint sparks when a breeze pushed them too close together. "I wouldn't touch anything in there if you can avoid it," Lucan said.

Kithri chuckled. "You don't need to be a ranger to see that."

The walls around the roof garden were as high as a man. Built along one of them was a long greenhouse with an enclosed stone structure set into a corner of the wall. Smoke began to curl from Biri-Daar's nostrils. Lucan, bringing up the party's rear with Paelias, nocked an arrow. "I hear something down there," he said. "More than just the wind in the plants."

As she set foot on the gravel garden path, Biri-Daar clashed her sword on her shield. "Road-builder!" she cried out. "I, Biri-Daar, paladin of Bahamut and dragonborn of Karga Kul, call on you to come out and render unto the Knights of Kul what is rightfully ours!"

Her voice echoed in the space between the walls and up into the earth-vaulted sky above. When the echoes had died away, there was a dragonborn standing before them. None of them had seen him approach. "Biri-Daar," he said.

She nodded. "Moula. I am here for the quill."

The dragonborn she had called Moula stood a head taller than Biri-Daar and wore armor of lacquered indigo with the totems of the Knights of Kul etched on his shield and helm. Noting this, Biri-Daar said, "And I am also here to tell you that you are no longer welcome in Karga Kul. Exile is one possibility. If I must kill you to recover the quill, however . . ." She clashed sword and shield again. "I confess to my god that I might take pleasure in such a killing."

"Careful, paladin. If you take pleasure in killing, you won't be a paladin for long." Moula set his sword down and tightened the straps of his shield over his forearm. "To the winner the quill," he said, picking up his sword again.

"Perhaps I might have an opinion on that topic," came another voice, dry and sibilant. The Road-builder emerged through a glass door in the greenhouse, closing it carefully behind him. Once he had been a strong man, and handsome. But in his undeath, rich rags draped and swept around his skeletal frame, and an inhuman light shone from the empty sockets of his skull.

"It is rare to find a group of adventurers clever and hardy enough to brave my tomb and my keep," he said. "Welcome. Although I fear that I must not let you pass on." He gestured around the garden, and Remy, following the gesture, saw that the garden beds were nourished by the bones of previous would-be heroes.

"Remy of Avankil," the Road-builder said. "Philomen did not tell me to expect you."

The vizier's name in the lich king's mouth struck a chill in Remy's spine. It was the confirmation of everything Biri-Daar and Keverel had been telling him from the beginning. Instinctively Remy's hand dropped to the pouch containing the vizier's box, as though the Road-builder might try to pickpocket him. The Road-builder laughed. "Fear not, boy," he said. "I will not need to take it from you. Soon enough, you will offer it to me."

"You will never touch it," Remy said.

The Road-builder laughed again, the sound like two stones scraping against each other. "Delightful," he said. "One forgets so easily the bravado of the living."

Moula laughed at that, mimicking his master. "Dog," Biri-Daar said. "Slave of Tiamat. You turn your back on the Order."

"I realize the destiny the Order has approached since the Solstice War," Moula said. "Tiamat would yet accept your service, I think; though she would prefer to accept your soul."

"Ah, the Solstice War," said the Road-builder. "I remember it with some fondness. O hardy adventurers, you do realize that you fight the latest battle in a war that has never really ended. It was the sorcerers of Arkhosia who first sealed the portal to the Abyss that opened beneath Karga Kul, halting the advance of the demons and devils who entered into a bargain with Bael Turath . . . and here, today, the fate of that city will be decided. Doubt it not. You are formidable, adventurers. But even if you might survive me, you cannot survive the weight of empires. The ghosts of Arkhosia and Bael Turath still contend for the mastery of this world . . . and through them, the Knights of Kul came to their crisis at Iban Ja's bridge, no? Now here we have Moula and Biri-Daar, ready to fight on for the right to claim the soul of the Order."

Returning his attention to Remy, the Road-builder held out a hand. "Don't," Keverel said before the lich could speak.

"Cleric, I will have it one way or another." The Road-builder pointed out and up, toward his greatest work. "If I could make that, do you imagine you can oppose my will now?"

Keverel drew out his holy symbol and held it high in front of him. The Road-builder dismissed him with a wave. "Now," he said to Biri-Daar and Moula. "Perhaps the dragonborn would like to kill each other at this time, for the honor of their enemy gods?" He turned to the rest of the group and added, "I will do my best to occupy the rest of you."

As he spoke the last words, bits of shadow began to detach themselves from the shadows among the garden beds, shaping into wispy versions of the Road-builder himself.

They formed a perimeter around the garden and closed in. "Vestiges," Remy heard Keverel say. "Don't let them near you if you can help it. They die easily, but kill easily too."

The clean, pure light of Erathis shone forth from his talisman as Keverel invoked the god's protection. Kithri, long since out of throwing knives, slowly swung a sling back and forth. "Wonder if the bones of that skull will crack," she said, and snapped off a shot. The Road-builder flicked the stone aside with a glance.

Ghosting in, the vestiges reached to apply their necrotic touch. Lucan's arrows tore through them as if they were tissue; every strike swirled them away into dissipating smoke, but more and more of them rose. Kithri's slung stones ricocheted from the garden walls after passing through the vestiges without resistance. A window in the greenhouse shattered. The Road-builder hissed. "Poor manners for a guest, halfling. Very poor," he said.

From his hands poured liquid shadow that spilled across Remy and Obek. Remy smelled death, the scent of corpses . . . the scent of his own corpse. Dullness afflicted his legs. Obek growled a tiefling oath and struck out, slashing vestiges to shreds and leaping to land a strike on the Road-builder himself. Even approaching the lich took its toll; Obek bared his teeth against the Road-builder's necromantic aura and struck again as black spots appeared on his flesh.

An entire quadrant of the vestiges blew away in a blast of light from Keverel's talisman. The light flared brighter and brighter still—and steel clashed on steel as, their preliminaries out of the way, Biri-Daar and Moula came together in a pitiless battle of former friends. The traitor landed the first blow, shearing off a piece of Biri-Daar's shield and cutting deeply into her upper arm. She shoved him back into a tangle of fleshy flowers, following with a barrage of blows that he barely held off. The flowers, sensing blood, grew excited. Their stalks stiffened and their petals reached and grasped like fingers.

But Remy could spare little attention for their duel. He pressed forward, striking at the Road-builder but finding his blows deflected by the power of his necromantic aura. It clouded the vision and the mind; only Keverel's incantations kept them from succumbing completely. One of Lucan's arrows struck true, opening a crack in the Road-builder's skull. He answered with a simple gesture, two forked fingers pointed like a snake's tongue—but something black burst silently, momentarily obscuring both Lucan and Kithri.

When it cleared, both of them lay still. There came a brief hush over the garden, a spot in time between blows and parries, shouting and the crackle of magical discharge. Into the silence came the Road-builder's voice.

"Do you feel it, Remy? What you've brought me? Or should I say—what brought you?"

What brought me? Remy paused. The hesitation cost him as one of the vestiges got too close. Remy started to feel thick, started to think he heard the voices of the flowers beckoning him closer . . . they were spirits. They had not just grown from dead men, they were the spirits of the dead.

"Remy!"

Light blazed through the curtain falling over him—the light of Erathis, as Keverel gave himself up to the power of the god working through him. Karga Kul was Erathis's city, one epitome of the law and progress that pleased the god. If the quill would save Karga Kul, Erathis would work through Keverel to bring it there.

The vestiges began to fall back, torn to pieces by the force of the light from Keverel's talisman. Moula fell back before a fresh sustained attack, pivoting around and retreating in the direction of the bridge over which the party had first come to the garden. Biri-Daar pressed him; she grew more resolute and he more desperate, and at the same moment they opened their mouths and engulfed each other in flame.

Fire of another sort, black and curling and cold, spewed from the Road-builder. It brought forth a fresh cluster of vestiges. Obek struck again and again at the lich, and Remy did too, reinvigorated by the blazing Erathian light. He felt his sword bite into the Road-builder's bones. Paelias, given a brief respite by the momentary destruction of the vestiges, returned to the battle with a fury. All of the undead plants surrounding the Road-builder uncoiled and sprouted into sinewy vines, spiked with long black thorns. Some of them caught at the lich's robe, some his legs, some snaked up his arms. The Road-builder tore some of them free; others died the moment they came within the reach of his aura. But Paelias grew more vines, the power of the Feywild momentarily overpowering the lich's compact with Abyssal forces. Slowly the Road-builder was overcome; slowly the sword strokes of Remy and Obek began to tell.

All of them gained strength from Biri-Daar, her paladin's charisma bathing them in its psychic glow. With every strike at Moula, she grew stronger. Light flared more and more brightly from her sword. Behind Moula, Lucan began to stir. He got to his knees before the dragonborn traitor stumbled over him and went down, knocking Lucan down again as well. Moula landed heavily on Kithri. Lucan, long daggers in both hands, sank one of them to the hilt in a gap in Moula's armor, behind his left shoulder. The dragonborn roared in his agony; Biri-Daar bore down and split his shield in two, severing his shield arm above the wrist.

The remaining vestiges, at a command from the Road-builder, raised their spectral arms. In the space above the Road-builder's head, a sphere of deepest empty black appeared. The incongruity of it, seen against the pleasing highland prospect that was their sky, was suddenly to Remy almost as horrible as the necromantic sorcery of the orb itself. He thrust, and his blade jammed in the hinge of the lich's jaw. Splinters of bone flew away from the impact as the necrotic orb hovered over toward Lucan and Biri-Daar. Paelias's vines caught one of the Road-builder's arms and pulled it off with a grinding crack. The Road-builder was speaking, the language long dead and sounding like death itself in Remy's ears. Dying, Moula got to his feet one last time, knocking Lucan aside. Biri-Daar swung and he raised his maimed arm, sacrificing the rest of it to deflect the stroke.

Kithri stirred. Her face was pale, her eyes struggling to focus. One of her hands felt blindly along the gravel, looking for her sling or perhaps another weapon. Moula sank back, waving the stump of his arm trying to get his balance. Biri-Daar broke his collarbone and brought a freshet of blood from his chest with her next blow. He swung, forcing her back . . . and then he looked at her, the traitor regarding the avenging paladin. Moula looked at her and a sick smile spread across his face.

He turned away from her and with the last decisive action of his life, Moula ran Kithri through, driving his blade straight down into the gravel.

Biri-Daar, a split second later, struck off Moula's head. At that exact moment, Obek and Remy hacked the unlife from the Road-builder's body.

A split second after that, the necrotic orb fell among them and detonated in a soundless explosion that was the most violent thing Remy had ever felt.

The vines died and their creator was flung back through the greenhouse wall in a shower of glass. Lucan and Biri-Daar collapsed, and Remy toppled over backward with the bones of the Road-builder falling around him. He couldn't focus. He couldn't breathe. His heart skipped, stopped, then raced. Obek was driven to his knees, eyes squeezed shut against the terror that necromancy held for the renegade tiefling.

And Kithri spun away, still impaled by Moula's sword, her body turning over and over as it fell past the Keep's outer walls up into the sky. The last thing Remy saw was Keverel reaching vainly after her.

 ❧ ❧

Consciousness slowly returned. Paelias came out of the greenhouse, bleeding from a number of superficial cuts. Lucan, looking out over the parapet, wept. Obek poked through the Road-builder's remains with the point of his sword while Biri-Daar and Keverel headed straight for the stone structure at the end of the greenhouse. "Everyone up," Biri-Daar commanded. "We have yet to finish this."

"Finish this?" Obek said. "What's to finish? The Road-builder is dead. The dragonborn is dead. Let's get the quill and head for Karga Kul."

"Phylactery," Keverel said.

Paelias nodded. "Any guess about what it might look like?"

"No." Keverel shook his head. "Often they are boxes with small slips of paper in them. But they can be anything. I will be able to tell if we find it."

"Who cares if we find it?" Obek said. Remy had been about to ask the same thing. They followed Keverel through the greenhouse and into the Road-builder's study, a shadowed space littered with stacks of drawings and plans, bound books and strange instruments. A single small window looked out in the direction of the keyhole, which hung like a star formation in the earthen sky.

"If we don't find the phylactery, the Road-builder will reappear. Could be now, could be in a few days or a week. No way to tell. But I'd like to make sure that he doesn't come back at all." Keverel started searching, digging through the furnishings in the Road-builder's study, picking up speed as he went. At first he looked carefully; then he began to tear the study apart. Ancient scrolls and sheaves of vellum spun to the floor, along with surveying instruments, bound books, delicate scale models of bridges, retaining walls, even the Keep itself.

"What would it look like?" Remy asked, several times, trying to get the cleric's attention.

Keverel swept clear the top of a drafting table, splattering ink across the maps and plans he had already flung down. He stood, shaking, a cut-glass paperweight held in his hand as if it was a rock he could brain an enemy with.

"Stop," Remy said. "It won't bring Kithri back." He caught the cleric's arm. Keverel dropped the paperweight. It rolled across the floor as the keep rocked in a tremor, perhaps an echo of its keeper's death.

Keverel looked at Remy. Then he looked down. "Your box," he said. "The seals are broken."

"How do you—" Remy looked down too and saw gelid light spilling upward from the pouch where he kept the box.

"The Road-builder's death," Keverel said. "Or the second orb. Perhaps a combination of both. The discharge of magic broke the seals."

"Catastrophe," Lucan said. "We were hunted before. Now we will be hunted, and all of the hunters will know where we are." He looked around as if expecting demons to rise from the stones of the Road-builder's garden. "The Road-builder knew of Philomen. One wonders if the vizier himself might be waiting for us when we return to the shores of the river."

Lucan's anxiety infected Remy, whose mind filled with imagined scenarios. Had he been meant to fall in with

Biri-Daar so all of them could be delivered to the Road-builder, decapitating the Knights of Kul at the very moment the city was most endangered by the thinning of the Seal? He couldn't know. All he could do was look back on what had happened so far and realize that if things had gone differently at any number of moments, Karga Kul would already be doomed.

If, that is, the suddenly unsealed box had not doomed the city all by itself.

Remy could remember feeling that Philomen was among the greatest citizens of Avankil, a leader of all the Dragondown Coast. Now there could be no doubt. He had not only sent Remy out into the deserts to die, he was engineering some kind of plot involving demons and the undead. "If I ever see Philomen again," he said over the Road-builder's bones, "I will kill him."

Overhearing, Biri-Daar came to them. "Let's not get ahead of ourselves. First we had best see what Philomen went to all this trouble for," she said. The rest of them gathered around and Remy set the box on the cleared drafting table. The sigils, both broken and intact, glowed a deep yellow, darkening toward orange. Remy opened the box. Within, set into a velvet bed, was a chisel perhaps eight inches long, octagonal in cross-section with each face carved minutely in long strings of runes.

"Ah," said Keverel and Biri-Daar simultaneously.

Another glow appeared from a writing desk in a corner of the study. Every head turned to see that it came from a quill in a jar. The quill was long and curling, cut from the tail feather of a phoenix and burning as brightly as if that bird was at that moment immolating itself. But it was not burning; it was aglow, fiercely, as if challenging the chisel that at that moment was rising from the box.

"Hold it, Remy," Biri-Daar said. "Steady it."

"No," Keverel said, but Remy had already caught the chisel. It was hot in Remy's hands, but not too hot. The cleric looked as if he might say something else, but he held his tongue and went to the writing desk. Gently he touched the quill and plucked it from the inkwell in which it stood. "It is as I feared," he said softly.

"What is?" Paelias asked.

"The Road-builder's phylactery is Moidan's Quill," Keverel said. "We must get to Karga Kul before he returns."

BOOK V
BETRAYAL

An hour after the Road-builder's death, the six survivors clustered just outside the portcullis at the Keep's main gate. "Obek," Lucan said for perhaps the fifth or sixth time. "You heard this from someone who claimed to have heard it from someone who knew the man who had no hands that claimed to have lost his hands in this very keep. Do I have that right?"

"Give or take one someone," Obek said.

"I don't believe it."

"Our alternative seems to be climbing back up the inside of the Road-builder's Tomb," Paelias said.

"Would you like me to go first?" Obek said. "I'm willing."

"How will we know it works?" Lucan asked.

"Enough," Biri-Daar said. She stepped forward and cast the rope off the broken bridge. It snaked out, falling into the sky, looking terribly frail and thin when it had reached its full length. Biri-Daar stepped back. "If you're still willing, Obek."

"Ah," he said. "Sacrifice the tiefling."

"The tiefling should perhaps remember that he offered."

Everyone stood around for a count of perhaps ten. Then Obek picked up the rope, swung it loosely around one gloved forearm, and lowered himself over the edge. They watched him descend until he was out of sight. "We should still be able to see him," Paelias said. "There is an illusion at work."

The rope appeared to swing loosely in the breeze below— above—the Keep. "Lucan," Biri-Daar said. "Then Keverel, then Paelias, then Remy, then me."

In that order they descended the rope and disappeared. "Probably the tiefling is killing us one by one as we appear . . . wherever it is that we appear," Paelias said as he swung over the edge. "Just remember as you die that I told you not to trust him."

"Those will be my last thoughts. Yes, they will." Remy cast his eyes to the heavens, and was unsettled when he found himself looking up the Whitefall rapids toward a spectacular waterfall, its curtain of mist picked out in the evening sun even though the bottom of the canyon was in darkness.

Biri-Daar nudged him. "Your turn."

With the rope in his hand, Remy paused. "The Road-builder knew that the quill was necessary to keep Karga Kul from being overrun. To keep the demons on the other side of the Seal."

"What better way to guarantee a long life?" Biri-Daar

said. "Or unlife. We'll talk this over when we're on the ground. Right now the goal is to get there. Go."

Remy went, lowering himself up into the sky. For the first time since coming out into the courtyard of the Keep, Remy felt strong vertigo. He shut his eyes and concentrated on letting himself down, hand over hand, bracing himself with a coil of rope around one foot. The thought occurred to him that he might open his eyes and find himself on the Astral Plane. But when he did open them, as his feet found solid ground, he was standing on the rune-scored stones of the keyhole. The rest of the group had already built a fire and set to having a look at some of the more interesting objects they had found in the keep. Paelias, Keverel, and Lucan read over some of the Road-builder's scrolls. Obek was tapping at the stone in a ring he had taken from the dead Moula. He also carried a satchel filled with other booty, such as they had found in their brief search of the Road-builder's study and other parts of the Keep on their way to the broken bridge.

No one had yet said a word about Kithri, but all of them felt her absence. When Biri-Daar appeared no one asked how it happened that they could climb down into the sky and end up where they had ended up. The Road-builder's magic, the magic of the Inverted Keep itself . . . some phenomena did not bear close examination. If they happened, they happened. They were to be experienced, not understood.

Paelias, crosshatched with cuts from his trip through the greenhouse window, was the first to address their situation head-on. They had eaten, drunk, passed around the last of a flask of spirits Lucan had picked up back at Crow Fork Market. The eladrin was whittling a small flute when in the middle of the task he broke off and said, "The way I understand things, our situation is thus. We are in possession of Moidan's Quill that is needed to reinscribe the Seal of Karga Kul. We are also in possession of a chisel that one assumes was intended to destroy that seal. Moidan's Quill cannot be destroyed except at the cost of losing the city of Karga Kul to demons; if the quill is not destroyed the Road-builder will appear in its vicinity at some indeterminate but not distant time. So our current task is to get to Karga Kul, talk to the Mage Trust, evade capture or death at the hands of the vizier of Avankil and his minions, and replenish the Seal so that the quill can be destroyed. Do I have that right?"

"In a general sense," Biri-Daar said.

"What about the chisel?"

"The chisel . . . Remy, let me see it," Keverel said. He inspected it for a moment before going on. "Those runes speak of service to the Demon Prince Orcus. He and his army are massed on the other side of the Seal, awaiting their chance to pour across any threshold into our world. Clearly Philomen has pledged his life and his service to the forces of the Abyss. Just as clearly, he hoped to get the chisel to Karga Kul, either via allies in Toradan or by other means we have not yet understood."

Keverel handed the chisel back to Remy. "The chisel and the quill must be kept apart. Philomen will be on the hunt for one; we must not let him capture both in the event that things do not fall our way."

"No. We were drawn together," Biri-Daar said. "Bahamut has made it so. Do you not see? The restoration of the Knights of Kul and the salvation of the city of Karga Kul, these are the same task. Bahamut has led me to destroy Moula, the apostle of Tiamat. Now he leads me on to finish the work against the demons of the Abyss that threaten the city of the Order's birth. Our two errands are the same. It is time to finish them together."

The two locked gazes. "I do not know if this is wise, Biri-Daar," Keverel said. "The breaking of the box will have alerted Philomen to our location. He will waste no time trying to get the chisel back. If we are to stay together, we need to move fast and be on our guard."

"To Karga Kul, then," Lucan said. "But we all knew that already."

"And how are we to get there before the Road-builder comes back?" Remy asked. "How far is it?"

"On foot, ten days. On horse, four."

"In ten days, we will have met the Road-builder again," Keverel said. "Perhaps even in four."

"Then we must travel more swiftly," Paelias said. "We must return to Iskar's Landing and trade on the hospitality of the halflings again. The river will take us to the cliff landing below Karga Kul in two days, will it not?"

"It will, but I fear those halflings will not be nearly so happy to see us now that Kithri is dead," Lucan said.

Keverel shook out his blanket and lay down. "That must

be balanced against another unhappiness," he said. "Orcus will be in a fury that we have destroyed the Road-builder. All liches pay their homages to the Demon Prince."

For a few minutes more, Paelias whittled. He sheathed his knife and blew an experimental note on the flute. "Orcus," he repeated. "The Demon Prince will chase us all the way to Karga Kul. So will Philomen's agents. And when we get to Karga Kul, we will have to contend with a disintegrating Seal and Corellon knows what else. Including, possibly, a reincarnated Road-builder whom our only chance of avoiding requires a boat trip with a tribe of potentially hostile, or at least indifferent, halflings."

He looked around at them. "Do I understand our circumstances?"

"Mostly you have the right of it, yes," Keverel said.

"Then as long as everyone knows what awaits us, let us await it no longer. What is it, half a day back down to Iskar's Landing?" Paelias rose and piped a note on the flute. "To the river, comrades."

Obek had said little since returning to solid ground. But he too stood. "I'm with the eladrin. Let's move if we're going to move."

"It is not your decision," Biri-Daar said.

Meeting her gaze, Obek said, "I didn't make a decision. I offered an opinion. The right to an opinion I earned up there." He pointed toward the spectral hulk of the Inverted Keep, somehow less ominous knowing the Road-builder was—however temporarily—dead. And the final blows, Remy thought, were struck by Obek and me. I helped to kill a lich. It was a story to dumbfound his fellow Quayside urchins back in Avankil.

Only Remy wasn't any kind of urchin anymore. Perhaps he had already been beyond that when Philomen sent him out on the errand he was never supposed to complete. Certainly he was beyond it now.

"Dragonborn and tiefling, the assembled humans and elves have no interest in your grievances." Keverel stepped between them, placing a hand on the back of each. "Obek, you fought well in the Keep, but we do not know you. Ask Remy about finding a place in the group. Biri-Daar, this quest is personal for you, and spiritual, and it will be the matter of great songs. But only if we survive. Obek willingly risked his life to join us, braving the Road-builder's Tomb on his own. He has earned our trust until he proves himself unworthy of it."

"That's what I would have said if I could have thought of how to say it," Remy said. Everyone looked at him and he realized what they were thinking. It was the first time he had claimed a voice in the group.

Biri-Daar cracked a smile. It was the kind of smile, Remy thought, he had seen on the faces of fathers at the sight of their children's first steps. Partly he was proud of himself and of her regard, and partly he was spurred on by its slight condescension.

"Let us go, then," she said. "And let us leave the memory of our comrade Kithri the halfling to Avandra. She, patron of halflings, the Lady of Luck and the spinner of fortune's wheel, she will bring Kithri's spirit to its rest." All of them realized toward the end of these words that Biri-Daar was offering up a prayer for Kithri. But before they could grow solemn, Biri-Daar was already walking away down the ridge toward the Tomb Fork of the Crow Road.

———◆——◆———

As Paelias had predicted and all of them had quietly assumed, Vokoun's band of river halflings did not greet them as long-lost brothers, or even as fellow seekers after a common goal. The river pilot was cold as he looked from one face in the group to another. "So," he said at last. "You have added a tiefling and left the halfling behind."

"She died in the Inverted Keep," Biri-Daar said. "Died well, in battle against the Road-builder himself."

"And we have a great need for the speed of your boat, Vokoun," Keverel added.

"Why would that be? Demons on your trail from the Keep? Dig up something hot from the Tomb?" The halfling, stout and resolute, stood with hands on hips confronting the human cleric and dragonborn paladin.

Lucan stepped forward. "Vokoun," he said. "Look." With sleight-of-hand tricks, he made gold coins appear, one after the other, seemingly from thin air. "All of us could use a little entertainment," he added, "and we need passage aboard your boat. Come now." He grew sober. "Kithri was a dear friend of mine. None mourns her more deeply than I—and yet there is no time to mourn. Not if we are to get to Karga Kul in time."

A new campfire blazed up on the sandy spit of Iskar's Landing. The sun had long since fallen behind the mountains.

Down by the river, it was nearly dark under a sky of rich violet streaked with orange near the horizon.

"Teach me that trick," Vokoun said. "And someone go find the upland men over by the creek. They have spirits. We can't run the river in the dark, so you have the night to convince me."

Later, around a fire of their own, Vokoun said, "Once I saved you folk from the yuan-ti. What am I going to be saving you from if I let you on my boat this time?"

"I believe we could have worked things out with the yuan-ti," Paelias said. "Perhaps the next time we are ambushed, you can observe instead of intervening."

"Perhaps I will, if only to shut you up, eladrin," Vokoun said.

"The Road-builder," Keverel said. "If it is the truth you desire and not a story that will let you pretend to be bolder than you are, there it is. We will carry the Road-builder's phylactery to Karga Kul. And there, once it has accomplished its last task, we will destroy it. And him with it."

Vokoun drank and started to speak. Then he thought better of the speech and drank again. After some time, he spoke. "The story is that the Road-builder became a lich."

"It is true," Keverel said.

"What happens if I don't let you on my boat?"

"One of two things. Either we destroy Moidan's Quill, which is also the Road-builder's phylactery, and Karga Kul falls to a horde of demons, or we try to get to Karga Kul on foot and run the risk of the Road-builder appearing again before we get there." Keverel reached out for the bottle and took a drink of his own.

Vokoun took it back, then remembered his manners enough to offer it around before drinking again. "And this phylactery. That's what brings him back?"

"Until it is destroyed," Biri-Daar said. "And it can't be destroyed until we use it in Karga Kul."

They told stories after that, in turns around the fire. Vokoun began, and spun a comic tale of his ancestors' first boat, up in the marshes around the great inland sea that was the source of the Whitefall. Paelias picked up the theme of sailing, and told of an eladrin hero who sailed the astral seas of Arvandor in search of a woman stolen from him by Sehanine. Remy listened the entire time trying to figure out if Paelias was talking about himself. When the star elf's story ended with its hero returning to the Feywild, and from there to the mortal world, without his beloved, Remy felt that he had learned something he might rather not have known. Paelias was a fine companion, and a strong ally in battle. His sorrow, once his story was known, belonged to the company.

He was thinking this while everyone looked at him and he realized it was his turn to tell a story. Having no grand yarns to spin, no epic lies to tell, Remy opened his mouth and said something he had never said before, to anyone. "Once I saw the City of Doors," Remy said.

It was a secret he had never told anyone, of the time when, running from a gang of older boys, he had leaped across a sewer ditch and skidded on the fog-slick boards he landed on, straight through an open street-level window. He had landed hard, flat on his back, and lain in the darkness trying to get his breath. Outside the window, he heard the other boys laugh—they'd only seen him lose his footing and skid out of sight. When their sounds diminished to silence, Remy rolled over onto hands and knees and looked around to get a sense of whose home or shop he had accidentally invaded. Probably he could climb straight back out with no one ever knowing he had been there; but what would it hurt to take a look around first? If, of course, he wasn't in the kind of place where a wandering youth could find more trouble than he bargained for. Avankil was full of such places.

Slowly his eyes adjusted to the dimness. The room was narrow and rectangular, with the window in one short side and two doors in the other. The short walls were stone and mortar, slightly damp with the normal condensation of a belowground room, while the long walls were covered with slotted shelves, as if someone had once stored bottles there. Remy could well understand why they no longer did; in this part of Avankil, anything within sight of a window and unprotected by magic or blade would be stolen the moment its owner turned his back. The room was empty now, but knowing Whisker Angle, Remy feared that anything might happen.

All the more reason, perhaps, to get moving and get out of there—but there were those two doors set into the far wall. One clearly led up. A sliver of daylight was visible at its bottom, between door and jamb, and Remy could hear human voices on the floor above, their sound reflecting down the stairs. Three voices, it sounded like, speaking a sailor pidgin Remy recognized but did not understand.

An argument was perfect cover, was it not, for a little exploration?

The second door—it was on the left, and the door met the jamb flush, with no hint of light, noise, or smell from the other side. Remy listened and heard nothing. He opened it, slowly, and when he had opened it halfway he stopped and stared, struck dumb by what was on the other side.

A fat tiefling in a butcher's apron sorted through a bin of severed wings. "You here about the knucklebones?" he asked gruffly. In one hand he held a long, reptilian wing, with stubby claws at its main flight joint; in the other, a cleaver.

"The what?" Remy said.

"Knucklebones. Wyvern knucklebones. If you're not here for them, what are you here for?"

"I just—" Remy gestured over his shoulder and glanced back.

The room he had just been in was no longer there.

He spun back around to see the tiefling grinning at him. "Never been here before? An adventurer." He waggled a cleaver in Remy's direction. "Lucky you don't have wings, boy. You'd have walked out of here without them."

The tiefling pointed to another door beyond an enormous butcher-block table. "Out is that way. Back to where you came from is somewhere out there. Luck."

"But—"

"Go, boy. Nothing stays in here but me and dead things."

Remy went. Out the tiefling butcher's door, he found himself on a strange street. It was wider than most of the squares in Avankil, and everywhere he saw doors. There were round doors with latches set in the middle, double doors made of stone or pebbled black wrought iron; there were doors in the street itself, and doors that seemed to hang just near a structure without being attached to anything. And among those doors moved . . . everything. Every race Remy had ever seen in Avankil, or read of in the illustrated scrolls he spied in ship captains' collections or the vizier's library, or heard stories of in tallow-stinking taverns or beneath an ancient pier swaybacked with age. Every monstrous humanoid or elemental presence, every glimmering manifestation of astral will, every lumbering undead hulk of the Underdark. Remy was in a place that seemed to have no beginning and no end. No sky arched over the doors and storefronts, no sun shone to cast a shadow. Yet there was light, and there were shadows. No vantage point let him see beyond the limits of the city . . . yet he could look up and beyond, and there he could spy stars and strange luminescent swirls, as if some deity had taken light and made it into icing for a vast and invisible confection.

He looked down again. A detail jumped out at him: next to the doors that he could see—dozens of them!—was carved a symbol. A hand, fingers up, with a teardrop in the center of its palm.

"Or," commented a passing elemental wisp, "a drop of blood. The Lady is quite taken with the falling of blood and tears."

Remy started. "The Lady?"

"Ohhh," crooned the wisp. It was the color of air, visible only as a distortion of what was behind it. Its eyes were blurs. "You are in Sigil yet you know not of the Lady. A delight! How has this happened? No, wait. You opened a door, did you not? In a city on the mortal plane, where you come from. And you found yourself here."

"Yes," Remy said. "But—"

"Where is here? Sigil! City of Doors! Crossroads of the Planes!" The wisp swept in on itself, curled into a spiral as if aspiring to the colors in the sky. "This is the place that is always between all places," it went on. "The place from which you can get to any other place in a single step. The place that holds Creation together. The knotted, beating heart at the center of all that exists."

Then it vanished. Its voice, lingering a moment longer, added, "Or perhaps not."

Remy walked through the city of doors, seeing in each of them a gateway to a world as large and various as his own. Could it be true? "Boy," a voice hailed from a half-open door set beneath an overhang carved with a large version of the Lady's symbol in yellow and red. Remy looked and saw a devil, three-eyed and four-armed, with a tail curling around its feet. "You don't belong here, do you, boy?"

"I'm here," Remy said.

The devil clapped, one pair of hands slightly later than the other, creating a delayed echoing effect. In the portion of the sky Remy happened to be looking at over its left shoulder and down a short alley beyond which Sigil apparently vanished quite soon, a star went out. "Excellent response," it said. "The only response that makes sense, which makes you quite out of character here. It is a point of pride among the citizens of Sigil that they make sense to outsiders rarely, and then only when they hope to gain something from it."

It clapped all four of its hands on Remy's upper arms. He tensed, fearing violence—how would he fight a devil in a foreign place, with no weapon and no friends?—but the devil laughed. "You walked through a door you had never seen before, in a place where you had reason to fear for yourself. Is that not so?"

"That's true," Remy said.

"True is a word I don't much like," the devil said. "So. That is a word. When one speaks of true, one is speaking of morality."

Remy wasn't sure what to make of this. "Ha!" the devil crowed. "A boy who knows when to keep his mouth shut. Would you like a way home?"

It waved a hand and the door next to it opened. Through the doorway Remy could see the waterfront of Avankil. The Blackfall meandered, wide and lazy, past the quays. A smell of slack water drifted through the door, becoming one more of the smells Remy had not had time to disentangle from the overwhelming savor of Sigil.

"What's it going to cost me?" Remy asked.

"You can either kill a man for me or agree to perform an unspecified deed at an unspecified time, which will be no more of a moral transgression than killing a man." The devil grinned at Remy, clasping all of its hands together. "What say you?"

Remy thought about it. He was thirteen, old enough to know when someone was trying to put something over on him but not quite savvy enough to know what it was. At this moment he knew that no matter what his answer, he was likely to regret it later.

And he very badly wanted to go home.

The door to Avankil shut and disappeared. Only the wall, blank stone grimed with interplanar soot, remained. The devil's grin spread until Remy thought its head might separate along an invisible axis defined by the meeting point of its upper and lower teeth. "There will come a time when an adventure-minded boy such as yourself might do me a great service. Here." She held out a hand, palm up. In the center of her palm was a single gold coin.

Remy took it, fearing the consequences if he did not. The moment he lifted it from her palm, the devil vanished. He looked at the coin. It was a perfect featureless disk, with no face of king or emperor on its face.

Remy wandered Sigil until his legs were heavy and his tongue thick. Once a merchant of glass jars offered him a drink of water, but he was afraid to take it. He looked down at the stones of the street and wondered how many different worlds they had come from. Something was coming loose in his head as fatigue took him over. He was unmoored, as Sigil itself was unmoored. Remy was everywhere at once. He was afraid of never finding his way home and afraid to ask anyone where the way home might be.

From the fog inside his head shone a sudden clear realization. If he did not take control, he was never going to find his way out of Sigil. Looking around, Remy saw other wanderers. How long had they been there? One of them, a hunchbacked dwarf woman with long braids tucked into her boots, caught his eye. She knew, Remy thought. She knew him for what he was. She was telling him not to make the error she had made.

He was in a darkened stretch of street. Ahead, several streets crashed together into a broad square, alive with light and smoke. Remy headed for it. He would either find his way home or . . . for the first time, he realized that he could make his way here, in Sigil, just as he could in Avankil.

All of the worlds were here, each behind a door. Sigil was not a prison; he was not lost there; it was a gate standing open before him. All he had to do was walk through. Remy had good shoes on his feet and a good knife in his belt. He could go anywhere. He would go everywhere. Some men looked for Sigil their entire lives without finding it. Remy had fallen in and now, he was thinking, he didn't want to climb out. "Pelor with me," he said softly, and turned to face the next door he saw.

It had no knob, no latch, no visible hinge. What it did have was a slot in the exact center. Next to the door stood a tall and bulbous humanoid who looked as if it had been constructed of potatoes. "The Lady of Pain desires that you leave now," it said. Roots curled around its mouth and its eyes were black cavities that Remy would have cut out of any potato he saw in a kitchen. Even its breath smelled of root cellars and freshly turned earth.

"No," Remy said. "I am going to . . ."

"Perhaps Sigil will welcome you another time." The potato-man smiled and gestured to the door.

Already Remy was aching for the lost opportunity of Sigil. If only he hadn't waited, if only he had seized the chance when he'd had it instead of running around like a child looking for his mother.

"Young man," the potato-man said. "You are awaited elsewhere."

I could carve you into chips, Remy thought. But he walked to the door and put the demon's coin in the slot.

And his hand came away damp from the condensation on the inside of the basement room's one stone wall.

Outside, in the Avankil street where Remy had fled the gang, the normal voices and sounds of the city echoed from storefront to storefront. From the floor above, he heard a man and a woman arguing. Home.

Remy sniffed at his sleeve. Earth, smoke, sulfur, perfumes distilled from plants that grew nowhere on this world . . .

Sigil!

❖

"Quite a tale, lad," Vokoun said. "Either there's depth to your character or a liar's skill in your tongue."

Obek clapped Remy on the shoulder, and in the same motion prevented him from leaning forward with a retort to Vokoun's provocation. "A tale-teller's skill," Obek said. "I've been to Avankil. What else do these boys have to do when they're lying around the docks with the rats all day?"

Laughter erupted around the fire, and Remy took the joke in good humor. Coming from Obek it was easier. There was no deceit in him. Nor was there any malice. Tieflings were notorious for both, which either made Obek unusual for his race or meant that the other citizens of the Five Cities didn't know tieflings very well. "Crow Fork Market reminded me a little of it, but I didn't want to say anything."

"Wise," Lucan commented. "We barely believe you now. Then, before we'd seen you in action, we'd never have taken you seriously."

"I wasn't even there, and I can agree with that," Paelias agreed.

"Is it true?" Vokoun said.

Remy nodded, looking into the depths of the fire. He fancied he could see a tiny salamander, a scout from the Elemental Planes sent to see if the suddenly exposed chisel was of interest to the elemental powers . . . then it was gone. "Yes," he said. "It's true. I've never seen it since. I would like to go there again."

"The Lady of Pain has walking potatoes for servants?" Vokoun looked as if that, more than anything else, was impossible to believe.

"I don't know what he was, really," Remy said. "That's what he looked like, though."

"The part that worries me is the devil giving you a coin," Biri-Daar said. Remy looked at her and could see her measuring him yet again, deciding where his obligations lay, and his loyalties. The story disturbed her, he could tell. It disturbed him as well; how was he to know whether some kind of spell or curse had been placed on him?

"Paelias," Remy said.

The star elf held up a hand. "Biri-Daar," he said, "devils have many reasons for doing what they do. There is no taint of the Abyss on Remy, save the chisel."

"How much more do you need?" Obek joked.

"Silence," Biri-Daar said. "We weigh the success of our quest here, and the survival of Karga Kul. It is no time for jokes."

"Every time is a time for jokes," Obek shot back. "Especially the most serious times." His sword sang out of its scabbard and hung perfectly level, its point an arm's length from Remy. "So. Do we kill the boy and take the chisel ourselves? Do we kill the boy and destroy the chisel? Or do we quit this arguing and go on to do what needs to be done?" At each question, Obek turned the blade of his sword, walking the gleam of firelight up and down its length. "Me, I just need to get back into Karga Kul. Whatever makes that happen faster, I am for."

"Put up your sword, tiefling," Biri-Daar said evenly.

He looked at her. "I am called Obek."

After a pause, Biri-Daar took her hand from the hilt of her own sword. "Put up your sword, Obek," she said.

The blade flashed once more as Obek reversed and sheathed it. "There," he said. "Done. Now let us go to Karga Kul." Then he looked at Remy, who had not moved during the whole exchange. "Joke, my friend. It was a joke. No one was ever going to get killed."

Maybe not, Remy thought. But he also thought that Obek was going to be in for a surprise if he ever came after Remy seriously. Remy wasn't a Quayside urchin anymore, or even the vizier's messenger. Somewhere along the Crow Road, he had become a warrior.

* * *

They pushed out into the lively current of the Whitefall an hour after sunrise the next morning, Vokoun at the tiller whistling an elf melody. The river was narrow and fast but mostly flat for the day, he said. "Just one bit of white water to get through, past the crook below Vagnir's Ledge."

"Sounds like there's a story in that name," Remy commented. He was just behind Vokoun, enjoying the feel of the boat on the water. The rest of the party was clustered closer to the middle of the boat, trying to stay out of the oarsmen's way.

"There's a story in every name," Vokoun said. "Most of them aren't worth telling."

The story of Vagnir's Ledge, Remy found out later, concerned a suicidal dwarf and a chance encounter with a griffon, after which the dwarf became a legendary hero among his people—who inhabited the caves along that part of the canyon. But before Remy ever heard that story, he and the rest of the group very nearly ran afoul of those dwarves' ancient enemies.

After a full day of riding the river, monotony broken only by the occasional nibble of a fish on the hooks they trailed behind the boat, they tied up to a leaning oak tree, its branches spreading a good fifty feet out over the water and its roots exposed at the river's edge. "In ten years it'll be a snag," Vokoun said.

"In ten years, you might be a snag too." Paelias jumped nimbly from the boat up to a low-hanging branch and swung into the tree. The rest of the non-halfling passengers disembarked onto the shore while the crew made the boat fast and cleaned out the day's trash. They clustered in a flat crescent at the base of a wooded mountainside, with the sound of a stream nearby and the forest canopy alive with the energetic songs of birds. "This would be a fine place to settle," Paelias said from his perch.

Some of the halflings hopped out of the boat and set to work building a fire at the shoreline. "Someone's been here before, and didn't like it," one of them said, holding up a skull.

"Maybe not such a fine place to settle," Remy said. He and Lucan scanned the edges of the clearing.

Keverel examined the skull while the halflings finished laying the fire. "Whoever this was, a blade killed him, and not two years ago," he said. Something crashed in the woods, some distance above them. The sun was low; already it was dusk in the trees and on the water, and the light falling on the other side of the Whitefall's canyon was darkening to orange.

More crashing from the trees put them all on guard. Vokoun and the four halfling rowers cocked small crossbows and clustered together. Remy drew his sword and heard the creak of Lucan's bowstring. "Erathis," Keverel murmured, and at the invocation of the god a dim glow spread from the edge of the woods. Remy could see it playing along the edges of swords and the curves of helmets. But it was not men they were going to fight.

"Death knights," Paelias said as the undead soldiers broke into the open clearing. The halflings cocked crossbows and the party fell into combat order, their backs to the river. Remy had heard of death knights. In the stories, a single one of them could tear through a company of marching soldiers as if they were farmhands. At the edge of the trees, he could count at least a dozen of them. Perhaps more.

One, a dragonborn, larger than the rest and clearly the leader, stepped forward and raised a hand to arrest the progress of its subordinates. They stood at attention, eyes dimly aglow along with the steel they wore. "Biri-Daar of the Knights of Kul," the champion said.

She stepped forward to face it. "Once you were Gouvou, were you not?"

"Once I was living Gouvou. Now I am a servant of Orcus and my name is no longer of any use."

"Yet I will call you Gouvou," Biri-Daar said. "Because that is the name attached to your treachery."

"What have I betrayed? Surely not the legacy of the Knights. That was formed at the Gorge of Noon, at the southern foot of Iban Ja's bridge. Moula carried it on. I carry it on." Gouvou opened his jaws wide, threw his head back, and roared. A column of flame, burning the color of shadow, or clouds on the horizon lit by distant lightning, erupted from his mouth—and the radiance of Erathis disappeared.

"It is their unholy fire," Keverel said. "He may think it has driven the light of Erathis away, but he will discover differently." The cleric touched his holy symbol to his lips, then drew his mace up and held it at the ready.

"He did not?" Remy said softly.

Keverel shook his head. "I could bring it back. But to what purpose? We can see them now."

Biri-Daar drew her sword. "Single combat," she said. "Hold your minions to it."

"You put me at a disadvantage. Will your fellows submit should I defeat you?" Gouvou laughed, a sound like the rattle of a snake. The sound hung in the air, against the backdrop of the river's rush.

Remy never saw the signal, but at some unspoken sign the two dragonborn, one living and one dead, came together, swords ringing against each other and striking sparks from decorations on armor. The halfling crew kept their crossbows at the ready, but Vokoun held them back from firing. Keverel did the same for the rest of the party. Remy had never seen a ritual single combat before. Fights on the Avankil waterfront did not have rules. Even when one party called a man-to-man duel, there was always someone willing to slip in from behind and change the odds. The only halfling Remy had known at home specialized in slipping out of crowds to hamstring participants in such duels. He made a fine income at it until his face became known and someone cut his throat in a crowd before he could come out of it to cut a tendon.

That was Avankil. This was the lower Whitefall, and the death knights stood back as did the living friends and comrades of Biri-Daar.

Gouvou fought with a speed and agility that belied the death of his body. Remy had never seen a living being move so fast; Biri-Daar kept up, but only just. She parried, and took the blows she could not parry at an angle, striking back enough to keep Gouvou honest . . . or so Remy thought until he heard Keverel chuckle. "She's learning," the cleric murmured. "In another moment . . ."

Biri-Daar flicked the death knight's blade aside and struck deep, through his armor and into the undead flesh below. Gouvou made a coughing noise and rang his blade off the side of Biri-Daar's helmet. Dented, the helmet tumbled away until one of the watching death knights stopped it with his foot. Biri-Daar wounded him again, under the arm—and again, at the joint of his hip. Gouvou stumbled, the rhythm of his combat broken. Biri-Daar opened his armor from collarbone to nipple on the right side.

In his extremity, the death paladin found a last well of strength. Gouvou blasted Biri-Daar back with a storm of unholy fire, the shadowy flames pouring over her and driving her to one knee. She held there. Remy started forward; Keverel stopped him—as the steady clear light of Bahamut shone forth from Biri-Daar's holy symbol, blazing through the unholy flames. She put her hand on her sword and rose slowly to her feet. The two faced each other.

"Biri-Daar, you fight for a legacy that never existed. This is the true legacy of the Knights of Kul," Gouvou said, spreading his arms as unholy flames licked along the rents in his armor. Behind and around him, the same flames played across the bodies of the other knights. They raised their swords.

Biri-Daar roared out a gout of fire, overwhelming the unholy flames and scorching the undead flesh from Gouvou's body. At the same time, Remy and Obek leaped forward. Obek shattered the death knight's sword and Remy his breastplate and the bones underneath. Gouvou went down, reaching for his sword, but Obek cut off the reaching skeletal hand. Remy drove his sword point through the hole in Gouvou's armor, feeling the blade punch through the armor on his back and sink into the ground. All around them, the subordinate death knights were attacking again. Remy spun away from a looping mace head, letting go of his sword and leaving it in the destroyed remains of what had once been the dragonborn paladin Gouvou. Obek cut down the death knight who had swung at Remy, and Remy reached to pick up a sword from the ground.

"No!" Lucan called. "It contains a soul!"

Remy's fingertips brushed the hilt and he heard—as clearly as he once had heard voices from Avankil through an open door in Sigil—the soul speak to him. Instantly he knew everything there was to know about this halfling who had become a death knight. He was from a small village in the highlands outside Furia. He had fought, and fought well, in wars against the enemies of his liege. He had married, and begat children . . . and then been corrupted. In Avankil.

By Philomen.

The vision vanished as Remy heard the thundering crunch of Keverel's mace. He looked and saw that Keverel had just crushed the final unlife from a halfling death knight in the act of reaching for the sword Remy's fingers had just touched. With the fatal blow, the soul had departed from the weapon that bound the death knight's essence.

More of them were coming from the woods. Two of Vokoun's halflings were down. Keverel's helmet was knocked off and the upper part of his left ear was hacked away. Biri-Daar bled from every limb, it seemed. Obek, Paelias . . . they were all wounded, and tiring, and the death knights still came from the trees.

Philomen had sent them. The vizier's power reached even to the lower Whitefall.

The halflings called from the shore. All three of them fired their crossbows in the direction of the boat. "More of them!" Vokoun called. "In the water!"

"To the boat!" Biri-Daar roared out. They fought a steady retreat, holding back the flood of death knights as Lucan turned and unleashed a barrage of arrows at targets Remy couldn't see. Two of the death knights reached the trunk of the leaning oak and began to climb.

Remy broke away from the group, seizing a long sword from the ground. He killed the first of the two death knights before it knew he was coming. The second, already clasping the tree's lowest branch, knocked Remy sprawling with a booted kick to the side of his head. When he got up, he could tell that one of his eyes wasn't focusing properly, and his ears rang. Still he jumped and grabbed the death knight around the legs. The branch broke off from their combined weight and they fell, the impact sending an agonizing throb through Remy's head. He shoved the death knight away, clearing space for a sword stroke that opened its throat. It grinned horribly through the blood and Remy barely parried its return thrust . . . but parry it he did, and the death knight overbalanced ever so slightly.

In the moment when it was extended, its sword too far out and its cut throat fountaining blood onto the forest floor, Remy struck off its head. He turned and headed for the river's edge, where the rest of the group were standing knee-deep and boarding the boat. Lucan's arrows helped to hold the death knights back, but some of them waded straight in, and Remy could see another emerging from the water below the tree. "Lucan!" he shouted, pointing—but too late. It severed the boat's mooring rope before three arrows punched down into it. Looking up, the death knight drew a throwing knife. A fourth arrow appeared to sprout from its armor, a perfect shot just to the left of the breastbone.

Its life force draining away, the death knight raised both hands and clapped them together. As it sank beneath the surface, the tree, and Lucan in it, burst into unholy flames.

Lucan screamed and leaped from the branch into the water, trailing the awful radiance of the unholy flames behind him. The tree burned as if it had been dead and seasoning for two winters, flames roaring up from it to cast flickering shadows on the combat at the shore. "Lucan's in the water!" Remy shouted. Over the roar of the burning tree, no one could hear him. He dropped his sword, got a running start past the leaning trunk, and dived out over the boat into the black water beyond.

It was cold and his armor was heavy, dragging him down so fast that he could see the bottom, dimly illuminated by the burning tree. Lucan was close enough to touch; the unholy flames were still dying on his body and his eyes were wide with shock. Remy caught him and kicked hard for the surface, pitting his strength against the weight of the armor. It was a struggle he would only win for a few seconds. The hull of the boat above was a leaf-shaped blackness against the infernal orange of the flames. Remy reached, and kicked, and did not know he had thrust one arm out of the water until strong hands grabbed it and pulled him the rest of the way up. "Remy!" Keverel cried. He held Remy's arm while Obek and Paelias pulled Lucan into the boat.

"Row!" Vokoun ordered. The boat was drifting, far enough out into the water that the death knights could not reach it—or reach up to it from the riverbottom. Remy could see seven of them still, grouped on the shore watching the boat.

Keverel began ministering to Lucan as Obek helped Remy out of the water. "Brave stuff there," the tiefling said.

"And stupid. Who jumps into water wearing a mail shirt and boots?" Vokoun shook his head. "Now that might be a story worth telling. If we live to tell any stories at all."

Two of the halflings were dead, and the necrotic magic of the death knights' weapons was working in every wound. Remy could see the flesh beginning to die even around the small nick across the back of his knuckles. Most of the others, cut much more deeply, were groaning and sick with the death rot. "Lucan's going to die soonest," Keverel said. "I have to see to him first. Anyone with a healing draught, what are you saving it for?"

Remy had one and gave it to Obek, who was wounded deeply in the side. There were three others for Paelias, Biri-Daar, and Keverel, whose head wound had exposed the bone of his skull just above the ear. The two remaining oarsmen were struggling against the current, which quickened as the river grew narrower and poured through a chute into another spot of flat water between sheer stone walls. "I need more oars," Vokoun said. Remy sat down at one of the benches and picked up an oar. Obek took another. Paelias joined Keverel at the prostrate Lucan, who was muttering and gasping in a burn fugue.

"If he catches a chill, he'll die," Obek said. "Elf or not."

One of the halfling oarsmen shrugged and said, "One less elf."

Remy looked at him. "You don't like elves?"

"He doesn't have to like elves," Obek said.

"I don't have to like him."

"Oarsmen!" Vokoun called out. "Shut up and row!"

"Whatever you want to call him," the halfling said, "if he catches a chill he's going to die."

Keverel knew that too, and kept Lucan under two heavy blankets while he brought all of the power of his healing arts to bear. Lucan's hair was mostly gone, his hands and face were badly burned and his chest and stomach were scorched where metal buckles had touched his skin as his clothing burned. Lucan shivered and muttered under the blankets, and Keverel muttered Erathian prayers and blessings back. Eventually Lucan subsided into an uneasy sleep. "Will he live?" Biri-Daar asked.

"I think so," Keverel said. "I'll keep doing everything I can." The cleric looked exhausted. Yet he went from person to person on the boat, making sure that the necrotic effects of the death knights' blades were arrested and that natural healing could begin. He spent extra time with Obek, who had been hurt more seriously than anyone knew. When he had made a round of the boat, Biri-Daar commanded him to get some rest. Keverel was asleep almost at once.

The banks of the river were lower around them, hilly and dark under the light of a gibbous moon that picked out occasional brighter rock features. "We shouldn't tie up again," Biri-Daar said. "In this wilderness, the only thing we're likely to see is more of Philomen's minions."

Remy watched the banks slide by, his oar across his knees, waiting for Vokoun's next order. Lucan would live, probably. And Remy had saved him from the two death knights, who would surely have killed him in the tree. *I put an end to Gouvou as well*, Remy thought. He was proud of himself even though he knew that he had done only what was expected of a warrior. He was proving himself worthy. Biri-Daar would accept him.

Another thought occurred to him. What need had he of Biri-Daar's acceptance? She had saved his life, yes, but he had long since repaid that obligation, and was now with them of his own free will. He had the chisel, and his personal errand was to make sure that it was never used . . . and also to make sure that Philomen received the death he had earned.

"Do you think the devil you saw in Sigil marked you out to carry the chisel?" Obek asked quietly.

Remy thought about it. "Perhaps. How would I know?"

His brief sojourn in the Crossroads of the Planes had happened shortly before Remy had come to the vizier's attention. That much was true. Whether one thing had caused the other . . . that was a question Remy could not answer.

"What else might devils have marked you for, Remy?" Obek was looking at the water, but Remy could tell he was tense and alert.

"It makes no difference," Remy said. "I am done being marked out for anything. I make my own marks now."

"I hope so," Obek said.

Paelias came back to sit with them. "Lo, star elf," one of the halflings said. "Your friend here is marked out by devils. Strange company."

Obek turned and stared at the halfling until he looked away. When he turned back, Paelias said, "Biri-Daar doesn't think it's safe to tie up anywhere."

"Didn't Vokoun say something about rapids?" Remy asked.

"I did. There are rapids. If we cannot tie up, then we will have to run the rapids at night," Vokoun said. Remy looked up to see the halfling pilot looking right at him, amused at Remy's surprise. "You do know I can hear anything anyone says on this boat? No matter how quiet. On my boat, all words come to me."

"Can we run the rapids at night?" Biri-Daar asked.

"Only if we don't mind drowning or being dashed to death on the rocks," Vokoun said. "If we want to live, we should find some place to haul the rafts out and walk them around. There are portages in this canyon." He listened and Remy grew conscious of an approaching roar. "Hear that? It's tricky in the daylight. At night? Madness."

"This whole thing has been madness," Paelias said.

"We run the rapids," Biri-Daar said. "It's too late to do anything else."

Vokoun surprised Remy then. Rather than refusing, or arguing, he shrugged and signaled the oarsmen. "Very well!" Vokoun said. "For dying, one day's as good as the next."

He might have said more, but the sound of the rapids reached them, and there was nothing else to say.

The moon was almost directly overhead. In its waxing glow, the rapids of the lower Whitefall glowed a nearly incandescent violet. The ten adventurers on the boat could have linked arms and spanned the distance from canyon wall to canyon wall—and the river itself was narrower yet by twenty feet of fallen boulders and gravel. Half a mile upstream, the river was more than a hundred feet wide. Squeezed down to one third of its width, it surged and boomed over rocks the size of houses, with the walls spray-wetted for twenty feet above the river's surface. Vokoun's boat moved faster as if chasing the current ahead. "Oars in the water!" he cried. Remy and Obek looked at each other, not knowing what he meant; simultaneously they looked at the two surviving halfling oarsmen, both of whom were dragging their oars at an angle away from the boat. Remy did the same, and the boat swung into the center of the channel, drawn by the pull of the water piling over itself into the first chute of the rapids.

Remy had always lived on flat water, the Blackfall Estuary that stretched miles wide away from quays of Avankil. He had never seen rapids like these. The water ahead, as far as he could see under the moonlight, was white foam intermittently broken by darkness that could be either water or stone. Vokoun leaned out over the bow. Paelias was up next to him; the halfling called out something Remy couldn't understand and Pealias looked back. "Row!" he shouted. "Row, for your lives!"

We want to go *faster*? Remy wondered. But the halflings were digging into the water, and they had survived this run before. He dug in, and saw Obek doing the same. The boat leaped forward again, and just as quickly swung sideways. Without warning Remy and Obek were on the downstream side of the boat. The halflings dug hard, trying to straighten out the boat as Obek and Remy dragged their oars. The boat started to pivot back—and an unseen rock tore the oar from Obek's hands. He lunged after it, overbalancing and dragging the downstream gunwale perilously close to the water level. Vokoun was shouting something that Remy couldn't hear. Remy hauled back on Obek, barely holding onto his own oar with one hand as he tangled the other in Obek's belt. "Back in the boat!" Biri-Daar and the halflings were screaming as Remy leaned back into the boat's middle and Obek hung over the edge grasping vainly after the oar that had already vanished into the darkness. Vokoun and Keverel joined the clamor as Biri-Daar got a grip on one of Obek's legs. The tiefling, knowing the oar was lost, was trying to get back in, but he had nothing to grasp and if he reached back his face dipped into the water.

"High side!" Vokoun screamed again and again.

The boat swung so close to a group of boulders that Remy could have reached out and touched them, had he a free hand—but Obek, closer yet to the rocks, shoved the boat away with both hands and used the same shove to arch himself back, getting just enough of his weight close enough to the boat that Remy and Biri-Daar could haul him the rest of the way in. "Row! Row! High side!" Vokoun and Paelias screamed.

Remy and Obek flung themselves up and across the width of the raft, bringing it back to level with a crash and fountain of spray. Some of their gear went overboard, but in the dark Remy couldn't tell what it was. After that everything was the roar of cold water over black stone, the sting of spray, the ache and tremble of muscles fighting the current. Remy slowly felt himself turning into a sort of golem, rowing when Paelias yelled row and doing anything else only when told . . . a rowing golem, made to move boats through dangerous mazes of broken stone and surging water. Spasms racked his back. His hands were partly numb and partly torn with blisters that broke, bleeding onto the oar and into the water. Yet he rowed when he was told. Beside him Obek tried to row with his shield, his harsh devilish features set in a mask of angry determination.

Everyone began to scream. Remy could not hear what they were saying. He looked up and saw that the entire river was pouring into a single chute, narrow enough that the boat turned sideways would dam it up, the water charging up the rock walls that bound it in tongues of spray taller than the obelisks at Crow Fork Junction. The boat seemed, incredibly, to rise as it rode the cresting volume of the river through this choked-off throat—Remy thought, in his exhausted golem's haze, of a rope swing that hung from a long cypress branch over a deep pool just upstream of Avankil's old city walls. When you swung, there was a moment of perfect stillness as you reached the top of your arc; the river spread below like a sheet of tin on cloudy days, like a blazing mirror when the sun shone; and you fell endlessly until you broke its surface and plunged through the deeper and deeper shades of greeny brown, the cold of the Blackfall's deepest belly just reaching your feet before you again hung suspended, weightless, and began to kick to the surface with burning lungs and schemes aborning about how to cut in line to do it again faster, sooner next time . . . .

And in the next moment they were gliding across the unbroken glassy surface of a deep, wide pool. The sound of the rapids was already fading. The boat turned in a slight eddy, finding its way to slack water in the shadow of a sheer rock wall that disappeared straight down into the depths. Remy reached out his oar to push the boat away from the wall. "Row," Vokoun said. His voice, worn down to a deathbed wheeze, lacked its usual commanding tone . . . but they rowed. The boat heeled around and pointed downstream again.

By dawn, they were in a stretch of river that Remy would have sworn was just upstream of Avankil, in a region known as the Striped Bank. There the steep hills on either side of the river, and looming steeply over the tributaries that ran cold and fast down from the hills, were horizontally streaked in fantastic shades that Remy had only otherwise seen in the frozen sherbets mixed in the keep for Philomen and others in the nobility of Avankil.

Here, too, the streaks in the canyon cut were visible, and in similar colors; and also here, the river itself ran smoothly between them, even if the smaller streams that fell into it tumbled over themselves in their eagerness. But downstream, Remy knew, was not Avankil but Karga Kul. They fled toward it with death knights on their trail, and Erathis only knew what other minions of Orcus.

Erathis. He had sworn by Erathis.

It was dawn. The rising sun picked out the colors in the canyon walls, blinding Remy with beauty on this morning he had not expected to live to see . . . and he was invoking another god. Empty of feeling, he examined this problem. Why had it happened? Would it happen again?

"Keverel," he said, but when the cleric looked his way Remy knew he could not say more about the true nature of the conflict he felt.

"Remy."

A long time passed. Keverel did not press him and the boat was silent. After the previous evening and night, none of them had much to say. Obek rowed with his shield until Vokoun told him to stop. "Remy can row worth the two on the other side—not," he was quick to add, "because they're halflings, but because they're lazy. Too lazy even to be killed by death knights when there's someone else who can do that for them."

They rowed in the dawn, until the sun shone over the diminishing canyon walls and Remy knew that whatever had come before, he was about to see the famed towers of Karga Kul. Paelias and Vokoun keeping lookout at the bow for snags and sandbars. After some time Remy said, "Philomen sent them, didn't he?"

"Yes," Biri-Daar said. She was trailing a hand in the water to soothe the burns from Gouvou's flame.

"He spoke of Orcus. Was that bravado, or true?"

"True. Orcus puts his touch on all of the death knights. And every lich as well. The Road-builder and his retinue were given over to the Demon Prince as well. I fear," Biri-Daar said quietly, as if she meant only Remy to hear, "that we have not seen the last of his actions yet."

"Philomen is the Demon Prince's man."

It was not a question exactly, and when Biri-Daar answered she was expanding on what Remy said. "If you can call him a man," she said. "He may have become something else."

In the few minutes of their conversing, the canyon walls had grown lower. "It is one year, almost to the day, since

I have seen Karga Kul," Biri-Daar said. "These riverbanks lower, and the city grows closer. At the moment when the left bank begins to rise, and the right bank grows still flatter—that is the moment when you may look to the horizon and see the towers of Karga Kul. From there they look as if they hang over the waters of the river; but that is only an illusion. As you draw closer, you see first that they are on the left bank, and then, as you come farther down the river, they disappear for miles. Only in the last few bends, as you near the landing below the bluffs, do the towers reappear again. It is a trick of perspective, of the rise and fall of mountains. But it breeds stories."

This was the longest Remy had ever heard Biri-Daar talk. She was coming home, coming to the end of her quest. And she was bringing him, with his demon-tainted chisel and his uncertain history . . . I have much to atone for, Remy thought. If not in the true situation of things, then certainly in the eyes of those who have endangered their lives to save mine.

Yet he was not the only one on the boat with something to prove, something to atone for, something to settle and make right. Biri-Daar had her own ghosts. "What did Gouvou mean about legacy?" Remy asked.

As soon as he had said it, Remy realized that it had come across as a match thrown into a hayloft. He lifted a hand and started to add something else, but he never got the chance. "Oh, I think he was clear about that," came Lucan's voice. Everyone looked around in surprise that the elf had survived the night and awoken coherent—save Keverel, who shocked

Remy by shooting him a look of pure anger. Remy hadn't seen the cleric that furious in any of their encounters with the minions of Orcus. "I just meant," Remy began, but he didn't get to finish.

"Yes, he was," Biri-Daar said, picking up from where Lucan had left off. Looking at the contours of scale and color on her face, Remy realized that he had learned to read the expressions of dragonborn on this journey—one more thing he had never expected to know, or thought could be known, or thought about at all. "He did not tell us anything that we did not know already. Since the battle at Iban Ja's bridge, Bahamut and Tiamat have been at war for the souls of the Order of the Knights of Kul. Ever since, in each generation, some of the Knights of Kul have been corrupted. And we no longer know who to trust."

Vokoun's boat beached with a crunch of sand against its keel and a last rush of water swirling around its bow. They looked across the river, where the main docks of the city bustled with larger ships in from the Gulf. Caravans of mules and camels carried cargoes up the switchbacking road that led to the city's main gate, far above and out of sight. Other merchants, willing to pay the outrageous fees to avoid that road, loaded their wares straight into a cave. "From there," Biri-Daar explained, "everything goes up, carried by tamed beasts. Those were once caves. Now they have been carved and worked into a dozen levels of basements and dungeons."

"The Seal is in there?" Remy asked. "Seems too easy to get to."

"You wouldn't say that if you'd seen what's inside," Obek said.

"The militias of Karga Kul make very sure that nothing goes in through that cave except what has been bought, paid for, taxed, approved, licensed, and inspected," Paelias said. "Or so I am told. A cousin of mine is a merchant of Feywild herbs. He rages entertainingly about the rules of this city and the Mage Trust."

"And there are magical entrapments throughout," Obek added. "Any invader will find the first caves coming down on his head the minute the Mage Trust snaps its fingers."

What a spectacle it was, Remy thought. The Whitefall, running slow and nearly a mile wide, pouring into the waters of the Gulf to their right. To their left, the canyons that channeled it, all the way upstream beyond the landing and up into the high lakes country where Vokoun and his people came from. Across the river, the zigzag road on the face of the cliffs, rearing high above the water.

And above it all, the towers of Karga Kul.

BOOK VI
KARGA KUL

They came to the front gate via the switchbacking road, which they climbed on foot, sandwiched between a brace of donkeys and a long string of angry camels. It was late in the afternoon before they reached the top of the canyon.

Flanked by forbidding watchtowers, the main gate of Karga Kul stood open. At the foot of its walls sprouted a semipermanent shantytown of itinerant merchants, tinkers, actors, and supplicants to the Mage Trust or one of the city's other authorities. "The unlucky ones who can't gain entry," Keverel said to Remy. "This is why Obek needed to come in with us." As they approached, some of the shanty dwellers came toward them bearing promises of fabulous wealth, forbidden pleasures, occult knowledge . . . they focused on Biri-Daar, recognizing her as one of the Knights of Kul.

"Noble paladin! I have lost my letter from the Emperor of Saak-Opole and the Mage Trust will not see me unless I am sponsored!"

Biri-Daar reached out a gauntleted hand to fend off the shouting, gray-headed madman. "There is no emperor in Saak-Opole, is there?" she asked Obek.

He chuckled. "Not these last five hundred years."

Closer to the gate, traffic was divided into commercial goods and individual entries. Biri-Daar held the blazon of the Knights of Kul high in the air and a functionary at the gate saw it. He waved them forward. "Number in your party."

"Six."

The functionary counted. "Number of the six who are citizens of Karga Kul."

"Two." Biri-Daar pointed at Keverel and then herself.

"Errand."

"A report from Biri-Daar of the Knights of Kul to the Mage Trust."

The functionary looked up at her. He was a stout and soft man, accustomed to a life of quill pens and couches. His sense of professional ethics, Remy could see, was nagging at him. Doubtless he was not supposed to let just anyone in to see the Mage Trust. But, he was likely reasoning, even if he did let them in and they went to the trust, there were further and more formidable barriers. That was the excuse he needed.

"Biri-Daar of the Knights of Kul, you and your friends are welcome here," the functionary said without a hint of warmth. He wrote on a sheet of heavy paper and handed the paper to Biri-Daar. "As I'm sure you are aware, your entry paper must be with you at all times during your stay."

"Thank you," Biri-Daar said, matching the functionary's tone. Then they were through the gate, the functionary already saying again behind them, "Number in your party . . ."

The first thing Remy noticed about Karga Kul was that it was clean. He had seen cleanliness before, in his mother's house and in sections of street and square in Avankil. There, money bought cleanliness and the threat of violence kept it. Here, in Karga Kul, he watched tradesmen pack up their storefront tables at the end of the day and pick up every last scrap of leather or wrapping canvas, every gnawed chicken bone or apple core that the day's business had deposited in front of them. He had never seen anything like it, and the question that he had eventually found its way to his mouth.

"Obek," he said. "Who do they fear?"

All of them were waiting while Biri-Daar conversed with the secretaries of the Mage Trust. They sat at long benches on a covered patio at one corner of the trust's offices, where the trustees spent their days hearing the complaints of the citizenry and their nights delving into the avenues of magical research—thaumaturgical, necromantic, wizardly, or elemental—that best pleased and piqued their natures.

Obek shrugged. "There are militias that enforce the will of the Mage Trust. One thing the Mage Trust wills is that Karga Kul be clean. I like it."

"What happens if someone doesn't clean up?"

"Try it and find out," Obek said. He walked over to a merchant packing jerked meats back into rolls of canvas and bought a fistful of long strips. Handing one to Remy when he came back, Obek watched the conversation between Biri-Daar and the trust's official. "Wonder if they're talking about me," he said.

"I would guess they're a little more worried about the fate of the city and the seal," Remy said.

Obek chuckled. "Think you? Perhaps. But I am known in this city, and there are those who despise me."

"You mentioned that when we met."

"Did I mention that I killed one of the trustees?" Obek countered. He watched Remy's face with a toothy grin on his own. "I didn't, did I? Well. We all have our secrets." He bit into the jerky and chewed. "Fear not, Remy of Avankil," he said around the bite. "The trustee in question deserved it. And so does his successor, although I fear Biri-Daar would disagree. A word of advice. Do not put the chisel in anyone's hands. When the time comes to destroy it, make sure you do it yourself." Obek bit off another mouthful of jerky. "I'll be there to make sure you make sure. Not because I don't trust you, mind; just because it's the kind of thing that cannot be allowed to go wrong."

"How did you just happen to find us?" Remy asked.

Obek nodded thoughtfully as he chewed. "Nothing just happens," he said, and might have said more, but Biri-Daar was coming over to gather the group back together.

"The trust will meet with us," she said. "But there is no guarantee that they will believe what we have to say."

"Why not?" Remy asked. "They sent you, didn't they?"

"They never expected us to succeed. And if I tell the truth, my story will make me look like a liar," Biri-Daar said.

Lucan, Paelias, and Keverel were just coming over to rejoin the group from a brief trip through the last dying corners of the day's market. "Liar?" Lucan said. "Has Remy been telling stories of Sigil again?"

"Much is at stake here," Biri-Daar said. "If the Mage Trust is not on our side, we are going to have to fight all the way to the Seal, and fight to inscribe it anew. How much time do we have before the Road-builder returns?" She looked to Keverel with this last question.

He was shaking his head. "There is no way to know. Lich magic is unpredictable. He may not return for days; or he may return before I finish speaking. But we must destroy the quill as soon as we can."

"Then let us get on with the conversation," Biri-Daar said, and led them into the Palace of the Mage Trust.

The civilization that founded the city that became Karga Kul was known only by its obsessive repetition of the numbers six and seven, always together. In the Palace, that repetition took several forms. There were six floors and seven rooms on each. The stairs between each floor numbered thirteen. The Palace itself was hexagonal in shape, with seven windows on each side of the hexagon, and so on. Guards conveyed them down a hall paved with hexagonal stones. As they walked, Remy counted, and sure enough, the hall was seven stones wide.

He wasn't sure what to think about Obek's revelations. It was certain that the tiefling's presence would be a problem for the trust—unless he had been truthful in his assertion that the trustee had deserved death, and the surviving trustees agreed with his perspective. Remy found this unlikely. Was it possible that Obek had already informed Biri-Daar of this? Remy couldn't decide. It was the kind of secret that, once revealed, might endanger the success of their quest, and for that, Remy knew, Biri-Daar would not hesitate to kill. On the other hand, the Mage Trust of Karga Kul was notoriously capricious; it was possible that a little fear might make them a little more tractable.

Not for the first time, Remy was glad that he did not share the responsibilities of leadership. He was free to act but no other lives depended on his choices.

Obek, walking in front of him, looked over his shoulder at Remy. It was strange to see a tiefling wink in a conspiratorial way, as if in getting to know Obek, Remy had somehow become tinged with the infernal himself. It made him nervous—but Obek had fought bravely since forcing his way into the group in the sewers of the Inverted Keep. Remy found that he trusted the tiefling, and could find no reason not to.

He winked back and they went on through the jumble of sixes and sevens until they came to the double hexagonal doors of the Council Chamber of the Mage Trust.

The council chamber was built in the shape of a six-pointed star, each arm of which was a small gallery of long-dead members of the trust. Around a seven-sided table in the center of the chamber were six chairs, and in those six chairs were the members of the trust. A seventh chair sat empty. The guards conducted the adventurers into the chamber and remained near the door.

Remy looked from member to member of the trust, seeing age and wisdom and fear . . . except on one face, a woman no older than his mother. Either she was a prodigy, or something had recently changed in the trust. It was impossible to think that someone so young had grown powerful enough in magical ability to warrant election to such a position. "This is Shikiloa," another trustee said, introducing her and then the rest of the trustees in turn, herself last. Her name was Uliana. Remy didn't remember the other names and the other trustees took no notice of him. All eyes were on Biri-Daar primarily, with leery glances reserved for Obek, who hung behind the group near the door. Remy wasn't sure whether the trustees were nervous about Obek himself or about tieflings in general, but whichever was the case, they surely did look discomfited by his presence. He faded back away from the table to stand next to Obek. "Don't worry," he whispered, moving his lips as little as possible. "I will speak for you even if no one else will."

"Biri-Daar of the Order of the Knights of Kul," Uliana said. She was one of the oldest of the Mage Trust and the longest-serving. "This trust sent you forth on a grave errand. Have you returned bearing good tidings or bad?"

"Both," Biri-Daar said.

"Which outweighs the other?"

"That yet depends on our actions," Biri-Daar said. "And on yours. We have recovered Moidan's Quill that inscribed the original Seal of Karga Kul."

"The quill your fellow knight stole," one of the trustees whose name Remy had forgotten said. He was a fat and red-bearded man with quick intelligence in his eyes and a goblet of wine in one hand.

"True, and disturbing," Shikiloa said. "You will pardon the directness of my speech; I fear that the desperation of the situation calls for a simplification of this body's normal rules about age and order of speech."

"You would feel that way, of course," Uliana said. "Arguments of protocol are a waste of time with the seal so thin."

"There is another problem," Biri-Daar said.

"Which is . . . ?" the red-beared drunkard prompted.

"Philomen, the vizier of Avankil, is in league with the Demon Prince Orcus," Biri-Daar stated.

There was a long moment of shocked silence. "How can this be?" Shikiloa said. "Avankil has been our staunchest ally, even when Toradan and Saak-Opole turned against us."

Biri-Daar pointed at Remy. "This is Remy, also of Avankil," she said. Then she looked at Remy and he knew he was expected to speak.

He took a few steps forward, to stand next to the empty seventh chair. He and Biri-Daar flanked it, with Lucan, Paelias, Keverel, and Obek in a gently curved rank behind them. "Since I was a boy," he began, "I have been a courier for Philomen. I do not know how it started. But he had always been good to me. A few . . ."

Remy faltered, realizing he had no clear idea of how long it had been since he left Avankil. "The last thing he asked of me was that I take something to Toradan for him," he went on. "And I could not know what it was. I was attacked on the road to Toradan by stormclaw scorpions. They killed my horse. I would have died too, in the wastes there, if Biri-Daar had not stopped and Keverel had not healed me. I have been traveling and fighting with them ever since."

"So you have betrayed your errand for Philomen?" Shikiloa asked.

"His errand betrayed me," Remy said. "He sent me with this, and knew that it would draw the kind of attention that gets messengers killed."

Holding the chisel's box carefully in both hands, Remy angled it so each member of the trust in turn could see the sigils carved into its lid and along the front near the latch. They recognized the enchantments, he could see; their eyes widened, and even the red-bearded trustee set his goblet down and made a sign. "What is in it?" Uliana asked. "We have no time for roundabout stories, and less for theatrics."

"A chisel," Remy said, and opened the lid.

"Designed by someone closely tied to Orcus," Keverel added. "Designed, I fear, to destroy the seal."

"Ridiculous," Shikiloa said. "Philomen is a scholar of languages, a peddler of petty court schemes, a bestower of favors upon women of little virtue. He has traveled thrice to Karga Kul in the last ten years. All of us have met him, and none has ever sensed anything ill about his demeanor. Yet you have this that you call proof?"

"There is more," Biri-Daar said. "Much more. Yet as Uliana says, we have no time. For our news is not yet fully given. Moidan's Quill," she went on, producing it from inside her armor, "is more than what it seems. Uliana. Note the symbols, carved so delicately into the barrel near the point. Do you recognize them?"

The trustee paled, her skin fading to nearly the off-white color of her hair. "A phylactery," she said. "It has been made into a phylactery."

"It was always a phylactery," Keverel corrected. "Was not the seal laid down at about the time the Road-builder disappeared and the Inverted Keep tore free into the sky?"

The Mage Trust was silent.

"We killed the Road-builder," Biri-Daar said. "But as long as the quill is intact, he will return. We must act immediately."

"Immediately? We must act decisively, yes, but not rashly," Shikiloa said.

"Begging your pardon, Excellency, but if the Road-builder returns you will find a brief hesitation to have been extremely rash," Lucan said as he stepped forward.

Redbeard raised his goblet. "So we have a quill containing a lich king, a chisel imbued with demonic powers, a secret enemy in control of Avankil, and an Abyssal horde about to break through the seal. There. The situation is described. Now let us address it."

Suddenly Remy liked him.

"Quite," Uliana said. "The seal is weakened almost to transparency. I fear it is too thin to reinscribe."

Redbeard set down his goblet. "Then—"

"Then we must inscribe a new one and destroy the old as we lay the new one in its place." Uliana looked at everyone in the room, each in turn. "Then we must destroy quill and chisel both, and before the return of the Road-builder. Guard!" she called.

The senior guard inside the door stepped forward.

"Close the gates to the city," Uliana commanded. "Both at the road and at Cliff Quay. No one shall enter or leave Karga Kul until the seal is replenished and our citizens and traders may safely go about their business again." The guard left and Uliana turned to Biri-Daar. "You have an unexpected comrade in your group," she said. "And I do not mean the boy from Avankil."

"I'm not a boy," Remy said.

"Ah, but you are," Redbeard said, "because you do not know when to keep your mouth shut." He gave Remy a salute with the now-empty goblet.

Shikiloa rose and paced. "As the successor to Vurinil, Mage Trustee of Karga Kul—"

"Daughter, I believe, is the word," Obek said.

She glared at him, a flush rising across the planes of her face. Remy had seen that look on faces before killing. "—Vurinil, who was killed by the tiefling Obek, may I speak?" she asked Uliana—a little too sweetly, it seemed to Remy.

"Certainly," Uliana said.

"Obek will certainly say that my predecessor was a usurper, and a betrayer of the trust between this city and the trustees. He may be right about this. It is also true, however," Shikiloa said, "that since his murder of Vurinil—my father Vurinil, a noble servant of the trust and of Karga Kul—the seal has rapidly deteriorated, there have been sightings of demons in the streets and in the lower portions of the underground keeps. Now Obek comes back, in the company of Biri-Daar, herself a member of the same guild that stole the quill! And with them comes yet another stranger, this Remy, bearing a demonic instrument for the destruction of the seal! Fellow trustees, it seems that we have not helped ourselves by entrusting our lives and the life of Karga Kul to these . . . adventurers."

"Yet what strange deceivers they be," Redbeard observed dryly. "Coming right to the front door and presenting themselves to us."

With a shock, Remy realized that the other three members of the trust, the ones who had not yet spoken in the debate, were asleep. Could this be the feared Mage Trust of Karga Kul, he thought—the trust that strikes such fear into its citizens that they pick up orange peels from the street?

"You are drunk," Shikiloa said. "As is your custom. Well, it is my custom to suspect the motives of those who preach unseen danger, when they might well simply be aggrandizing themselves. You, tiefling. Murderer. You risked your life entering this room, did you not?"

Obek nodded. "I did."

"If we kill you now, will your risk have been worth it?"

"Erathis is the god of this city, and I am an adopted citizen of Karga Kul," Obek said, standing erect and fearless, not looking over his shoulder at the guards who awaited Shikiloa's command to strike him down. "I returned to fight for this city, and as far as I pledge myself to any god, it is to Erathis."

"And I'm sure he is glad of your devotion. It's Erathis we need, and Bahamut too, and perhaps the Lady of Pain thrown into the bargain, if the Knights of Kul are to do us any good," said Shikiloa. "I expect neither the gods nor the dragonborn to offer us any assistance we might wish to accept."

A pained expression crossed Biri-Daar's face at this mention of the Knights. "When the Knights of Kul are needed, they will rise to that need," she said.

"That is my hope as well." Uliana turned to the window.

Shikiloa smiled. "Will you go and ask them yourself? Perhaps you could bring them news of Moula and the quill as well."

"If that is your wish, I am willing," Biri-Daar said, in a tone of voice that indicated she was willing only, and just barely at that.

"Do not," Uliana said. "Not yet. Instead let us see what the minions of Orcus are planning. I do not believe the Road-builder's return is imminent. I would feel it. So we have a moment to gather knowledge, and perhaps even to use it wisely." The last was directed at Shikiloa, in whose eyes burned something more than anger but just slightly less than hate.

She is afraid, Remy thought. He caught Biri-Daar's eye, and Keverel's, and saw that both of them thought the same thing. But of what?

———◆———◆———

The Black Mirror of the Trust was a circular pane of obsidian, polished and laid into a frame of burnished copper so that it could stand vertical or be laid flat. Each position lent itself to different methods of scrying. Uliana laid it flat. The rest of the Mage Trust spread around her and the mirror. Remy and the rest of Biri-Daar's group mingled with them, Biri-Daar closest to Uliana and Obek on the opposite side. A visibly skeptical Shikiloa and an obviously drunk Redbeard were closest to Obek, where they could watch Uliana. From a chain around her neck she took a tiny crystal vial. Three drops of clear fluid fell from the unstoppered vial onto the polished obsidian. Whispering an incantation under her breath, Uliana moved her hand in a smoothing motion, a few inches over the obsidian. The drops spread into an invisible layer—and as they spread, an image emerged.

First came color: black warming through red to a fiery molten orange flecked with brilliant white. Then motion, the shapes of figures . . .

Remy saw Obek turn his head, ever so slightly. He followed the tiefling's gaze and saw that Shikiloa was doing something with her hands. Looking back to the mirror, Remy watched the figures resolve. They were all shapes, all sizes, the nameless hordes of the Abyss under the control of their ruler Orcus. Orcus, the Demon Prince of the Undeath, sworn enemy of all things living. Goat-legged, dragon-tailed, with the horns of a ram and the fiery eyes of the greater undead. Bearer of the Wand of Orcus, with its skull of a dead god, Despot of Thanatos—his presence loomed over everything they saw.

"It is as I feared," Uliana said. She spoke with her eyes closed, since to channel the vision into the mirror she could not see it herself—at least not with her eyes. "They are gathering. They know that the seal weakens. They know . . ."

Motion drew Remy's attention away from the mirror and back to Shikiloa. He saw her hands move. She brought a hand to her face, kissed something she held between finger and thumb.

When she drew it away again, blood glistened on her lower lip.

Shikiloa extended her hand over the mirror. "Father," she said, her voice low but clear in the nearly silent room. "As you bid me."

As she opened her hand, Obek was reaching to catch the bright bloody sliver that fell from it. Redbeard, his eyes bulging from their sockets as he saw what she had done, flung out an arm and shoved her back away from the mirror, the action instinctive but futile as the sliver fell through Obek's hand as if it was not there.

Obek clutched at his pierced palm, roaring with pain. Blood spurted from it as if it had been pierced by a spear rather than a sliver no thicker than a needle. Drops of that blood fell with the sliver onto the mirror's surface. The color of the blood spread like a glaze across the scene of Orcus's dominion. When it had covered the entire surface of the mirror, the entire surface flipped up to the vertical. Behind the bloody glaze, figures loomed closer. Something crashed into the finish.

"Traitor!" Obek roared, his bloody hand thrust out at Shikiloa. "Like your father."

Another crash against the glaze left a crack exactly the size of the sliver that had fallen from Shikiloa's hand. She met his gaze, cold and distant. "You are a traitor to all humanity. And your kin, the demons, are coming to claim you."

"Fool," growled Biri-Daar. Another crack appeared in the surface of the mirror. The Mage Trust, save Uliana, fell back toward the shadowed galleries in the points of the star-shaped room. "Who turned you against the trust?"

A chip of the mirror came loose and plinked on the hexagonal stones of the floor. Sound came from it: a profusion of roaring and screeching, the scraping of what sounded like claws on the other side of the mirror.

"No one turned me," Shikiloa sneered. "I am my own creature. My choices are my own. The tiefling dies if the city has to die with him."

"How did you know he would be here?" Remy asked.

From the look on her face, he knew the answer.

"Philomen," he said.

She did not deny it. She raised a short staff, its head transforming before their eyes from a crescent moon to an iridescent green skull.

"No," Uliana groaned. Her eyelids fluttered as she tried to open her eyes and get free of the vision. "No," she said again—and then she reached out her left hand, pointed unerringly at Shikiloa, and incinerated the youngest trustee before Shikiloa could defend herself.

At that moment the mirror exploded in a hail of obsidian shards. They stung and sliced across the exposed skin of Remy's face and hands, tearing also at the leather of his tunic and boots. He ducked away, hearing the fragments ricochet around the room. Already there were screams; the unprotected and unprepared trustees were badly cut and slashed.

The demons that came through the opened portal were about the size of dwarves, but a burnt red in color with cruel wide mouths and four-fingered hands ending in ragged black claws. They tumbled over one another coming through the mirror frame. Behind them, the fiery hellscape of Thanatos belched its miasma into the council chamber.

"Demons aren't my kin," Obek snarled, and cut two of them in half before their feet had found the floor.

Since leaving Avankil, Remy had seen many things he'd never seen before. Most of them he had no name for, but these he recognized. They were known as evistros, or carnage demons. Remy had heard stories of them rampaging in packs near places where Abyssal energies spilled into the mortal world. They existed only to destroy. And they were destroying now, tearing the Mage Trust to bits as the embattled trustees, few of whom had ever fought with anything other than words, found themselves overrun by the savage demons who clawed and bit and rent them without mercy. They died despite the best efforts of Biri-Daar and Remy and the rest, who cut down the evistros nearly as fast as they could pour through the violated mirror.

Of the Mage Trust, only Uliana fought with courage. Her first victim had been Shikiloa the traitor, but in the moments since she had cut a swath through the evistros as she fought to close the portal they had opened. With the mirror destroyed, she opened her eyes and began to lay waste to the enemies of the trust and her city.

"Eladrin!" she shouted above the infernal yowling evistros and the sounds of steel on demonic flesh and bone. "With me!"

The star elf vaulted clear of the melee, leaping to catch a wall sconce and swinging up to brace against a timber supporting the vaulted ceiling. Grimly and with absolute calm he began to destroy the evistros that approached Uliana. Remy too fell back to protect her, as did Obek from the other side. Keverel swatted a leaping demon out of the air as it cleared the portal. It scrambled on the ground, but before it could find its feet he broke its back and turned to the next, the name of his god repeated over and over again on his lips.

The second focus of the battle was Biri-Daar, who stood alone, her enchanted blade describing an arc of maiming and death around her. Lucan's arrows whispered through the air to catch those evistros that got out of the portal past Keverel and Uliana. They were everywhere, in frenzied groups dismembering the dead and swarming over the living. Some, caught up in the bloodlust, turned on one another, splattering their black and sulfurous blood to mix with the spilled red of the Mage Trust.

Something tugged at Remy's belt, pulling him off balance. He looked down and saw one of the demons, gnawing on his belt—and the pouch where he had carried the chisel across the long miles from Avankil. Remy flicked his knife out of his sleeve, the way he'd learned back home on the waterfront, and stabbed it through the eye. It lashed him across the face with one claw and kept digging for the chisel with the other. He twisted the blade, feeling the bones of its skull crack. Malignant light still shone in its remaining eye, but with the twist of the blade its arms and legs fell limp and it dropped away as a blinding flash brought tears to Remy's eyes. When his vision cleared, he saw tumbled and blackened bodies of evistros all around, yet he was untouched save for the fading afterimage.

"Mind the chisel, Remy," Uliana said. "If they get their hands on it, the seal is as good as destroyed."

Looking down, Remy saw ragged claw marks scored into the leather of his belt and the pouch containing the chisel in its box. Then the evistros came again in another wave, and he lifted his sword to meet them. Over his head, Uliana's magic swept and flared, the evistros falling back before it as slowly—slowly, and with the help of Paelias, whose fey magic was anathema to the carnage demons—she choked off the open portal. The evistros came through fewer and fewer at a time, Keverel and Lucan exacting a terrible toll at their emergence; then they came through one at a time, wriggling through a diminished hole too small to admit a full grown man; then, as Keverel caved in the snarling face of a last single demon, Uliana closed off the portal, severing the dying evistro at the waist.

Still there were dozens of them in the Council Chamber. Cut off from Thanatos, they knew they could expect no mercy—not that they knew anything of mercy in Orcus's realm. Gathering into knots of three or four, they banded together and fought to the death. Lucan ended the fight with a final arrow through the gut of an evistro that had already taken a half-dozen blows from Obek's sword.

Of the Mage Trust, Uliana alone survived. She bent to pick up a large sliver of the Black Mirror, slick with the commingled blood of the rest of the trust. "Karga Kul will never be the same," she said quietly. "And things may yet become more desperate. Remy of Avankil."

Remy took a step forward.

"Have you the chisel?"

"I have it," Remy said. He remembered the stubby, grasping fingers of the evistro feeling along his belt, and shuddered at the thought of what might have happened.

"At least some of the evistros knew of it, and you may yet meet more adversaries who will. Yet you must keep it," Uliana said. "You have brought it this far under terrible pressure and with commendable courage. Now you must keep it a little longer, for there is no one else who can be trusted to do it."

"I would trust any of them to do it," Remy protested, extending his arm to encompass his companions.

"Which speaks well of you. Yet you have brought it this far, and we do not know whether that is luck or strength. It would be foolish to risk a change now. You will keep it until the time comes to destroy it. Biri-Daar."

Biri-Daar offered a shallow bow.

"You will select six Knights of Kul, the six whom you would most trust to uphold the precepts of the order. You will go with them to the guard at the Cliff Quay and you will give him this." She wrote on a parchment and pressed it shut with her seal. "Quickly. Meet us in the Chamber of the Seal. You have the quill, yes? Make sure you keep it with you."

Without a word, Biri-Daar took the letter and left, shards of obsidian crunching under her boots. Uliana was moving at the same time, but in the other direction. She passed her hand over a blackened iron lock bolted into the wall, which fell open. As it did, the outline of another door appeared. "We must go now," she said. "It may already be too late."

The door opened to a narrow passage that angled down. "There are few ways to the Chamber of the Seal," Uliana said. "This, and one other from below that only the trust knows of. At least I believe that is so."

Remy could easily touch both walls of the passage without extending his arms all the way. The stone was cold and smooth, the angle down into the interior of the cliff from which loomed the towers of Karga Kul consistent even as the passage doubled back on itself, zigzagging down and ever down. Remy touched the walls every so often, because it kept everything real. He had seen so much in the past weeks—how long had it been since he had left Avankil? He thought perhaps only a month—that he found it difficult at moments like these to believe in even the simple reality of stone.

They reached a landing, hexagonal in shape, with doors in each of the six walls. "You would not want to open the wrong door here," Uliana said. She walked slowly in a counterclockwise circle, touching the center of each door as she passed it. After a complete circuit, she stopped at the door directly underneath the staircase. Before she touched it, the door opened, disappearing into the wall. As they passed over the threshold, Remy looked and could see no sign that the door had ever existed.

Down they went again. "We are at the deepest levels of the ancient chambers cut into the cliff," Uliana said. "Soon we will be below the level of the sea. I have not been this way since my initiation into the Mage Trust. I hope I never come here again."

Remy thought he could smell the sea, but all he could see was the immediate length of the passage in front of him. The floor glistened in the Erathian light sparkling from Keverel's helm and the head of Uliana's staff. When they came to a branch in the passage—the first they had encountered since going through the door—Uliana nodded toward it and said, "The knights, if they come, will come from there."

"They will come," Keverel said.

They passed the branch and Remy looked to see if he could detect any light from approaching dragonborn paladins. The branch was dark. "They will come," he echoed, and they passed on.

The roof of the passage grew higher, and vaulted. "Now we are in an ancient level that existed long before Karga Kul was called Karga Kul. Archives in long-dead languages mention this place as myth. It is possible that the builders of the first of these labyrinths opened a portal to the Abyss intentionally."

"Never a good idea," Lucan said.

"Your sense of humor is inappropriate," Uliana said.

Paelias winked at his elf cousin. "But appreciated," he said softly.

Next they came to a massive stone door, polished to a gloss that shone in the near-darkness. It was built of fourteen panels, seven black and seven red. "The colors of our vanished forebears," Uliana said. "Red for blood and war, black for ink and knowledge."

"Blood and ink," Keverel said. "Books and killing build cities."

Lucan looked surprised. "Irreverent, holy man? That's unlike you."

"Proximity to the Abyss, perhaps, pollutes my demeanor," Keverel said, gritting his teeth.

"Leave him alone," Remy said.

Lucan looked to him, flashing a bit of the suspicion Remy had seen in him right after joining the group back at Crow Fork Market. Then he looked away. "All of us need to back down," he said. Flicking an arrow from his quiver, he spun it through his fingers like a baton and slipped it back in, choosing his saber instead.

The rest of them dropped hands to hilts as Uliana worked an invisible charm that opened the fourteen-paneled door. It swung silently back, revealing a great chamber, its ceiling lost in darkness and its walls writhing with ancient relief sculptures. They entered, and for a moment looked on in astonishment. "A marvelous people they must have been," Uliana whispered. "I mourn them though they have been dead for thousands of years. The world is impoverished by their absence."

Remy listened to her, and wondered what it must be like to think so deeply about the past. The present was more than enough for him to handle. The sculptures on the walls were of great heroes, three times the height of a man, depicted in postures of combat against demonic enemies. "They built this place as a shrine and a warning," Keverel said. "How long has the seal lasted?"

"How long since the Road-builder shed his mortal life and became a lich?" Uliana answered. "The records become partial, then fragmentary, then . . ." She gestured up at the sculptures. "Then they are gone. Perhaps someone, somewhere, knows. I fear, though, that the only beings who know the true history of the seal and the city that became Karga Kul are . . ."

She pointed to the center of the room, as the sound of the approaching knights echoed down the passage outside.

The portal between Karga Kul and the Abyss was a circular stone door, set into the floor and without visible hinge or spring. The seal itself was a rectangular stone the size of a coffin lid and perhaps two feet thick, laid over the narrow gap between portal and bedrock floor. Once it had been a mighty stone, carried in by six dragonborn Knights of Kul who held it down while the first of the Mage Trust carved the first characters in the first seal.

None of them had known that already the Road-builder had made Moidan's Quill, with which Uliana stood ready to write, the seat and repository of his treacherous soul. At last, they would replenish the seal, destroy the quill, get permanently rid of the Road-builder, save Karga Kul, and restore the status of the Knights of Kul.

Or they would all die.

Six hand-picked knights held the replacement seal, which could not touch the portal until the old Seal was removed; doubling the seal would have the effect of canceling both. So there would be a moment when the portal, necessarily, was open. The gods alone knew—and perhaps not even they—what would come through during that time.

"Hold it so that it overlaps from the seal to the floor," Uliana ordered. "Exactly as the other one." She looked over at Biri-Daar, who stood at the head of the ceremonial guard carrying the new seal. "The last time this was done, it was the abbot of the Monastery of the Cliff who held the quill. Or so it is hinted in the oldest records we have yet found."

"Those same monks are now corrupt," Keverel said. "They are a canker on the city of Toradan. When this is done, they are our next task."

"When," Paelias said. "The certainty of the holy man."

"Quiet, please. It is time to write." Uliana held up the quill. Remy had noticed something odd about her voice and looking at her he realized what it was: she was quietly weeping as she spoke. Before he had more than the briefest moment to wonder why, she thrust the quill into her left eye.

A low, quivering noise escaped her but she remained perfectly still. Removing the quill from her eye, she bent over the new Seal and began to write.

Each sigil burned as she inscribed it, blood and fluid from Uliana's sacrificed eye dripping from her chin but her hand never wavering from its task. The quill moved in broad sweeping curves across the seal. The Knights of Kul looked away from her as she approached each of them in turn, working letter by agonized letter through the inscription that would reseal the portal to Thanatos. And as she wrote, the quill began to burn. Remy's pulse quickened. If it burned away before she finished, would the Seal hold back the hordes of Orcus?

And would . . . ?

Shadows began to form and pool in one corner of the room, farthest from the door. Biri-Daar saw Remy looking. She turned her head and saw exactly what Remy saw. She took a step around the edge of the portal to position herself between Uliana and the gathering shadows. They ballooned, piled on each other and grew up along the wall. Remy thought he saw a humanoid shape emerging.

Uliana, the flaming quill in her hand, added the last characters. The shadows on the wall had acquired a human silhouette. "Quickly," Keverel said as Remy drew his sword and faced the silhouette. "Remy. Not yet. We need both of your hands."

He sheathed his sword and joined the rest of the group at the edges of the fading seal. Its sigils were burnt-out, blackened as if by the fires of the hellish plane they held back. The six of them got their hands under the edges of the seal. Remy looked at Biri-Daar, awaiting a cue. "Hands under the edge," Biri-Daar said. "Ready. Three. Two. One."

They lifted. The Seal came away from the portal and the chamber floor, surprisingly light in Remy's hands. As it did, sulfurous smoke boiled around the edges of the portal and under his feet. Remy felt it begin to slide and rise. It tilted. He fought for his balance. He and Biri-Daar, still on the portal itself, slipped farther from the edge. If they did not let the Seal go, they would pull it out onto the portal . . . and their straining comrades with it.

Remy and Biri-Daar flung the crumbling Seal away, clearing the boundary between portal and floor. The air around him burned and shimmered and he saw that the portal was starting to sink into the floor. A clear gap emerged on the opposite side of the portal. Demonic shapes scrambled up through it. On the side closest to Remy and Biri-Daar, the honor guard of the Knights of Kul stepped out onto the portal. "Now!" Uliana cried out, her ruined eye leaking tears and blood.

"Now or never," Biri-Daar growled. She cut down the first demon out onto the portal.

A shape resolved from the shadows along the wall—tall, cadaverous, bearing a staff . . .

No, Remy thought.

It was not the Road-builder, returning at the last moment as his phylactery the quill burned away to nothingness in Uliana's hand. Where Remy had expected the Road-builder stood Philomen, vizier of Avankil. But it was a Philomen transformed—his skin pallid, eyes alight with a fire like the fire that bled around the edges of the portal and flicked at the legs of the demons who continued to pour through the gap. The head of his staff, which back in Avankil was a seven-pointed star worked in emeralds and gold, was now a pale green iridescent skull. Like Shikiloa's, Remy saw—a replica of the Wand of Orcus.

With a flick of one hand, Philomen froze the Knights carrying the Seal. "Look at me, noble dragonborn," he said, voice low and inviting.

"No!" Biri-Daar roared, but they were looking . . . and they were falling, unconscious, the seal banging to the floor and crushing one of the knights beneath it. He lay, his life bleeding out of him, eyes unfocused, the pain not reaching through the vision of death Philomen had laid over them. More demons vaulted up through the gap. Remy joined Biri-Daar at the gap, cutting the insectile limbs from a mezzodemon as Biri-Daar slashed the wings and the head from a vrock flapping up behind it.

Philomen called out a word in a language Remy did not recognize. The demons stopped, not advancing but not retreating either. "Remy," Philomen said, almost kindly. "My most trusted courier. You have completed your errand at last . . . although not without some unfortunate detours along the way. Come now. All is forgiven. I will take the chisel now, and events will run their destined course."

Remy removed the chisel from its case, where he had kept it despite the breaking of the magical seals. He let the case fall to the floor and held it up as if it were a knife. "Was it you that time, in Sigil?" he asked. "Did you send me there, mark me, send me back?"

"It wasn't so direct as all that," Philomen. "Surely you know that I seldom act so straightforwardly."

"Until now," Uliana said.

The hierophant nodded with a glance at the last surviving member of the Mage Trust of Karga Kul. "Until now."

Uliana stepped forward and confronted him. "This, Philomen, is an act of war by Avankil against Karga Kul. Know that in your lust to serve your master you have doomed not just the people of Karga Kul but the people of your own city as well, since war never leaves either side utterly untouched."

"Uliana, I fear that I am beyond caring what the Mage Trust thinks. My master made his wishes known; I am pledged to bring those wishes about. Thus the chisel, and the final breaking of this moribund seal, which for too long has prevented the real powers of the planes from taking their rightful place at the head and throne of this world."

Keverel spoke to both of them. "Uliana, you reason with a man who is beyond reason and no longer a man. Philomen, you command this rabble as though you were a hierophant, one of the death priests of Orcus. Surely one so powerful as a hierophant may simply do away with us and go about his business of flooding our world with demonic savagery."

"Wait," Remy said. "Philomen. Why do I need to give you the chisel?"

Philomen's eyes narrowed. "You stand on a very thin edge, Remy. A word from me and you go into Thanatos. Mortals do not return from thence."

Remy brandished the chisel. "This is what you want," he said.

"Remy, you mustn't," Uliana said. Biri-Daar reached out to him; Remy flinched away.

He faced down the vizier. "Philomen, mortals do not return from Thanatos. Do chisels?"

In Philomen's face, Remy saw that he was right. "You want the chisel for yourself. If it goes into the Abyss, you'll never see it again."

Philomen drew himself up. "Boy. This bravado of yours will fade quickly when you find yourself looking into the face of Orcus."

The sneering Remy could have stood. The threats were nothing new. But after what he had done during the past weeks, after the betrayal and the bravery, the horrors and the magnificence of the comrades in whose company he had fought his way across the Dragondown . . . he was not a boy, and would not be called one.

"Boy?" he repeated.

Pivoting, he drove the chisel like a knife through the slack face of the nearest demon. Its skull burst like a rotten fruit and it dropped without a sound. "Boy?" Remy said again. He kicked the demon, rolling it over. "I am no boy to lead by the nose and leave in the wastes to die. Not anymore."

Another kick sent the demon, and the chisel protruding

from its head, over the edge of the portal slab and into the midnight fires of Thanatos.

Philomen said nothing aloud, but Remy's mind lit afire with necrotic agony as the demon-beholden vizier, once a man and now a death priest hierophant, smote him to his knees. The invading demons sprang back into action and from deep inside the agonized reaches of his brain, Remy heard the sounds of desperate battle. He looked up into the looming maw of a hezrou, the size of a troll—and three arrows, one after another, *thwocked* into the side of its head. Galvanized, Remy sprang back from its fall, which shook the portal slab. His sword was in his hand and a battle surged around him, tilting and swaying the slab as the combatants ebbed and flowed across its invisible axis.

A flash, gone in an eyeblink but brighter than the sun for the moment of its existence, closed Remy's eyes. He turned to see what had happened; the talons of a hopping vrock raked down his back; he swung blindly, felt the blade of his sword grate along bone, and saw that Uliana had unleashed some force . . .

She had brought down the lightning. A thousand feet underground, Uliana had brought down the lightning. Demons lay blackened and unmoving all around. It was, Remy saw, as if the spell she had invoked to protect him from the evistro was a bee sting. Even Philomen staggered—and staggered again as Paelias began to work his fey magic, weaving a thicket of living thorns around the hierophant's legs. It grew; Philomen killed it with a necrotic touch; it began to grow again. Obek leaped out onto the portal slab, bringing it for a moment nearly level. A plan presented itself to Remy. It depended on a great many things going right—in other words, on luck . . . "Paelias!" he cried. "It's luck we need!"

"And luck you shall have!" the star elf cried in return, the silvery and lethal charms of the fey flicking from him like raindrops to dazzle and weaken the demonic foes. Turning his attention back to Philomen, Paelias called out a charm in the liquid Elvish of the eladrin—Lucan, his bowstring broken, and rushed across to join the melee, snapped his head around, eyes widening at the audacity of his eladrin cousin—and Remy felt a reckless flood of certainty.

Yes. It was daring. It was bold. It would work. Paelias had stolen the hierophant's luck. It was the great trick of the fey warlocks, dangerous and fickle. There was no telling how long it would last.

Philomen turned to the star elf. "O fey," he chided. "You would have my luck? We are far past the time when luck could save you."

Seething necrotic energy arced out from Philomen's staff and struck Paelias down, the tatters of the eladrin's fey aura swirling away into the darkness. Keverel fought back, his mace crunching into the vizier's back, but it was too late. With a wail Paelias covered his face with his hands and pitched over on his side, his legs scissoring along the floor. A hulking goristro demon fell upon him, heedless of Lucan's arrows—and Remy was too far away.

Paelias had known luck would not save him, Remy thought. That is why he handed it off to me. The footloose eladrin, unwelcome among his own, had died saving the lives of strangers.

Remy charged toward Philomen, the agony of betrayal too much to bear—but luck intervened. A vrock scrabbling through the opening between worlds caught the hem of Remy's tunic in its beak. He lost his balance on the angled surface of the portal slab, and fell. The vrock raised a talon; he parried it; the vrock let go his tunic and bit into Remy's shoulder, the hooked tip of its beak punching through armor and muscle straight to the bone. With the hilt of his sword he hammered at the side of its head, again and again, breaking its beak and then shattering its skull. It fell limp and he kicked it back through the gap whence it had come.

"The seal, Remy!" Biri-Daar called. "Now!"

Remy ran to help. Reaching the corner of the seal nearest him, he dropped his sword and found purchase for his hands in the grooves of the deeply cut runes. The magic pouring from them tingled in his fingertips; the wound in his shoulder pained him less, although still terribly. With every pull on the seal, the muscle in his shoulder tore a little more.

The floor of the chamber was polished to a fine gloss, and the seal too was smoothed by the attentions of long-dead artisans. It moved much more easily than a stone of its weight should have . . . until it hit the raised lip at the edge of the tilted portal slab. "Lift," Remy said through gritted teeth—not to Biri-Daar, stronger than he was, but to his shoulder, which screamed out in his head as he bent his legs and strained upward with everything he had. The seal came up off the ground.

Around them the battle surged, Lucan and Keverel and Uliana and the recovered Knights of Kul arrayed against a host of demons that grew with every moment. Uliana's greatness, Remy realized, would never be known. She brushed aside the demons like flies, destroying them with a thought. Only Philomen was a worthy opponent for her.

And she was slowly, surely, getting the better of him as well. He could draw on the strength of Thanatos, on the awful power of the Demon Prince of the Undeath—but she drew on the power of the very stones from which the city of Karga Kul had been hewn, the unknown thousands of years that men had struggled to keep the demonic hordes from overrunning the mortal plane. All of that—all of what made Karga Kul, Karga Kul—was with her. Philomen struck at her with necrotic horrors, visions of the damned; she struck back with the elemental rage of mountain and sky. Keverel, the holy man of Erathis, fought with her, the strokes of his mace and strength of his faith slowly taking their toll. In Uliana's remaining eye shone the grim and somehow ecstatic determination of the warrior who knows that she will not survive the day, but knows too that a more important enemy will die with her.

The Knights of Kul killed and killed, also knowing that they were to die. So brave, Remy thought, seeing one of them at last overrun by a swarm of evistros, killing them even as they tore the life from his body. Let me be worthy of that bravery and that sacrifice. And Paelias's sacrifice of luck.

It was a prayer of sorts, and whether any god heard it—Pelor or Corellon or Erathis or any other—the act itself restored Remy's resolve and strength. With Biri-Daar on the corner of the seal nearest him, Remy braced his feet on the other side of the raised lip of the portal slab, hauling the seal out over it as Obek pushed from behind and the Knights of Kul gave their lives for their city and the honor of their order. But still the slab and the seal did not meet flush, and the sigils began to flicker. The magic, given its potency by fleshly sacrifice, faded just as fleshly life did—only much faster. "To me, Knights!" Biri-Daar called out, and the four remaining Knights of Kul leaped to her, seeing at once what needed to be done.

They came down on the edge of the slab, forcing it down level with the floor—and the luck fled. Fleeing vrock demons, seeing their last chance, dropped from the darkness above, their sudden weight enough to pitch the slab over to an opposite angle. The seal hung out over the gap created by the tilt. Biri-Daar was left dangling at the end of the Seal, and Remy scrambled back from the sudden appearance of the endless, despairing waste of Thanatos spread out below him. The vrocks scrambled through the gap and were gone . . . all except one.

It craned its vulture's neck and bit down on Biri-Daar's leg. She growled and kicked at it with her other leg. It flapped its great wings and tugged, adding its two claws to the grip on her leg.

The seal began to overbalance and slid, grinding along the edge of the hole between the mortal plane and the infernal Thanatos.

Remy saw it all happening before it happened. Biri-Daar looked up at the seal as she felt it shift. She looked down at the vrock. She looked up into the darkness, toward the towers of Karga Kul that whitely reflected sunlight far above in a world that—Remy realized as Biri-Daar looked back down, and over, and directly at him—she would never see again.

She let go at the vrock's next tug, and was gone through the infernal gap. Remy cried out, wordless and anguished, lunging for her—but she swung a powerful arm and knocked him away, his extended hand just brushing and tugging at her breastplate and down the length of the arm that shoved him back. Biri-Daar fell, eyes open, sword out, killing the vrock even as its companions swooped up from the black crags and Remy lost sight of her, the world lost sight of her. He scrambled back toward the center of the portal slab, still screaming even as he felt the slab's inexorable swing, and it closed against the Seal with a boom that rolled up into the invisible heights of the chamber and out into the ends of the hall, far above in the quiet space of the council chamber of the decimated Mage Trust.

Uliana died knowing that the Seal was restored. Paelias, bluish pallor seeping into the skin around his mouth, lay dead near the figure of Philomen, who was on hands and knees.

Remy approached the vizier. There was something in his left hand. He looked at it and put it in the pouch where for the last weeks he had carried the chisel. Then he looked down at the drawn, corrupt face of his former mentor. This, he thought, is the man who got me out of Avankil. For that, despite everything else, I owe him a debt.

"Would the monks at the Monastery of the Cliffs have killed me?" he asked. "If I had lived to reach them? Or would they have taken me to the Road-builder themselves? How did you imagine me dying, Philomen?"

"You did not have all the luck," Philomen said. "Boy."

Wordlessly Remy ran him through, leaving his sword where it stood at an angle out from the ribs of the desiccated corpse of the man who had given Remy his first job. But that was when he had still been a boy. He looked around. "Lucan," he said.

The elf was kicking over the corpses of demons and killing whichever of them stirred. "Remy."

"Where's Obek?"

"Here," came the tiefling's voice from the other side of the Seal. "Who do you think kept pushing when you were out on the carousel there?" Obek came into view—their light was much diminished, and Remy could barely see him until Keverel, his voice hoarse with exhaustion, invoked the name of his god one last time, the word Erathis spreading through the chamber, bringing light to the shadows.

"Philomen," Keverel mused. "Vizier of Avankil." He walked to the vizier's body, rolled the staff along the floor with his foot, prodded the many sashes and pouches of the vizier's robe. "It is a very dark day. Biri-Daar was the greatest of the Knights of Kul. Her memory may yet restore the order to the greatness that is its rightful legacy." The cleric's gaze roved over the carnage in the Chamber of the Seal, and came to rest on the Seal itself. "This is now the tomb of Biri-Daar," he said. "Though few will ever see it." He made a gesture of blessing over the seal, and it seemed incongruous to Remy, who had seen what lay beneath the floor.

Keverel saw him looking, and must have read the expression on Remy's face. "Blessings are not for those places that are already holy," he said. "Surely you have learned this now."

"Learning," Obek said. "I am sick of learning. Let us go away from this place to somewhere else, a place where there is nothing to learn."

The four of them were coming closer to each other, not intending it so but under the power of an impulse to draw together, the four survivors of a journey long and treacherous. "You did well, tiefling," Lucan said.

"Oh, praise from the elf," Obek said. He looked at the Seal and at the body of Paelias. "None of us did well enough."

"But we did," Keverel said. "Karga Kul stands, and will stand. That, at least, we have done."

They were quiet for a long while after that, in the glow of Erathis that silvered the bodies of the living and the dead.

BOOK VII
NEXT

The sun on the Dragondown Gulf did as much as anything could to dispel the memories of what had happened inside the cliff. Remy looked up from Cliff Quay. "It's time to leave this place for a while. There will be unrest in the absence of power," he said. "The Mage Trust is dead. The seal is restored. Enemies remain. Our victory is partial."

On Remy's other side, Obek and Lucan leaned against the railing of a pier, looking not up at the city but down at the ship they were about to board. They were paying in gold for their passage south to the Cape of Toradan, where the city of that name still stood looking out over the waters of the Dragondown Gulf. Remy considered that he had seen two of the Five Cities. Toradan would be the third, Toradan whose native sailor sang to raise a wind to bring them home more quickly:

Spires of Toradan, spires of Toradan
Let the golden fires of the sun
On your rooftops guide me home

Remy regarded the gold-filigreed fragment of eggshell in his palm. He had it from a paladin of Bahamut, one of the great leaders of the Order of the Knights of Kul. He shook out the chain and looked at the broken links. Any jeweler in Toradan would be able to repair it. The boat rocked and groaned in rhythm with the swells on the outer Cape Kul, and Remy turned his mind forward, to Toradan. Avankil would no longer be safe for him. Like Biri-Daar, perhaps, he was growing into a citizen of the Dragondown; all of this land's mystery, wonder, and danger were his to explore.

Philomen's agents survived—in Avankil, and Toradan, and in the Monastery of the Cliff. The threats that lay below and behind the visible world were still dangerous. But where there were threats, there was adventure. And glory.

And, of course, the treasures of lost civilizations whose remains were everywhere . . . if one knew how to look. Remy saw Obek and Lucan gambling with another pair of passengers, and Keverel looking out over the bow into the limitless reaches of the gulf beyond the harbors. These three, and four more who had died along the way, had begun to teach Remy to see.

The world would yet teach him more.

The coffers of Karga Kul had produced a handsome price in gemstones for the staff of Philomen. The vizier's other treasures included a ring Remy wore on his right hand index finger. Lucan said it was a ring that brought luck. Remy thought that he had seen how luck operated in the last moments of Paelias's life, and wasn't sure he wanted more luck around. He'd always survived with the luck he'd been born with.

But the ring was his, and in the pouch where he had carried the chisel, next to Biri-Daar's gilded eggshell, Remy carried a drawstring bag filled with more money than he had ever seen in one place in his life. His first impulse when Lucan had given him his share had been to give it back, to say that the lives of his comrades were not worth gems and gold.

Lucan had seen the argument brewing in Remy's eyes. "Remy," he'd said. "It never was a trade. You don't get to choose one or the other."

And Remy had taken the treasure. Kithri, Iriani, Paelias, Biri-Daar . . . I only knew them a few days, or weeks, Remy thought. Yet they will be more alive to me in my memory than anyone I knew in Avankil. This was what destiny felt like, he decided. When everything around you—every sensation and experience and memory and expection—when all of it was more real than anything you'd ever felt, that was destiny. That was how you knew you were walking the path your life had laid out for you.

Remy would walk the path. He jingled the pouch. He would learn to experience sadness and the thrill of victory at the same time. Over his head, the sailors sang, and the ship turned south away from the Quay of the Cliff, heading for open water and the towers of Toradan.

ABOUT THE AUTHOR

Alex Irvine is the award-winning author of five original novels including *Buyout* and *The Narrows*, two short story collections, and several shared-world and media-related projects, such as *Batman: Inferno* and *The Vertigo Encyclopedia*. His comics work includes *Daredevil Noir*, *Iron Man: The Rapture*, and *Dark Sun: Ianto's Tomb*. He has worked as a reporter for the *Portland Phoenix*, and was part of the writing teams for the ground-breaking ARGs *The Beast* and *I Love Bees*. He lives in Maine.

APPENDIX

THE BLOOD OF IO

As with all stories that deal with the ancient past, tales about the birth of the dragonborn are hazy in their details and often contradict one another. Each tale, though, reveals something about the dragonborn that is true, regardless of the historical accuracy of the legend—and it often reveals much about the teller.

One tale relates that the dragonborn were shaped by Io even as the ancient dragon-god created dragons. In the beginning of days, this legend says, Io fused brilliant astral spirits with the unchecked fury of the raw elements. The greater spirits became the dragons, creatures so powerful, proud, and strong-willed that they were lords of the newborn world. The lesser spirits became the dragonborn. Although smaller in stature than their mighty lords, they were no less draconic in nature.

This tale stresses the close kinship between dragons and dragonborn, while reinforcing the natural order of things—dragons rule, dragonborn serve.

A second legend claims that Io created the dragons separately, at the birth of the world. Io crafted them lovingly to represent the pinnacle of mortal form, imbuing them with the power of the Elemental Chaos flowing through their veins and spewing forth from their mouths in gouts of flame or waves of paralyzing cold. Io granted them the keen minds and lofty spirits shared by other mortal races, linking them to Io and to the other gods of the Astral Sea.

During the Dawn War, however, Io was killed by the primordial known as Erek-Hus, the King of Terror. With a rough-hewn axe of adamantine, the King of Terror split Io from head to tail, cleaving the dragongod into two equal halves. No sooner did Io's sundered corpse fall to the ground than each half rose up as a new god—Bahamut from the left and Tiamat from the right. Drops of Io's blood, spread far and wide across the world, rose up as dragonborn.

This tale separates the creation of dragonborn from the birth of the dragons, implying that they are fundamentally separate. Sometimes, those who repeat this legend suggest that dragonborn are clearly less than the dragons made by Io's loving hand. Other tellers, though, stress that the dragonborn rose up from Io's own blood—just as the two draconic deities arose from the god's severed body. Are they not, therefore, this tale asks, like the gods themselves?

A third legend, rarely told in current times, claims that dragonborn were the firstborn of the world, created before dragons and before other humanoid races. Those other races were made, the legend claims, in pale imitation of dragonborn perfection. Io shaped the dragonborn with his great claws and fired them with his breath, then spilled some of his own blood to send life coursing through their veins. Io made the dragonborn, the legend says, to be companions and allies, to fill his astral court and sing his praise. The dragons he made later, at the start of the Dawn War, to serve as engines of destruction.

This version of the tale was popular during the height of the Empire of Arkhosia, though it was subversive at the time—it proclaimed that dragonborn should be the masters of dragons and not the other way around. It also highlighted the superiority of dragonborn to other races, which was a common theme in the rhetoric of ancient Arkhosia.

One common theme binds all these legends together, though—the dragonborn owe their existence, in some fundamental way, to Io, the great dragon-god who created all of dragonkind. The dragonborn, all legends agree, are not the creation of Bahamut or Tiamat—their origin does not naturally place them on one side or the other of the ancient conflict between those gods. Therefore, it's up to every individual dragonborn to choose sides in the eternal struggle between the chromatic and metallic dragons—or to ignore this conflict completely and find their own way in the world.

CHOOSING SIDES

The common people of most races are unaligned, with few making a conscious effort to choose a good life or an evil one. Dragonborn, however, are much more likely to choose sides in the cosmic war between good and evil. Dragonborn often tell the story of Io's death and the birth of Bahamut and Tiamat as a moral tale intended to emphasize the importance of standing on one side or the other.

"Io didn't die so we could stand in the middle," they say. "We're not called to ambivalence. The choices stand before you—Bahamut's way or Tiamat's. The only wrong decision is refusing to choose."

Of course, more dragonborn choose Bahamut's path than Tiamat's. The pathways of justice, honor, nobility, and protection are more conducive to society's smooth functioning than those of greed, envy, and vengeance. Those who follow Tiamat's ways usually keep their choice quiet, worshiping the Chromatic Dragon in secret shrines while going through the motions of fulfilling social expectations.

Choosing sides isn't just a matter of a one-time choice of alignment, however. Every moment of crisis calls for a decision, and dragonborn are inclined to see those decisions as a matter of stark extremes. When wronged, a dragonborn can choose the path of Bahamut and seek to bring the wrongdoer to justice. Or the victim might choose the path of Tiamat and swear vengeance. Even good-aligned dragonborn who are devoted to Bahamut sometimes choose the latter path—not out of impulsive rage, but because it's the best course to take in that particular situation.

A few dragonborn reject the idea of choosing between Bahamut's way and Tiamat's, notably the followers of the Temple of Io's Children. These dragonborn are often unaligned, but their position is a decision not to choose sides, rather than a sign of ambivalence. They view the distinction between the gods as a false dichotomy, a choice between two sides of the same coin, not really different from each other.

This disdain for ambivalence extends beyond choosing alignment. While dragonborn appreciate the virtue of listening to both sides of an argument, they don't respect anyone who hears both sides and can't choose between them. Decisiveness is a mark of strong character.

This attitude makes compromise more difficult for dragonborn to reach or accept than it is for other races, but not impossible. In fact, sometimes dragonborn reach compromise all the more quickly because they realize that each side is committed to its own position and won't be persuaded to alter its perspective, making some kind of compromise the only possible solution.

Reprinted from:
Player's Handbook Races: Dragonborn
James Wyatt
ISBN:978-0-7869-5386-8

WELCOME TO THE DESERT WORLD
OF ATHAS, A LAND RULED BY A HARSH
AND UNFORGIVING CLIMATE, A LAND
GOVERNED BY THE ANCIENT AND
TYRANNICAL SORCERER KINGS.
THIS IS THE LAND OF

CITY UNDER THE SAND
Jeff Mariotte
OCTOBER 2010

*Sometimes lost knowledge is
knowledge best left unknown.*

FIND OUT WHAT YOU'RE MISSING IN THIS
BRAND NEW DARK SUN® ADVENTURE BY
THE AUTHOR OF *COLD BLACK HEARTS*.

ALSO AVAILABLE AS AN E-BOOK!
THE PRISM PENTAD
Troy Denning's classic DARK SUN
series revisited! Check out the great new editions of
The Verdant Passage, *The Crimson Legion*,
The Amber Enchantress, *The Obsidian Oracle*,
and *The Cerulean Storm*.

Follow us on Twitter @WotC_Novels

RETURN TO A WORLD OF PERIL, DECEIT,
AND INTRIGUE, A WORLD REBORN IN
THE WAKE OF A GLOBAL WAR.

TIM WAGGONER'S
LADY RUIN

She dedicated her life to the nation of Karrnath.
With the war ended, and the army asleep—
waiting—in their crypts, Karrnath assigned her
to a new project: find a way to harness
the dark powers of the Plane of Madness.

REVEL IN THE RUIN

DECEMBER 2010

ALSO AVAILABLE AS AN E-BOOK!

Follow us on Twitter @WotC_Novels

RICHARD LEE BYERS

BROTHERHOOD OF THE GRIFFON

NOBODY DARED TO CROSS CHESSENTA...

BOOK I
THE CAPTIVE FLAME

BOOK II
WHISPER OF VENOM
NOVEMBER 2010

BOOK III
THE SPECTRAL BLAZE
JUNE 2011

...WHEN THE RED DRAGON WAS KING.

"This is Thay as it's never been shown before . . . Dark, sinister, foreboding and downright disturbing!"
—Alaundo, Candlekeep.com on Richard Byers's *Unclean*

ALSO AVAILABLE AS E-BOOKS!

Follow us on Twitter @WotC_Novels